What people are saying…

"This makes it so easy to build your vocabulary through reading! I majored in English and as a word lover myself, I recognized many of the words in this book but still found myself looking at the definitions that were provided just to be sure I understood their meaning. Especially with all of the dumbed-down and questionable literature being published for young adults these days, such a series has tremendous potential to actually enhance their knowledge while upholding positive moral values."

—Teri Ann Berg Olsen, *Knowledge House*

"Burk's style is easy for the reader and geared to teenagers in the high school years. This book has 300 words that, for the most part, will be new to the reader... What an incredible way to increase the writing and speaking skills of your student!"

—Jennifer Barker, *The Old Schoolhouse Magazine*

"There are very few better ways to quickly read and actually remember 300 high-level words, such as "ruminate," "lachrymose," "salubrious" and "pulchritude." Some of the words may be recognized by many readers, but even this reader was learning new words throughout."

—Chloe O'Connor, *The Signal*

"Besides being an excellent tool to enhance vocabulary and language development, pre-teens and teens will find the story engaging. Best of all, the story steers clear of offensive language and unsavory themes."

—Anne Gebhart, *Heart of Texas*

Books in VocabCafé Series

The Summer of Saint Nick

I.M. for Murder

Operation High School

Planet Exile

Highway to Hollywood

The Wandering Watkins

The Wandering Watkins

By Judah Burk

Maven of Memory Publishing
Hurst, Texas

The Wandering Watkins

ISBN 978-0-9833277-2-1

Cover and layout by impact studios

Printed in the United States of America

To my friends and professors at Ouachita Baptist University, thank you for pouring into me your time, energy and wisdom. It was because of you that I learned the value of sisterhood, ethnical journalism, foreign cultures, American literature, good philosophy and psychology, and most importantly studying and living Christianity. The four years I spent in Arkadelphia were some of the most challenging but rewarding years of my young life, and I promise to carry the lessons I learned throughout the rest of my life. It was a true pleasure to learn under your tutelage.

An Introduction to VocabCafé

The purpose of the VocabCafé book series is to encourage the development of vocabulary knowledge. At Maven of Memory Publishing we believe that a good understanding of vocabulary words is crucial to lifelong success. Contained inside this novella are more than 300 words that can be helpful in improving the vocabulary of any reader, which can lead to better reading, writing, and speaking skills. It can also help improve test scores for students intending to take standardized exams.

Every vocabulary word is placed in the context of a narrative story. The storyline and sentences surrounding the words should help readers easily deduce their meanings. For easy reference and instant reinforcement, the literal definitions of every word are at the bottom of each page. At the end of each chapter there is a review of the vocabulary words featured in that section. We recommend that you go over this word review immediately after finishing the chapter in order to study the definitions while their context remains fresh.

These books were written with an intended audience of high school teenagers, although many parents find them appropriate for younger students. As a family-based company, our goal is to make a quality product that can be enjoyed by everyone. These stories contain no magic, sorcery, swear words, or illicit situations. Nonetheless, we recommend that parents read every book (not just ours) that they give their children to make sure the messages and themes coincide with their beliefs and standards.

Accompanying flash cards organized by chapter are available for purchase and highly recommended to help ensure success. Each card has the word definition and its use in the story. Reviewing these will help you in your quest for mastery of vocabulary words.

We hope this series is instrumental in helping you advance your proficiency with the English language.

Good Luck!
The VocabCafé Team

The Wandering Watkins

1

A SOLEMN GOOD-BYE

The thick black rain clouds gathered momentum as they swept across the prairie sky, swallowing any semblance of the sun's joyful rays. Along with their dark, ominous presence, the clouds carried an arctic chill to the Midwest American plains. Thunder and lightning crackled in the distance. It was March 1856 in Wyoming. The outside temperature dropped quickly as the wind grew stronger. Without saying a word to one another, the members of the small caravan knew they needed to reach their destination soon, before the weather made it impossible to do that which they came to do. The darkness in the sky perfectly reflected the ***abject*** despair experienced by the group of travelers. Everyone walked in silence as the wagon full of precious cargo rolled beside them. The journey they made had one purpose, and rain or shine, it must be completed that day. With the torrential weather looming overhead, the party carried on.

Days like this were always some of Anna Watkins' favorite times on the prairie. To her there was something magical about spring rains on the open fields of Wyoming. The gray skies blended in with the vast mountains making it look like the horizon went on forever. The mighty winds rushed against the blue grass, tossing the blades back and forth like waves in the sea. On any other day, the

---

Abject (ab-**jekt**) – ADJ – utterly hopeless

15-year-old would be standing on her front porch giggling as she twirled in the wind, letting the great gusts whoosh her golden ringlets into her face. She loved the electrifying effects of a thunderstorm. But this day was different. Anna was not dancing on her front porch but marching among the crowd. Instead of bouncing wildly in the wind, Anna's golden curls were tied neatly behind her head with a simple black ribbon, one that matched her somber frock. Her left hand held tightly to the petite, white hand of her three-year-old brother Charlie; her right hand lifelessly touched a cold wooden box. It was one of two identical wooden boxes that rode gently on the bed of the uncovered wagon. Her older brother Jacob sat on top of the wagon next to the driver. As much as Anna hated the thought of touching that ***abysmal*** container, she dreaded the moment she would have to let go. For Anna knew once the wagon came to a stop it would be time to say her final good-byes.

A child of western expansion, Anna had experienced her share of separations. Although she was only five when her parents decided to move the family westward, Anna vividly remembered the experience of leaving their home in St. Louis. Even as a small child she understood that once her family moved west, things would never be the same. By the 1850s, St. Louis had grown into a bustling city of over 70,000 people. Travelers came from all over to experience the city, culture, and cuisine. Originally famous for its riverboats, St. Louis grew in popularity as frontiersmen and women moved westward. It was an exciting time to be there, as scores of emigrants passed through looking to find their own prosperity. The city was alive with colorful characters from all across the world

---

Abysmal (uh-**biz**-muhl) – ADJ – awful

searching for new fortunes, lives, and adventures. Out west, settlers could transform the featureless and ***amorphous*** plains into their own American dreams. So many people traveled through the Missouri town that St. Louis became affectionately known as the "Gateway to the West." It did not take long for Anna's parents to also become infected with the westward bug. Promises of better futures, cleaner air, and rich ***agrarian*** homesteads lured the Watkins toward Oregon just like everyone else. However, even with her experience of leaving the only other home she ever knew, nothing in her short time on earth had prepared young Anna for the farewell she was facing.

Thomas Watkins, Anna's father, had lived in St. Louis all his life. His mother died shortly after giving birth to him, and his father, stricken with grief, took to drinking to ease his pain. Charles Patrick Watkins, Anna's grandfather, soon became a ***dipsomaniac***, unable to resist the temptation of drink. He never took the time to get to know his only son, turning instead to his bottle for comfort. He barely had the energy to grant his wife's last request of naming the boy Thomas after his own father. To the devastated man, the little boy was an unfortunate reminder of what he had lost. Charles couldn't forgive either the child or himself for the death of his beloved wife. Bitter and hopeless, he never recovered. Thomas's last memory of his father involved his eighth birthday and a licking he would never forget. Little Thomas had asked for money to buy a sugar candy to celebrate turning eight. Drunk and angry, Charles

---

Amorphous (uh-**mawr**-fuhs) – ADJ – lacking definite form; having no specific shape; formless

Agrarian (uh-**grair**-ee-uhn) – ADJ – rural; agricultural

Dipsomaniac (dip-suh-**mey**-nee-ak) – N – a person with an irresistible craving for alcoholic drink

raised his voice and his belt to the boy. October 10th wasn't a joyous occasion that necessitated sweets, but a day of stiff drinks and mourning for the loss of his dear wife. Enraged by the seemly callousness of his child, Charles wanted to teach his son a lesson. Thomas's backside remained sore for the next three days. His father later left the house to purchase some whiskey. He never returned.

It is likely the young Thomas would have chosen a path of rage rather than redemption had it not been for the kindness of his older sister, Anna Marie. His elder by twelve years, Anna Marie took over the responsibility of raising Thomas after their mother's death. Caring for him with love and affection, Anna Marie knew how to ***countermand*** the effects of their father's harshness. Wise even for someone twice her age, the young mistress steered the small boy toward healthy avenues to express his hurt, frustration, and confusion. The most important place Anna Marie led him was to the church. Under the sagacious guidance of the ***Decalogue***, Anna Marie educated her younger brother with the same conviction and gentleness her mother had raised her in learning and applying the ten "thou shalt nots." The two were nearly inseparable until Thomas turned fourteen. By then Thomas was old enough to care for himself, so with the encouragement of her brother, Anna Marie accepted the proposal of an older gentleman, Theodore Perkins, from Maryland. Mr. Perkins was in the train business and had come to St. Louis to look into the possibilities of expanding the railroads westward. Although it would take some years to complete the tracks,

---

Countermand (**koun**-ter-mand) – V – to revoke or cancel
Decalogue (**dek**-uh-lawg) – N – Ten Commandments (Exodus. 20:2–17)

Mr. Perkins instinctively knew that soon everything would be heading west; he wanted his company to be first to get there. While Mr. Perkins' trip was initially meant to last no longer than a month, upon meeting the lovely Anna Marie Watkins, he found ways of extending his visit. Convincing his superiors that a full investigation of the investment potential of the Missouri town required a minimum of three months, Mr. Perkins made for himself the time to court and woo his newly beloved. Upon his arrival to Maryland after his three months in Missouri, the fifty-six-year-old seasoned gentleman returned with a pretty twenty-six-year-old bride. Anna Marie left Thomas's education and adolescence in the hands of St. Peter's Catholic Church. There he planned to study to become a priest. His sister's departure to Maryland meant a permanent separation of the siblings. Thomas would always miss his sister and was forever grateful for her kindness. Without Anna Marie, he would have carried the exhausting burden of his hatred for his father for the rest of his life. However, Anna Marie had shown him that forgiveness, not vengeance, was the true path to freedom and healing. It was in her honor that Thomas had named his only daughter.

Thomas spent the majority of his young adult life at the all-boys school at St. Peters. He studied, ate, worked, and lived there. Unlike the majority of his pupils, Thomas loved every minute he spent at church. When he was there, he felt like he had a purpose. He felt safe and secure. For the other students, St. Peters was just a boarding school; for Thomas, it was his only home, and the priests were his only family. Since the age of 14, Thomas had never questioned his destiny of becoming a priest; never, that is, until one Sunday afternoon in June. It was the summer before Thomas was to take his vows, and he could hardly wait to officially join the order. Although he had been certain about his decision to join the church for years, he was required to spend one year ***extramurally***, "out in the world," before he could become a priest. This was not a decision to make flippantly; the Fathers at St. Peters wanted Thomas to understand what he was giving up before he made his commitment to dedicate his entire life to the church. Thomas was annoyed that he had to wait to fulfill a commitment he had already decided upon. However, the priests were wiser than he; they understood that zealous youth often make hasty commitments which they later regret. While Thomas was the type of man who would have fulfilled his commitment regardless of any adjusted feelings, the other fathers knew that a frustrated priest makes for a bad priest. So it was agreed that Thomas, upon completing his studies at St. Peters, would live one year outside of the church. At first Thomas protested; after all, he loved working at the church. So the priests relented and allowed him to work part time at St. Peters and in his remaining time he worked at a small grocery store in town. Thomas was convinced that his year would simply ***corroborate*** his already firm decision to become a priest. However, Thomas could never imagine the events that would transpire one Sunday afternoon and dramatically alter the course of his life.

Morning Mass had finished and Thomas went into town to run errands for the fathers. Working part time at the monastery, Thomas found himself doing all the little chores that none of the other fathers wanted to do. Today was his turn to ask for donations for a new church roof. Thomas didn't mind though; he loved doing the things

---

Extramurally (ek-struh-**myoor**-uhlly) – ADV – outside the boundaries of

Corroborate (kuh-**rob**-uh-reyt) – V – to make more certain; confirm

that needed to be done. Taking his usual place on the corner of Main Street and Rose, right in front of the city park, Thomas pulled out his can and held it out. As people passed and dropped coins into his can, Thomas responded to them with a simple thankful ***benediction.***

"God Bless," he uttered humbly.

After standing at the corner for about an hour, a ***Croesus*** passed his way, dressed in his finest black suit and hat of rich fabric. Thomas had never seen a man who was so clean that his shoes rivaled any mirror's reflection. Compared to Thomas in his humble robes that were well worn, the businessman looked like a king. Thomas did not care much for the way the man was dressed and probably would have looked right past him, as the man did to Thomas, if it hadn't been for the angelic creature who accompanied him. A delicate youth wrapped in the finest silk fashion hung gently on his arm. Dressed in a cool blue, the young lady with ivory skin, green eyes, and golden blond curls resembled a ***dryad*** of Greek mythology. The contrast of the graying wrinkles of the gentleman and the bright youthfulness of the woman convinced Thomas that the man must be her father or grandfather. He certainly couldn't be her husband. While the man walked briskly past Thomas, the fair lady released her grip and stopped. Standing in front of the young clergyman, she pulled out all the funds she held in her purse. She didn't stop to count the bills as so many before her had done, but simply placed all she had in the simple can. Struck by her generosity and beauty, Thomas had lost his words. Unable to think clearly,

---

Benediction (ben-i-**dik**-shuhn) – N – an utterance of good wishes
Croesus (**kree**-suhs) – N – a very rich man
Dryad (**drahy**-uhd) – N – a deity or nymph of the woods

he choked out the first thing he could think of to say.

"Would you like to come to Mass at St. Peters tonight?"

Ms. Charlotte Huntington was taken by surprise at his humble request. Flattered by his consideration, Charlotte dared not tell the man that she was not Catholic.

"I'll have to check with my father," she replied with a shy smile.

With that, Charlotte scurried off to catch up to the older gentleman, who ***admonished*** her for taking so long. Charlotte paid no attention to her father's rebuke. She was too embarrassed by the lie she had just told a man of God. Not in this lifetime or the next would she ever ask her father if she could take the night off to go to a Catholic church. Raised in a strict Baptist home, she knew the very idea of her going to Mass would be considered heretical in the Huntington family. It would have been better for her to politely decline, yet there was something about the unassuming man that made it nearly impossible for her to refuse his invitation. It was strange, but the eighteen-year-old felt compelled that evening to break from tradition and go to the cathedral.

Charlotte had been in St. Louis only two weeks before her brief encounter with Thomas Watkins that Sunday afternoon. The young lady had come with her parents to St. Louis from New York on account of her mother's declining health. Although the doctors were never quite sure what was the matter with Isabella Huntington, they were all agreed that a move south with the warmer climate and cleaner air would do wonders for the ailing woman. Despite lacking hard scientific evidence to support

---

Admonish (ad-**mon**-ish) – V – to scold

this course of treatment, Isabella's doctors believed this ***holistic*** remedy was her best option for recovery. While the effectiveness of the prescribed treatment is debatable, the one thing the doctors had unquestionably accomplished was the relocation of their most difficult patient. The pride and stubbornness of Isabella Huntington were legendary. Her doctors spent more time arguing with the ***hypochondriac*** than treating her imagined illnesses.

As the Huntington's only child, Charlotte moved with her parents to help her mother through the most traumatic experience of the woman's lifetime. One of New York's finest society ladies, Isabella believed the doctors' orders to move relegated her to the uncivilized South. Convinced of the backwardness of the Missouri people, she could barely stomach the idea of breathing the same air with those Southerners. If it had not been for the insistence of her husband Harold, Isabella would have chosen an excruciating death in Manhattan to the supposed healing ***panacea*** of the southern climate. Isabella did not take the move well. However, she was comforted by the congenial presence of Charlotte whom she believed to be the most angelic creature in the whole world, despite the numerous imperfections which Isabella was quick to point out. After all she was a Huntington, and no less. Charlotte loved her mother; however, there wasn't a person she wanted to be like less than she did Isabella.

Holistic (hoh-**lis**-tik) – ADJ – of or relating to the medical consideration of the complete person, physically and psychologically, in the treatment of a disease

Hypochondriac (hahy-puh-**kon**-dree-ak) – N – a person who worries or talks excessively about his or her health

Panacea (pan-uh-**see**-uh) – N – a remedy for all disease or ills; cure-all

Whether by chance or divine providence, the encounter on the street corner would not be the last time the pair would meet. That evening Charlotte managed to evade the watchful eyes of her skeptical guardians under the pretense that she was leaving the house to attend Sunday evening service. Her parents naturally assumed she meant at the local Baptist church, and she simply chose not to correct that notion. ***Absolving*** herself from her lie of omission, Charlotte reasoned that God didn't care what building she went to as long as she went to worship Him. To avoid unwanted suspicion from her chaperones, Charlotte had invited them to come along with her. Had they said yes Charlotte would have abandoned her plans to go to Mass. However, she was fairly confident that their obligation to their faith was satisfied with one service per week. While they were thrilled to encourage the piety of their daughter, any more religiousness on their part would have been a burden. As she suspected, they declined.

Naturally inclined for adventure, Charlotte was excited about the prospect of experiencing St. Louis without her excessively attentive parents, even if it was just one new building not far from her house. Stepping into the carriage, she instructed her driver to head to St. Peters. Ignoring the man's perplexed look, Charlotte gazed toward the street with a self-satisfied smile. For a daughter of New York ***affluence***, visiting a different domination was just about the most daring thing she had ever done in her short life. It, however, would be her first of many visits to St. Peters, and the start of a journey that would lead her toward many future escapades.

Absolve (ab-**zolv**) – V – to free from guilt

Affluence (**af**-loo-uhns) – N – an abundance of wealth, property, or other material goods

To say Thomas was surprised by the arrival of the young lady at that evening's service would not be entirely true. While pleased by the sight of her, something had prepared him to expect her. If asked, he couldn't explain it, but somehow he knew she would come. Once she was there he felt compelled to get to know her. It wasn't her beauty or her obvious wealth that captivated him—his lessons in priesthood had taught him to look beyond such outer trimmings. It was her countenance that allured him. He had noticed it that afternoon in the genuineness of her donation. She didn't stop to give her money out of some ill-conceived notion of guilt or self-righteous spirituality. She gave out of sincere compassion. Within the few moments of seeing her, Thomas was more impressed by her unpretentious kindness than he was with the pompous religiosity of his entire congregation. Thomas instinctively understood that if what he saw was only a small expression of her character, then her inner beauty would far surpass that of her outer. True integrity is a rare treasure, and Thomas found himself profoundly attracted to the young blonde sitting in the middle pew of that holy ***sanctum***. He was determined to introduce himself upon the closure of the service.

Their second meeting was only a bit longer than their first. Ever aware of the ***circumspect*** eye of her parents, Charlotte knew they would worry if she stayed out too late alone. The young New Yorker politely refused Thomas's offer to walk her home because she needed to return home with her carriage. Saddened by the missed opportunity, Thomas was at a loss for another excuse to get to

---

Sanctum (**sangk**-tuhm) – N – a sacred or holy place
Circumspect (**sur**-kuhm-spekt) – ADJ – watchful; cautious

know Charlotte better. Noticing his hesitation and disappointment, Charlotte seized the moment to offer another suggestion.

"Since I am new in town, perhaps sometime you can show me around," prompted Charlotte.

"Tomorrow I am helping out at the Farmer's Market; if you like, you could come to the center of town tomorrow afternoon and we can start there," responded Thomas. "Once a month all the farmers come from all over Missouri to sell their products. As a visitor, it is definitely something you should experience."

"I typically spend the afternoon reading while my parents take their nap, but I think I might be able to get away from the house for a couple of hours," said Charlotte. "At the very least a nice walk in the clean air should do me some good."

"Then I will look for you there," he smiled.

The two said their good-byes. Thomas watched the delicate beauty climb into her carriage. Conflicted by the myriad of feelings, Thomas didn't know what to think. For the first time since coming to St. Peters he felt that there was more to life than his peaceful ***arcadia*** in the church.

Charlotte did manage to leave the cloistered ***aegis*** of her parents to make it to the Farmer's Market. Thomas had undersold its beauty. As if by magic, the entire city center was transformed into a traveling open air grocery. Rows and rows of fresh fruits, vegetables, and plants lined the center. The freshness of nature surrounded the visitors, and the smells of summer engulfed them. So many colors

---

Arcadia (ahr-**key**-dee-uh) – N – any real or imaginary place offering peace and simplicity

Aegis (**ee**-jis) – N – protection

filled the center, with an array of produce of a variety of shapes and sizes. Types of food Charlotte had never seen were staked by the dozen, and things she was familiar with up north appeared twice the size of any she had seen before. After only a short time in Missouri, she was starting to believe the doctors were right about the southern climate. At the very least, her new home offered a host of opportunities that were unavailable in its northern counterpart. Although vastly different than what she was used to, there was something in the atmosphere that made Charlotte feel at home. She had always loved New York, but something about St. Louis seemed to fit her better. Perhaps it was the cleaner air or warmer weather, or maybe it had something to do with the shy man who stood before her with a handful of freshly picked wildflowers. The scent of the flowers was a beautiful ***ambrosia***; she could almost taste the delicate petals. Charlotte couldn't help but blush when Thomas gave them to her. In the past she had received numerous gifts from potential suitors. With her looks and family fortune, many men had tried to impress her with the finest delicacies, jewelry, and gifts from around the world. However, nothing was as ***compelling*** to her as the humble gesture of this handpicked bouquet. Yes, it seemed that everything about the southern way of life suited her. Thomas and Charlotte soon left the market to explore the town.

After only a few weeks, the spark that drew them to each other transformed into a desire for ***connubial*** bliss.

Ambrosia (am-**broh**-zhuh) – N – something especially delicious to taste or smell

Compelling (kuhm-**pel**-ing) – ADJ – having a powerful and irresistible effect; requiring acute admiration, attention, or respect

Connubial (kuh-**noo**-bee-uhl) – ADJ – of marriage or wedlock

Neither one was expecting it, but it didn't take long before they both realized that they never wanted to be apart. After the first day at the market the two found ways to spend almost every day that summer together. As a native to St. Louis, Thomas afforded Charlotte a rare glimpse into the hidden side of the city. He recounted the city's history and expansion. He told her about the progress of the steamboat line and how every day the city was growing more and more modern. The two shared stories of their own pasts, vastly different from one another, and expressed hopes about the future. Thomas, who until very recently was planning on becoming a priest, found the possibilities of a previously uncontemplated life beguiling. Charlotte found peace in the opportunity to live simply. While on the outside they seemed the most unlikely pair, on the inside they couldn't be a better fit. Despite the obvious obstacles, Thomas and Charlotte decided to marry.

The news of Charlotte's most unconventional courtship and engagement to an almost-priest nearly unhinged the very being of Charlotte's mother, Isabella. Outraged by the obstinacy of her child, Isabella threatened to pack Charlotte up and send her not back to New York, but to her relatives in England. If Charlotte refused to leave, then Isabella would have nothing more to do with her. Isabella was a true ***curmudgeon***, tormenting her daughter for falling in love. Having her only child marry a poor Catholic was not the future she had planned for Charlotte, and therefore it was not the future she would allow to happen. Despite Charlotte's pleas and tears, Isabella would not budge. Either Charlotte would agree to leave St. Louis,

---

Curmudgeon (ker-**muhj**-uhn) – N – a bad-tempered, difficult, cantankerous person

or she would leave the Huntington family altogether. Marriage to Thomas would cut her off from all family ties and wealth. To further dramatize her point, Isabella stated that whatever day Thomas and Charlotte chose to be their wedding day Isabella would count as Charlotte's funeral. Harold Huntington, while not in the least pleased with Charlotte's choice for a husband, was a little more gracious to his only child. After trying to ***expostulate*** with Charlotte to change her mind, he conceded to a private compromise with her. If Charlotte married Thomas, she would indeed be cut off from the Huntington family; Isabella would make sure of that. However, Harold offered her a small portion of her inheritance as a dowry on the condition that the young couple would never try to contact the family again. When Charlotte refused, Harold insisted. To this day, no one knows the father's motivation for offering the money; whether it was done out of true love for his child or to ease his guilt will remain a mystery. However, the young couple made a ***concert*** to marry, so her future in the Huntington family was sealed with this pact. Despite living only a few minutes from Isabella and Harold Huntington by carriage, after being wed Charlotte never saw them again.

Thomas and Charlotte were married in a private ceremony in St. Peters just three months after they met. The two exchanged their vows with only the other priests to serve as witnesses. In a matter of a couple of months both their lives had dramatically changed courses. Thomas was no longer to be a priest and Charlotte would never again

---

Expostulate (ik-**spos**-chuh-leyt) – V – to reason earnestly with someone against something that person intends to do or has done

Concert (**kon**-surt) – N – agreement of two or more individuals in a design or plan; combined action

be wealthy. Thomas's year away from the church turned out to be an unexpected blessing. Not only did he have the opportunity to get to know Charlotte, but he was also able to continue his work at the grocery store after they were married and soon became the store's manager. The money which the couple received from Charlotte's father had enabled the pair to purchase a small house near St. Peters and still put some money away for the future. It wasn't long before the couple had their first child, a son they named Jacob. The arrival of Jacob was bittersweet. While excited by the growth of their family, the new addition was a stark reminder that neither Thomas nor Charlotte had any other family members to share with their joy. Several times Charlotte wanted to take her precious bundle to her parents' house, but each time she tried, the memory of their rebuke stopped her. Whether right or wrong, she had chosen a different path for her life, and the sad reality was that it was a life her other family would never be a part of. Content with leaving the past behind, Charlotte turned all her energies toward her new family. Two years after the newlyweds welcomed Jacob, they were blessed with another surprise in the form of Anna. Overjoyed at having both a healthy son and daughter, the growing Watkins family had everything they could have wanted. Thomas worked hard in the grocery store and Charlotte cared for the children. For several years the small family lived a simple but happy existence in St. Louis.

Time changed both the family and the city. As the forefront of western expansion, St. Louis grew rapidly with the influx of speculator traffic. Settlers needed supplies, and as the manager of the largest grocery store in town, Thomas often felt that he was always on the front lines. Contentment with raising his family in the city waned as Thomas heard stories of never-ending prairies beneath

cyclopean blue skies. While life was good in the south, it could be great out west. Places like Oregon were fresh and ripe for the harvest. The more Thomas imagined his family's cabin on their own homestead, complete with livestock and fields, the more he grew dissatisfied with their dingy two bedroom brick house. By 1844, the once glittering modern city now resembled a dirty relic of the past. Like everyone else, Thomas was convinced that the future of the United States was out west.

Charlotte Watkins, on the other hand, was less convinced than her husband of the prosperity that lay before them in the western part of the country. She, too, had heard stories of settlers looking for fortunes, but in her versions the prospectors found diseases instead of panacea, and destitution rather than wealth. For a young mother of two, the adventure of going beyond the borders of civilization was littered with peril. *After all, hadn't she already made her great western expansion when she moved from New York to St. Louis?* Along with the dangers of traveling and living outside the borders of a city, a more personal reason held Charlotte to Missouri—her parents. Although Charlotte hadn't spoken to either Harold or Isabella for years, she still clung to the hope that one day the family would be reunited. When they lived only minutes away, she knew there was a sliver of a chance for reconciliation; a move out west would completely kill all hope of it. In fact, the last news Charlotte ever received concerning her parents would arrive shortly after the Watkins family had settled out west. It came in the form of a newspaper article. Although the Watkins' Wyoming farm was far from the center of civilization, every several months the local store

---

Cyclopean (sahy-kluh-**pee**-uhn) – ADJ – gigantic; vast

would get newspapers from back east. The news was hardly relevant by the time it reached the Watkins' small town, but Charlotte always enjoyed the slim connection to the life she had once led. While browsing an outdated St. Louis paper, a certain headline caught the attention of the curious reader. *Wealthy Couple Dies from Influenza and Leaves All Their Money to the Local Baptist Church.* Charlotte almost fainted when she recognized the description of the generous philanthropists. There blazing before her in bold, black ink were the names of Harold and Isabella Huntington. Since they were not known for their generosity in life, Charlotte could only assume her parents' substantial contribution to the church was one last snub to their wayward daughter. She had married an almost-priest in a Catholic church, it only seemed fitting that her sullen parents give away her inheritance to the Baptists. The ploy was classic Isabella—showy, egotistical, and subtly cruel.

It took more than two years for Thomas to persuade his wife to see the positives of his plan to move, arguing most forcibly for the welfare of the children. Jacob had just turned seven and Anna was almost five. Both were past the critical ages of contracting deathly infant diseases but were in their prime ***formative*** years. Besides, he hoped that he and Charlotte would have more children and he was persuaded it would be easier for the family to move now before they came along. Unbeknownst to the couple, the family would soon grow with the addition of their second son Charles. Thomas was convinced that Jacob, Anna, and any future children needed space to roam and explore. On their own homestead the children could

Formative (**fawr**-muh-tiv) – ADJ – pertaining to formation or development

learn all kinds of skills that weren't available in the city. They could learn how to build a house, care for livestock, farm, and so on. Thomas was excited that he could teach Jacob how to hunt and Charlotte could show Anna how to garden, while ignoring that he didn't know how to hunt nor Charlotte how to garden. What better way to spend the rest of Charlotte's dowry than on a new life for their family. Thomas urged Charlotte to forget the past and the family that so coldly ***extruded*** her from them and to embrace a new future under the western sky. Eventually Charlotte relented, and the Watkins family packed up their belongings and left St. Louis for a new life, not knowing that it would sadly be cut short.

Anna soon became keenly aware of the end of the journey as the carriage came to a halt.They had reached their destination. Jacob and the driver climbed down from the rider's seat and made their way to where Anna and Charlie were standing. Four other men joined them and gently lifted one of the wooden boxes off the carriage bed and delicately placed it into a pre-dug hole in the ground. Then the men came for the one Anna still grasped. Jacob gave her a somber nod, signaling that the time had come to let it go. Hesitant, Anna withdrew herself from the carriage. Although only seventeen, that day Jacob looked far older. The anguish of the past several weeks had furrowed his brow, and the ***melancholy*** he wore on his face eclipsed all his youthful vitality. Sadness had stolen his naivety.

When both boxes rested safely in the ground the afternoon ceremony commenced. Father Andrews took his

---

Extrude (ik-**strood**) – V – to thrust out; force or press out; expel

Melancholy (**mel**-uhn-kol-ee) – N – a gloomy state of mind, especially when habitual or prolonged; depression

place at the front of the congregation and began his sermon, his voice ***declaiming*** his somber message. He spoke of life and death, sadness and hope. The minister challenged the melancholic group not to wallow in their sadness but to rejoice in the remembrance of those departed.

For weeks to come people would marvel over the wisdom of Father Andrews's speech, hailing it as a "mighty fine sermon." But from neither the day of the funeral nor any that came soon after would Anna remember a single thing that was uttered as the scene before her played out like a Grecian tragedy. Her swollen red eyes fixated on the chiseled ***epitaph*** that lay on the gravestone before her.

Here lies:
Thomas and Charlotte Watkins,
Beloved Father and Mother.
May God grant them Peace.

As the minister closed with his final prayer, the crowd began to dissipate. If it had been possible, Anna would have stayed in the graveyard forever, for she could not image going on without her parents. Thoughts of remorse, sadness, and guilt circled in her head. If only she hadn't told her mother that she hated the dress she had made for her; or rolled her eyes when her father told her the same ol' story of how he shot his first buck. Every fight, every mistake, every hateful thought came flooding back to her mind, followed by the memories

---

Declaim (dih-**kleym**) – V – to speak aloud in an oratorical manner; make a formal speech

Epitaph (**ep**-i-taf) – N – a commemorative inscription on a tomb or mortuary monument about the person buried at that site

of things she would never get to do again with her mother and father. There would be no more lazy Sunday afternoon walks after church. Never again could she help her mother in the kitchen, or run swiftly into the arms of her father for a great big bear hug. The last thought made Anna's eyes swell with tears. Just imagining the warmth of her father's strong arms wrapped around her was almost more than she could stand. Anna wanted to run, scream, sob, and forcefully express every emotion that was ***seething*** inside of her. Yet she remained still, paralyzed by her own grief.

Soon only three figures remained before Thomas and Charlotte's final resting place. The ***forlorn*** faces of the miserable children were fixed on where their parents had so recently been buried. The freshly dug graves with the newly cut tombstones seemed strange in such a desolate place. The richness of the overturned dirt starkly contrasted with the dullness of the rest of the grounds. Many of the other headstones were dirty or broken; Thomas and Charlotte's was shiny and unsullied. The distinction was remarkable. These other burial sites, now long forgotten, at one time had also been fresh wounds for their mourners. And like the others in the cemetery, the memory of Thomas and Charlotte's funeral would dull with time.

Jacob, who stood a head taller than Anna, moved closer to his other siblings. In a gesture to offer his grieving sister comfort, he gently put his arm around Anna's shoulder. However, Anna found no comforting ***solace*** in Jacob's embrace. His actions felt cold and mechanic.

Seethe (seeth) – V – to surge or foam as if boiling

Forlorn (fawr-**lawrn**) – ADJ – desolate or dreary; unhappy or miserable, as in feeling, condition, or appearance

Solace (**sol**-is) – N – something that gives comfort or relief

Since their parents' death, Anna had seen a new side of her older brother, one that made her shudder with disgust. To her, the new Jacob was virtually emotionless and unmoved by the passing of his mother and father. Yet Anna had mistaken Jacob's lack of tears for cold-heartedness. Blinded by her own uncontainable expression of her feelings, she could not see the evident sorrow he carried with him. As the eldest of the three, Jacob now bore the responsibility of looking after the young family. Whatever ***stoicism*** Anna perceived from Jacob was his attempt to put his own feelings aside and care for his younger siblings. Although Anna did not understand it then, Jacob recognized that he needed to be strong for her and Charlie. While he could never replace their parents, for the time being he was their only ***surrogate***, and he had big shoes to fill.

Perceptions have an odd way of distorting reality, and what Jacob had meant to help Anna instead was warped in her mind as something cold and harmful. As time passed, Anna grew angrier with her older brother. Unable to grasp Jacob's intentions, Anna continued to misread his actions. Thus, out of his stoicism grew ***dragon's teeth*** of lasting conflict. Like an ember among dry pieces of kindling, Anna's resentment toward Jacob sparked a small fire. If left unattended, her embitterment would soon engulf her.

"Come," said Jacob. "It is time to go home."

Stoicism (**stoh**-uh-siz-m) – N – a school of philosophy that teaches people should be free from passion and unmoved by joy or grief

Surrogate (**sur**-uh-geyt) – N – a person who acts in place of another

Dragon's teeth (**drag**-uhnz teeth) – N – the seeds of conflict

"*What home?*" thought Anna silently to herself. They had no home anymore. Without their parents, the cabin on the Wyoming property was just a shelter. It was a poor semblance of the life they had enjoyed for the past ten years. They had already sold the majority of their livestock to pay the exorbitant doctors' fees their parents' illnesses had accrued. Considering the Watkins family a bunch of ignorant ***rustics***, these specialists charged extra for their house calls in what they considered the outskirts of civilization. Over the six months her parents were seriously ill, Thomas and Charlotte had seen a total of four different doctors.

From the onset of her parents' illnesses, Anna had prayed ardently for some sort of magic ***elixir***, either from the doctors or God, to make the sickness disappear. However, instead of remedies, the Watkins children received more physicians and their bills. Anna's petitions remained unanswered. The last doctor finally identified the disease which ferociously assaulted Anna's parents' immune systems as Consumption. Even with the diagnosis the doctor couldn't explain why only the parents and not the children had caught the horrible disease. By the time the doctor finally arrived at a diagnosis, the only thing he could do was make Thomas and Charlotte comfortable as they awaited the inevitable. The inevitable came three weeks later.

Once all the bills were paid, the only possessions the Watkins family had left were the property, the cabin, and Thomas Watkins' prize stallion which he had won in a gambling match. Named Samson, for his incredible

---

Rustic (**ruhs**-tik) – N – an unsophisticated country person

Elixir (ih-**lik**-ser) – N – a panacea; cure-all; sovereign remedy strength and beauty, the horse was treated more as a beloved house pet than a barn animal. Samson was a remarkable creature. Even when the money began to get tight at the Watkins' homestead, Thomas was unable to part with the beautiful black and white horse.

It was dusk when the Watkins children returned to their small cabin. The long walk from the cemetery to the Watkins' property had been a tumultuous one. Although the storm had passed over without a single drop of rain, remnants of the turbulent weather lingered. By the evening, the wind had amassed into a gale and Anna had to fight to keep from being thrown backwards. Charlie, long since exhausted from the day's undertaking, slept peacefully in her arms. This ensured that the task of walking was that much more daunting. Jacob soldiered on before them. They made the journey in silence. Nothing either Jacob or Anna could say would ease the burden which had befallen them. All they could do was walk one step at a time. Jacob was the first to arrive on the porch, followed shortly by Anna and her precious cargo. Fatigued, they quietly entered their house. Although neither said it, they both had the same thought–tonight would be their first night as orphans.

WORD REVIEW

Abject
Absolve
Abysmal
Admonish
Aegis
Affluence
Agrarian
Ambrosia
Amorphous
Arcadia
Benediction
Circumspect
Compelling
Concert
Connubial
Corroborate
Countermand
Croesus
Curmudgeon
Cyclopean
Decalogue
Declaim
Dipsomaniac
Dragon's Teeth
Dryad
Elixir
Epitaph
Expostulate
Extramurally
Extrude
Forlorn
Formative
Holistic
Hypochondriac
Melancholy
Panacea
Rustic
Sanctum
Seethe
Solace
Stoicism
Surrogate

2

A CARELESS MISTAKE

Mornings on the prairie always started early. The self-sufficient nature of the West required settlers to make the most out of their days. The morning following the funeral was no different. Although there would be a melancholy sense of ***gravitas*** to each task, chores still needed to be done. Regardless of Anna's feelings, the earth didn't stop spinning. The night had been restless for Anna, so when 5:30 rolled around she was already wide awake. The sounds of morning filled her room as she quietly lay in bed. She heard the back door open and close; no doubt Jacob was on his way out to gather water from their well. She heard birds chirping outside her window. The gaiety of the lark made her stomach turn. Unable to bring herself to get up, Anna threw the covers back over her head hoping that she might be able to wake from this terrible nightmare. Ten minutes passed before Anna slowly uncovered herself from the blankets. She inquisitively looked around to see if anything was different. Much to her dissatisfaction everything remained the same. There was no horrible dream to wake up from, this was her life. Sad ***plight*** or not, she had to find the energy to get out of bed.

Gravitas — (**grav**-i-tahs) – N – seriousness or sobriety, as of conduct or speech

Plight — (plahyt) – N – a condition, state, or situation, especially an unfavorable or unfortunate one

Anna found that strength when she glanced down at a small bundle on her floor. In the corner slept Charlie on a small, improvised bed. Because of his age, the toddler used to sleep with his parents. However, he was moved into Anna's room after their parents' sickness got worse instead of better. As evidenced by the haphazardness of the little cot, Charlie's bed in the corner was never meant to be a permanent solution. Charlie had protested at first, but the doctors insisted that a toddler in the bed was by no means conducive to a swift recovery. So off Charlie went to Anna's room where it was easier for her to look after him. Had Thomas and Charlotte known they had only a few months to live, they would have chosen to do things differently. Over the last several months Anna had taken over full responsibility for the tiny tyrant. She made sure that he was washed, dressed, and fed every day. Some days he worked with her, but most days he didn't. Charlie wasn't necessarily a bad child; he was just strong-willed. Even at three he knew exactly what he wanted and fought hard to get it. Although he was stubborn and ***intractable*** when awake, Anna had grown very close to her little brother. Even when he was at his worst, Charlie could get himself out of trouble with his infectious smile and sparkling green eyes. One could only stay mad at him for a short while.

Like her, Charlie had a head full of curls, but instead of golden blond, they were amber brown. Charlie's coloring resembled both his father's and Jacob's. It was unusual to see Charlie with curls, because their mother typically kept his hair very short and neat. After all, she had been raised Baptist, and a man with long hair was unheard of. Like most

---

Intractable (in-**trak**-tuh-buhl) – ADJ – not easily controlled or directed; not docile or manageable

other things, however, the illness had dramatically altered the way hygiene and appearances were managed around the Watkins' home. Anna made a mental note that she would soon have to attempt tidying up Charlie's locks. That is how Mother would have wanted it.

Anna gave herself five minutes longer to stay in bed. Then she would offer her ***succor*** in attending to the morning chores, and Jacob was likely already frustrated by her prolonged absence. Soon Anna arose from her self-made cocoon. Careful not to wake up Charlie, Anna gently folded her blankets back and placed her feet on the floor. As quietly as she could, Anna gathered her belongings and left her room behind. She had succeeded in her first task of the day—keeping Charlie unmoved by her proceedings.

Once on the other side of the door, Anna tripled her speed. Moving to and fro, she attempted to make up for her lost time. The faster she went, she reasoned, the more effective she would appear to Jacob. Even to her, the fallacies in her logic were glaring; however the self-delusion made her feel better. In reality, it didn't matter whether or not Anna went fast or slow that morning for Jacob had long left the house to take care of some family business in town. He went by foot so the journey would take the better part of the morning. Had he taken Samson, the trip would have been a lot quicker, but he found it senseless to use their only good horse for a journey that could easily be done with walking. The time alone would help him clear his head, allowing him to tackle the bothersome duties that come with the deaths of loved ones. Wills needed to be taken care of, deeds signed over, and financial responsi-

---

Succor (**suhk**-er) – N – help; relief; aid; assistance

bilities turned over to him. As Jacob would soon find out, death brings not only sadness but also an insurmountable number of errands.

It didn't take long for Anna to realize that Jacob was no longer in the vicinity. Her speed slowed, but her motivation to be efficient remained the same. The outside chores needed to get done, but first she took a few moments to ***plait*** her hair in a single braid to keep the curls out of her face while she bustled around. Then Anna grabbed her jacket and work boots and headed straight to the barn which was set several yards behind the house. Although it wasn't a particularly long distance, on certain frigid mornings Anna swore she walked a full ***furlong*** to get there. This was one of those mornings. The wind remained sharp from the previous day and the sun had not yet risen from its cloudy bed. The darkness of the morning made the distance between the house and the barn seem that much longer. Once again Anna quickened her speed.

The temperature inside the barn was not much warmer than outside, but the absence of the wind was welcome. Upon entering the large stable, Anna lit the gas lamps that hung around the barn. The lamps produced only a foggy glow, but gave Anna enough light to complete her work. She turned to the side mow to grab a bundle of hay that had been put aside for Samson's breakfast. In the past she would have needed three to feed all of the horses, but now one was more than enough. Along the way to feed Samson she passed several empty stalls where the various livestock had once been housed. The soft flicker of

---

Plait (pleyt) – V – to braid something, especially of hair or straw

Furlong (**fur**-lawng) – N – a unit of distance that is equal to 220 yards

the sparse lantern light illuminated the hollowness of the Watkins' barn. This ghost-like appearance was unnatural. Since the day the barn had been completed, it was Anna's responsibility to take care of the morning feeding. A once raucous place full of animal sounds now was filled with silence. Occasionally Anna heard muffled noises coming from the back of the barn reminding her that she had a purpose for carrying the bundle of hay.

Despite the need to sell off the rest of the livestock, Samson was not alone in the barn. Quietly lying in the next stall was a smaller than average milk cow, whom Anna affectionately called Dolly. Dolly did not belong to the Watkins, but was a ***gratuitous*** loan from Mr. Forrester, the dairy farmer in town. Although Mr. Forrester had never personally met the Watkins before he lent them Dolly, after hearing of their misfortunes he felt it was his Christian duty to offer a helping hand. He wasn't a man of exorbitant wealth—he himself had only a dozen milk cows—but he knew he could spare one of his younger cows to assist a family in need. In this time of extreme trial Dolly had been an unmistakably gracious blessing. Mr. Forrester had made it quite clear that she was at their disposal for however long she was needed; it was a fact that he had reinforced to Jacob at the funeral. Mr. Forrester showed through his generous gift that he was indeed a kind ***benefactor***.

Upon reaching Samson's stall, Anna quickly set to work starting with the most unpleasant task, which was clearing out the soiled straw. Anna loved working with the beautiful horse, but absolutely hated this grimy aspect of

---

Gratuitous (gruh-**too**-i-tuhs) – ADJ – given, done, bestowed, or obtained without charge or payment; free; voluntary

Benefactor (**ben**-uh-fak-ter) – N – a person who confers a benefit; kindly helper

the job. Holding her breath as she worked, Anna imagined pleasant distractions to make the job go faster. Once the hardest task was done she could enjoy feeding, watering, and brushing Samson. It was enough motivation for her to finish in record time. Anna soon completed her duties with Samson and went on to take care of Dolly. Initially skittish upon her arrival, Dolly had grown very comfortable in the Watkins' barn and had developed a fondness for Anna. At the Forrester's farm Dolly had just been another milk cow, and not a very productive cow at that. While Mr. Forrester was never mean to Dolly, Anna was able to give her undivided attention. Anna liked Dolly, and it appeared that Dolly understood it, for she wouldn't let any other member of the Watkins family milk her.

That morning Dolly was especially excited to see Anna. With all that had been going on over the past couple of days, Anna had been unable to milk Dolly properly. Dolly was antsy and could barely wait for Anna to sit down. More than once the poor cow kicked over Anna's bucket before she got a chance to start. While Dolly normally did not produce a ***cornucopia*** of milk, today's output nearly overflowed Anna's container. With two fewer mouths to feed, Anna would have to work quickly to use all of the milk. She would need to make butter, cheese, and perhaps even have enough for some sweet cream. With Dolly's bounty, the day was starting to look up.

Anna could barely close the lid of the milk pail when she was finished. Dolly, who seemed satisfied with her work, lumbered away to lie down in the corner. Anna removed both the bucket and her stool from the cow's stall.

Cornucopia (kawr-nuh-**koh**-pee-uh) – N – an abundance of something good

She would let Dolly rest awhile before she took her out to graze in the pasture. Closing the stall door behind her, she left Dolly to herself. Anna's milk container was far heavier than the bundle of hay she had moved around earlier. She attempted to carry it with one hand but soon found that it was a task that required two. Several times she almost dropped the container, nearly spilling its contents. She would pick it up only to quickly set it back down again, unable to get a good grasp. Full of milk, the bucket seemed to weigh fifty pounds. While contemplating the best way to bring the container back to the house, Anna decided to make an ***extemporaneous*** visit back to Samson, who had been curiously watching her as she struggled with her cargo. Leaving the bucket, Anna grabbed a handful of oats as a special treat for the horse. Like Dolly, he too had been neglected over the past several days and Anna wanted to give him some extra attention.

Carefully opening the door, Anna eased her way back into the small area that housed the beautiful horse. Caution was always needed when entering Samson's stall. Anna had once made the mistake of opening the door widely and having the mighty horse push past her and run out of the barn. On the reins Samson was a gentle giant, but off them he could be as wild as a mustang. Anna had almost no hope of catching the beast once he got past her. Samson loved his freedom so much that Thomas had installed a special latch to keep the strong horse in his stall. That morning Samson didn't try to fight to pass Anna. Instead he quietly backed up, allowing her to effortlessly come into the stall. Anna rarely returned in the mornings after cleaning the pen, and her presence suggested she

---

Extemporaneous (ik-stem-puh-**rey**-nee-uhs) – ADJ – impromptu

had something special. He eyed Anna's closed palm with intense curiosity. Slowly Anna opened her palm to reveal the tasty oats. Samson instinctively responded by stretching his head toward her open palm. He nearly inhaled the treats. Standing next to Samson, Anna enjoyed the gentle whimpers of the excited horse. The huffs and puffs he made while he ate were ***euphonious***, and made Anna chuckle softly. What an odd creature she thought to herself. This ***behemoth***, who was ten times her size, was tenderly eating out the palm of her hands. Samson had more than enough strength to crush her with one swift kick, yet he was docile enough to let her stroke his mane. It really was an incredible thing to think about. In that moment Anna felt both unbelievably powerful and exceptionally small.

Anna knew she couldn't stay long with Samson. Her chores in the barn usually took about an hour, and Charlie was due to wake any minute. Brushing her hands of oat dust and Samson saliva Anna rushed out of the stall. She quickly grabbed her bucket, which hadn't gotten any lighter, and waddled her way back toward the house. The-three year-old would be terribly frightened if he awoke in the house alone. In an effort to hurry back to Charlie, Anna forgot to secure Samson's special latch. Unfortunately for Anna, that latch was the only thing that would ***forestall*** an escape attempt from Samson. However, her mind was elsewhere as she raced to beat Charlie's awakening.

Anna had just made it into the kitchen with her

Euphonious	(yoo-**foh**-nee-uhs) – ADJ – pleasant in sound; agreeable to the ear
Behemoth	(bih-**hee**-muhth) – N – any creature or thing of monstrous size or power
Forestall	(fohr-**stawl**) – V – to prevent, hinder, or thwart by action in advance

container full of milk when she heard the robust calls of her younger brother.

"Mommy!" called out Charlie.

Rushing to put the container out of the way, Anna stowed the milk in the corner.

"MOMMY!" continued Charlie.

"I am coming," yelled back Anna.

Anna entered her bedroom to find a very alert Charlie ***bristled*** up in a standing position on top of the covers. He was in his underwear. At some point in the night he had thrown off both his shirt and pants. Like most toddlers, Charlie found it rather confining to wear clothes. He continued to cry out in a loud voice.

"Mommy!"

"I am here," replied Anna.

"You're not my mommy," replied Charlie bluntly.

Anna was speechless, and didn't know how to respond. Charlie was right; she wasn't his mommy, but she was the best he was going to get.

"Well, I am the one who is here," said Anna.

"But I don't want you. I want Mommy," continued Charlie.

Standing as tall as when Anna had first come in, Charlie stubbornly continued to call out for his mother. Anna didn't have the heart to explain the truth, but she also didn't have the energy to tackle his stubbornness. It was obvious by the way he was acting that today everything with Charlie would be a battle. Wanting to curtail his ***belligerence*** before it became an all-out war, Anna decided

---

Bristle (**bris**-uhl) – V – to be visibly roused or stirred (usually followed by up)

Belligerence (buh-**lij**-er-uhns) – N – a warlike or aggressively hostile nature, condition, or attitude

to sidestep the whole mommy discussion and to distract the small child.

"Hey, Charlie," began Anna. "Did you know that we have strawberry jam?"

"Really!?"

"Yeah, and if you hurry to the table you can have some with your bread for breakfast."

Anna's distraction worked. With glee Charlie jumped off his covers, still only in his undergarments, and raced toward the kitchen table. Anna knew that sooner or later she would have to explain the situation to the toddler, but now wasn't the time. Right now he was content with the thought of having fresh strawberry jam on his bread and Anna was happy that she was able to ***circumnavigate*** the unpleasant conversation with her distraction. Breathing a sigh of relief, Anna followed the bouncing child into the kitchen.

Now physically circumnavigating the toys he had left on the floor, Charlie made it to his favorite stool in just a matter of seconds. Climbing up by himself, he impatiently tapped his fingers on the table, signaling to Anna that he was clearly ready for his breakfast. Anna couldn't have been more than a minute behind Charlie, but to a child of only three it felt like an eternity. Ignoring the eager looks from her younger brother, Anna went straight to the cupboard to pull out the sole jar of homemade strawberry jam that was hidden in the back like a buried treasure. Anna almost hated the thought of opening the jar; it was the last of the preserves their mother had made the previous summer. Upon moving

---

Circumnavigate (sur-kuhm-**nav**-i-geyt) – V – to go or maneuver around

to Wyoming, Charlotte Watkins had begun to dabble in ***horticulture***, achieving some success with her planting and harvest. Over the years she became rather good. Without fail, every year her small garden could always produce a crop of delicious summer fruits, which she would promptly turn into an assortment of delectable jams and jellies. These never lasted long in the Watkins' house, regardless of whether Charlotte had made a few or a few dozen. Knowing that her children had a penchant for sweets, the sagacious mother soon began to hide a handful of jars in the cupboard for later consumption. This way the family could enjoy the jams year-round, and not just during the last months of summer. It did not take long for Jacob and Anna to recognize their mother's cunning. However, they enjoyed the seemingly never-ending supply of homemade jams too much to compromise her hiding spots.

Now Anna held in her hand the last jar of preserves her mother would ever make. Tucked away safely in the back of the cupboard, this strawberry jam was both a sweet reminder of Anna's past and a sour foreshadowing of her future. She was conflicted between opening the jar and enjoying the delicacy, and hiding it away to save it. Nothing she did would change the fact that it would be the last batch from her mother. Anna couldn't even harvest this year's crops because her mother hadn't been able to plant any. ***Immured*** inside her bed because of the illness, Charlotte had missed her favorite time of the year. Tears rolled down Anna's cheeks as she contemplated the consequences of simply opening a can of preserves. Opening or

---

Horticulture (**hawr**-ti-kuhl-cher) – N – the cultivation of a garden, orchard, or nursery

Immure (ih-**myoor**) – V – to shut in; seclude or confine

not opening the jar wouldn't dramatically alter any part of the Watkins children's lives, but the jam still held a sense of significance. Hesitantly putting the jar back into the cupboard Anna turned to look at Charlie. Wiggling with excitement, he could hardly wait for his breakfast. The only thing that the small boy had on his mind was the savory taste of strawberry jam. Anna couldn't disappoint him. The jam had been made in love to be enjoyed. While it might have made her feel a little bit better to hang on to the small memento of her past, in doing so Anna would miss out on the intended enjoyment of it. Perhaps, she thought to herself, she could find another way to keep the memory of her mother forever alive. So with a firm resolve Anna pried off the tin lid.

"Pop" sounded the lid. At the noise Charlie squealed with joy. Anna removed the sealing wax and took a moment to smell the freshness of the homemade jam. It smelled exactly like it had the day her mother first made it. She was sure it would taste even better. Grabbing the butter knife and two slices of bread, Anna made Charlie's breakfast. It didn't take long for the toddler to devour all that was set before him. Soon his hands and face were pink. When he was finished, Charlie looked up at his sister with a self-satisfied strawberry smile. Smiling back at Charlie, Anna handed him a tall glass of fresh cow's milk. The warm drink went perfectly with the toast and jam. Looking at the joyful Charlie, Anna instantly knew that opening the jar was the right decision.

After breakfast, Anna did not have to convince Charlie that he needed to wash up. Charlie might have been a free spirit when it came to whether or not he liked wearing clothes, but he was a stickler for being clean. He loved everything about strawberry jam, including making a mess with it, but he hated the sticky feeling it left on his skin. As soon as he was done he climbed down and went straight for the wash bucket; leaving behind a trail of strawberry handprints for Anna to clean up. Once she got Charlie settled, Anna started on the other household chores.

It was around midday when Anna remembered that she still hadn't let Dolly out of the barn. Feeling a little guilty for forgetting the poor animal, Anna gathered her rope and work boots. Not wanting the cow to suffer from ***dystrophy***, Anna made her way to the barn to let Dolly out to graze. Charlie was down for his afternoon nap and she had the opportunity to take the time to let the cow into the pasture for a while. Halfway to the barn Anna noticed a peculiar sight. The barn door was wide open. Thinking back over the morning, Anna remembered that in her rush to get the milk to the house before Charlie woke up, she had forgotten to close the door. While leaving the barn door open wasn't the wisest idea, especially in the winter when the cold wind could be dangerous for the animals, it wasn't the worst mistake she could have made.

As soon as Anna arrived inside the barn she realized her ***flagrant*** mistake. Upon reaching the end of the barn she saw a ghastly sight. Like the barn door, the door to Samson's stall was wide open. It would have been one thing if just his door had been opened, or just the barn door, but together they afforded Samson the gateway to his freedom. Exchanging Dolly's rope for Samson's bridle, Anna dashed outside the barn. Panicked because she didn't see the

---

Dystrophy (**dis**-truh-fee) – N – a condition caused by inadequate nutrition

Flagrant (**fley**-gruhnt) – ADJ – shockingly noticeable or evident; obvious; glaring

horse, Anna was ***frenetic.*** She had no idea where Samson had gone, or even what time he had gotten out. The sky was still dark when she had left the barn that morning, and now the sun was high in the sky. Samson had a possible six hour head start on her. Nevertheless she had to try to find him. At that moment, Anna needed her older brother and vehemently wished he hadn't gone away that morning. He would have known what to do. She had no idea when Jacob would return; it was more than likely he would be gone the entire day and not come back until late in the evening. If she waited for him, chances were she would never find Samson. Thankfully, Charlie had just gone down for his nap, which gave Anna a good two hours to search for the lost horse. It wasn't long, but she had to try and find the runaway stallion.

Not knowing where to start, Anna decided to search the periphery of the house. Samson loved to eat, so it seemed logical to check the garden and the pasture first. Hopefully Samson's stomach had lured him somewhere Anna could catch him. Anna ran back and forth to every spot a troublemaking horse could go. She checked the garden—nothing; next the compost—still nothing. She went to the well and fields. Anna called and called. There was no answer. As time passed Anna grew more and more panicked. There was no sign of him anywhere. A ***battery*** of questions filled Anna's mind. *What would she do if she couldn't find him? What if he were hurt and she couldn't help him? What would Jacob say?* These questions circled around her head like a Midwest tornado. She went back and forth

---

Frenetic (fruh-**net**-ik) – ADJ – frantic; frenzied

Battery (**bat**-uh-ree) – N – any large group or series of related things

from silently praying for help to cursing herself for entering Samson's stall this morning. The guilt of her mistake was ***incisive***, cutting straight to her very core. Samson was the only animal they had left to their family name. He had been their father's most prized possession, so much that even on his deathbed Thomas refused to sell him. She had lost him in a moment of carelessness. The weight of her blunder made her sick.

Anna ran so fast up and down the property that the scenery began to blur. She had never covered so much ground in such a short amount of time. Breathless from all the running and shouting, she stopped to compose herself. Her head was spinning as hot nausea filled her stomach. Her feet throbbed with pain from the blisters. She hadn't bothered to put stockings on and her work boots ***galled*** her feet.

After nearly two hours of searching, Anna had to give up her quest. Samson was gone. Dejected, she made her way back toward the house, where no doubt Charlie would be getting up from his nap. She had accomplished nothing in that time except to increase her feelings of guilt and prove that she should be ***inculpated*** for the loss of Samson. Exhausted and drenched in sweat, Anna returned home frightened to face her older brother.

Incisive	(in-**sahy**-siv) – ADJ – penetrating; cutting; biting; trenchant
Gall	(gawl) – V – to make sore by rubbing
Inculpate	(**in**-kuhl-peyt) – V – to charge with fault; blame; accuse

WORD REVIEW

Battery
Behemoth
Belligerence
Benefactor
Bristle
Circumnavigate
Cornucopia
Dystrophy
Euphonious
Extemporaneous
Flagrant
Forestall
Frenetic
Furlong
Gall
Gratuitous
Gravitas
Horticulture
Immure
Incisive
Inculpate
Intractable
Plait
Plight
Succor

3

A DAY IN TOWN

The anxious afternoon turned into an apprehensive evening. It was well past seven; Anna sat on the floor playing with wooden blocks with Charlie. The day's supper sat cold on the table. Charlie had long since eaten, but Anna waited patiently for Jacob to return. As the hours passed, she practiced and rehearsed her explanation of the morning's events. Anna had developed a rationalization deflecting her culpability, but it was not complete. Nothing she could say would exculpate her, but she hoped to ease the strife Samson's disappearance would bring. Over and over again she silently practiced her speech, all the while trying to suppress the nausea in her stomach.

Oblivious to his sister's anxiety, Charlie blithely played with the wooden blocks on the floor. Anna would build a tower with the blocks, and then Charlie would promptly knock it down. Charlie wasn't so much interested in the building aspect of the game as he was in the demolition. Anna enjoyed the mindlessness of it all. Charlie was entertained, and she was able to concentrate on something else.

It was nearly eight when a sound of galloping hooves could be heard in the distance, arousing the pair from their play. Anna was getting ready to put Charlie to bed when she heard the noise. Fear grabbed her. The sound of an approaching horse during the afternoon signified the visit of a friend, but the noise of racing hooves in the evening indicated trouble. Either some stranger was quickly approaching the cabin, or something was wrong with Jacob. As Anna was only 15 she felt unable to handle either situation alone. However, Anna had something else to worry about. Before she could tell Charlie to go wait in the bedroom, he had sprung from the floor and rushed straight for the door. Charlie knew no fear, and to him nobody was a stranger. In his mind the sound of someone approaching was always something to get excited about. His view of humanity was ***pristine***, not yet blemished by experience. Not knowing any better, he rushed to the foot of the porch and waited with the front door wide open.

Anna quickly followed Charlie, horrified at the sight of the three-year-old standing there defenseless. She looked first to Charlie and then toward the figure he was so intensely gawking at. The sun was just setting over the pasture, and the sky was painted a rainbow of red, gold, and orange. Despite the darkness of the setting sun, Anna could clearly see the ***Olympian*** figure—there Jacob sat nobly on the back of Samson. Anna was dumbfounded. She rubbed her eyes twice just to make sure that she was really seeing what she was seeing. Sure enough, there in front of her was the lost horse.

Soon Jacob arrived at the front of the house and Charlie ran up to meet him. Anna followed, her mind full of questions. She desperately wanted to ask Jacob where and how he had come across the horse, but the ***deprecating*** look on his face advised otherwise. Jacob might not have known the exact story of how Samson got out of his stall,

---

Pristine (pris-**teen**) – ADJ – having its original purity; uncorrupted or unsullied

Olympian (uh-**lim**-pee-uhn) – ADJ – majestic

Deprecate (**dep**-ri-keyt) – V – to express earnest disapproval of

but he intuitively knew who was at fault for his escape. Choosing not to test her older brother, Anna stepped back from the horse, allowing Jacob to secure him in the barn. Now was not the time for questions; now was the time to be thankful that both Jacob and Samson were home safely.

When Jacob returned from the barn, he said goodnight to Charlie. It was late and Jacob was feeling ***lethargic*** after the exertion of his afternoon adventures. Anna took charge and put Charlie to bed. Jacob stirred the fire in the stove and began to warm up supper. It had been several hours since Jacob had last eaten, and he was anxious to try Anna's venison stew. Jacob would have eaten dinner cold if he hadn't had to ride home in the evening wind. Warm stew was just what he needed to relax and let the stress of his day slowly melt away.

Dinner was back on the table, piping hot, by the time Anna was finished with Charlie. Jacob had already ladled himself a large bowl of stew when she sat down at the table to join him. Anna longed to ask Jacob about his day. It had to be interesting. He had gone into town to take care of their parents' affairs and returned home with a missing steed. There had to be a story to tell. Story or not, Jacob remained silent. After a day of tedious errands, he was happy to sit in the quiet. So for the remainder of their meal there was only silence.

Jacob put his bowl down after he had finished his third helping. Normally he would not have eaten so many servings. However, the events of the day had made his hunger ***autonomous***, taking on a life of its own. Satisfied

---

Lethargic (luh-**thahr**-jik) – ADJ – drowsy; sluggish
Autonomous (aw-**ton**-uh-muhs) – ADJ – not subject to control from outside

with the peaceful dinner, he was now ready to tell Anna the tale she had been longing to hear. Knowing that Anna was only interested in the ending, Jacob decided to start at the beginning. This way she would pay attention to the entire story. So he began, leaving the part where he caught the ***fractious*** Samson until the end.

"It was still dark out when I left the house this morning," Jacob began. "I think you were still in bed and I tried not to wake Charlie. I know what a bother he can be when you are trying to get chores done. Since you were going to be alone all day, I left Samson here. That way if there was an emergency you could get into town quicker."

The mention of Jacob's leaving Samson in her care made Anna tense. She expected the next words out of Jacob's mouth to be some form of criticism or rebuke. She quickly remembered her rehearsed explanation to help Jacob understand what had really happened. There was no need. Jacob didn't yell or even comment on the events that had passed; he simply continued on with his tale.

"I made it into town around eight," said Jacob. "Most of the businesses that I needed to visit were still closed so I walked over to the general store. Mr. Daniels had just opened up, so I went in to hear the latest news in town. He asked about you and Charlie, and how we were doing since the funeral. It was a just small talk, but it was nice of him to ask. Oh, that reminds me. Mr. Daniels wanted to know if you would let his little Andrew come over to play with Charlie. It seems he is driving Mrs. Daniels some kind of crazy, and she could use some time by herself."

Anna nodded in agreement, not really caring about the Daniels or setting up some play for Charlie.

Fractious (**frak**-shuhs) – ADJ – refractory or unruly

"Good," continued Jacob.

"Where all did you need to go?" asked Anna, hoping to hurry the story along.

"Everywhere," answered Jacob. "Mom and Dad had business all over town that needed tending to."

Prolonging Anna's anguish wasn't exactly the nicest thing Jacob could have done to his sister, but he felt a little bit justified since she was the one who had lost the horse. She could wait a little bit longer. Jacob even thought it might be fun to ***digress*** from time to time just to keep the story going.

"I left Mr. Daniels a little after nine to head to the bank. Although I was the only one there at that time, I still had to wait 30 minutes before I could meet with our parents' banker."

The bank which Jacob was referring to had long had a reputation of being slow. When their father was alive he often came home with similar stories of the inordinate amounts of time he spent waiting for the bank managers. Thomas Watkins often attributed the slowness of the service to the ***gerontocracy*** of the aged bank managers. Jacob had inherited his father's sarcasm in his storytelling. He went on to describe the process of changing over their parents' accounts into his name. Although it seemed like a simple task, it took over three hours for the process to finalize. If Jacob thought changing over the bank accounts was a hassle, the process of signing over the Watkins' land deed was a nightmare. Despite the fact that everyone in town knew the elder Watkins had passed away, Jacob had to sign

---

Digress (dih-**gres**) – V – to deviate or wander away from the main topic

Gerontocracy (jer-uhn-**tok**-ruh-see) – N – a governing body consisting of old people

paper after paper proving that he was indeed the heir to the Watkins' estate. At one point the whole process came to a halt when the bank teller asked Jacob for his parents' death certificates. Given that the funeral had only been the day before, Jacob hadn't received them. Nothing else could be accomplished until he left and got a signed paper from the local judge stating clearly that both Thomas and Charlotte Watkins were indeed dead. The slow, step-by-step ***gradation*** of the entire system was enough to drive anyone crazy.

"They acted like I had made up the whole death of our parents," remarked Jacob.

"What did you do?" asked Anna.

"The only thing I could do," replied Jacob. "I left the bank and went to the courthouse. Of course by the time I left the bank it was already noon and the judge was out to lunch. So I went and grabbed somethin' to eat at Elba's. When I was finished I went back to the courthouse."

"Was the judge there when you went back?" asked Anna.

"No, but I only had to wait about 10 minutes before he came in," replied Jacob.

When Jacob left the courthouse he was in better spirits than when he had arrived. Judge Weston was far more congenial than the bankers and Jacob was in and out of his office in no time. With all the right papers in hand, Jacob headed back toward the bank. He made it about halfway to his destination when he came upon a boisterous

---

Gradation (grey-**dey**-shuhn) – N – any process or change taking place through a series of stages, by degrees, or in a gradual manner

fracas in the street. A couple dozen people stood before him making a to-do about something. The commotion had gotten the attention of everyone in town. Curious, Jacob approach the small crowd to see what was going on.

"I couldn't see anything from where I was standing," said Jacob. "So I had to push my way through the crowd. And do you know what I saw when I got to the other side?"

"What?" asked Anna.

"Samson running back and forth down the street like a moonstruck horse," replied Jacob. "And I thought to myself, how on earth did he get there?"

Anna blushed. She felt embarrassed for a number of reasons. The most obvious was for letting Samson out in the first place, but secondly she blushed because Jacob had found Samson before she even knew he had gone missing, a fact she would not share with her older brother.

"Sure enough, the crowd had formed because the old oaf was causing a ruckus," said Jacob. "You know how he gets when he doesn't have a bridle on. He acts like Charlie when he's gotten into mama's stash of sugar candy. With his size and speed, no one was able to catch 'm."

Anna knew all too well how both Charlie and Samson acted when they had their freedom. She could just imagine Samson ***cavorting*** back and forth down Main Street, taunting anyone who tried to stop him. With every failed capture attempt, Samson only proved that he was more cunning than the townsfolk. Samson might have been crafty, but Jacob knew all of his tricks. After all, this wasn't his first time to go after the free-spirited horse.

Fracas (**frey**-kuhs) – N – a noisy, disorderly disturbance or fight; riotous brawl; uproar

Cavort (kuh-**vawrt**) – V – to prance or caper about

Samson was smart, and Jacob would have to find just the right moment to strike. There were still things to get done, and Jacob didn't have the time to play cat and mouse with the horse.

"The right moment came when I noticed Samson eying the watering trough in front of Mr. Daniels' store," continued Jacob.

"Did you sneak up behind him?" asked Anna.

"No," replied Jacob, "I jumped on top of him."

Anna was confused, and her puzzled look made Jacob chuckle. Jacob knew that sneaking up behind the horse would never work. Samson was keenly aware of what was going on behind him. So in a moment of ***derring-do***, Jacob had climbed on top of Mr. Daniels' store and jumped on the back of Samson. Had Jacob truly thought about what he was about to do, he probably wouldn't have done it. Jacob was almost as surprised as Samson when he actually landed on the horse. The successful jump incurred great ***acclamation*** from the approving crowd. Shouts and applauds came from all around. It took a few minutes for Jacob to calm the excited Samson, who was bucking and snorting rowdily because of the rider's sudden appearance. With calm words and a controlled presence Jacob was able to reassure the animal. Soon Jacob could ride proudly around the circle of spectators on the back of a well-behaved steed. Samson happily pranced to and fro basking in all the attention.

With Samson under control, Jacob was presented with a new dilemma. Samson was free of a bridle, and the

---

Derring-do	(der-ing-**doo**) – N – daring deeds; heroic daring
Acclamation	(ak-luh-**mey**-shuhn) – N – a loud shout or other demonstration of welcome, goodwill, or approval

moment Jacob jumped off the horse Samson would have his independence again. The shrewd horse would only once be fooled into submission by a surprise attack. Naturally, Jacob could have simply ridden Samson back home, but to do so would lose half of his day to travel, and he still had things to get done. However, if Jacob were to get off the horse, he would lose Samson. Jacob faced a quandary.

"Mr. Daniels would have gladly lent me a bridle," explained Jacob. "But he was fresh out and wasn't going to get any more until his next shipment of wares. He was out of rope, too, on account of the last big band of settlers who just left town. They had purchased everything that could even remotely resemble a bridle."

"Did you borrow one from the other townspeople?" asked Anna.

"By the time I realized I needed one it was too late to ask anyone because most of the crowd had ***dissipated***," answered Jacob. "Those who were left didn't have anything with them. I finally spoke with old man Gerald, who said he had a spare one in his barn and would fetch it for me."

"That was nice of him," replied Anna.

"Nice, yes, but it took the man forever to get the thing. Old man Gerald is probably sixty, but he walks like he is a hundred. I waited nearly half an hour on Samson's back for him to return before I realized that the bank would soon close."

It was Friday and the bank closed early for the weekend and wouldn't be open again until Monday morning. Having walked all that way, Jacob did not want to have to return home without completing his mission at

---

Dissipate (**dis**-uh-peyt) – V – to scatter in various directions; disperse; dispel

the bank. He also wouldn't have been able to finish any of his other errands in town without the necessary paperwork from the bank. The hassle of the proper paperwork was the ***bane*** of his entire day.

"What did you do?" inquired Anna.

"The only thing I could do," replied Jacob. "I rode Samson into the bank. You should have seen the bank manager's face when I arrived at his office on the back of Samson. They had to hold all of the paperwork up to me so I could sign it. Serves them right too for making me jump through all of those hoops. And when I was done, I casually rode him back out."

Jacob ***delineated*** the events perfectly, in vivid words that brought the day's events to life. Anna could just imagine the look on the bank manager's face when her brother rode a horse into his building. The whole scene was quite comical and she burst into laughter. Jacob was the type of person who never met a problem he couldn't solve. While some of his solutions were rather unorthodox, Jacob always got the task done.

"Once I left the bank, old man Gerald returned with the bridle," continued Jacob. So I was able to tie up Samson in front of Mr. Daniels' store and finish the tasks that needed to get done. Once I was finished with my errands, Samson and I headed home."

"Well, I am glad everything worked out all right," replied Anna.

Anna's comment referred to Jacob's encounter with the bank manager, but unknowingly she had opened up

---

Bane (beyn) – N – a person or thing that ruins or spoils

Delineate (dih-**lin**-ee-yet) – V – to trace the outline of; sketch or trace in outline; to portray in words

the one subject she had meant to avoid: Samson's escape. The smile on Jacob's face disappeared and he looked at his sister with seriousness. Not wanting to ***carp*** about Anna's mistake, Jacob approached the subject delicately.

"I am sure you didn't mean to let him out," began Jacob, "and I don't really want to know how it happened, but given our present situation we have to be more careful. It is just the three of us now, and we can't afford any more serious mistakes. Just imagine the consequences of not having Samson anymore. I mean what if something happened to you or Charlie? We would have no fast means of transportation into town. I know you try your best, but let's be honest, you don't always think things through. You have to be constantly aware of how your actions might affect yourself, me, or Charlie. Like it or not Anna, you have to start acting like an adult!"

Anna remained silent and just listened to her older brother. While everything he said was true, she didn't appreciate his ***candor***. She did act like an adult, or at least she thought she did. And what did Jacob mean when he said she needed to be aware of how her actions would affect him and Charlie? She was always thinking about her family. Anna found Jacob's speech not enlightening, but rather condescending. Like everything else since their parents' sickness, Jacob had managed to turn this situation into an opportunity to assert his dominance over her. Not once had he stopped to ask her about what happened, or whether or not she had "acted like an adult" today. He said it himself; he didn't EVEN care how Samson got out. Finally Anna

---

Carp (kahrp) – V – to find fault or complain querulously or unreasonably

Candor (**kan**-der) – N – the state or quality of being frank, open, and sincere in speech or expression

decided that Jacob was just arrogant. The anger toward Jacob which had been planted earlier began to take root and the seeds of resentment started to bloom.

Once again Anna had let her emotions take control of her thoughts. The mixture of embarrassment and pride had blinded her to the truth that Jacob was saying. He wasn't being mean or selfish. Perhaps his simple language was a little ***gauche***, but he was simply trying to impress upon her the seriousness of their situation. They were two kids who had suddenly been thrown into adult circumstances. Neither of them was yet eighteen and they would have to figure out a way to not only fend for themselves, but also take care of a toddler. Life on the prairie, for all of its promises, was hard. Danger lurked everywhere. Somehow the Watkins children would have to do the best they could to survive.

Gauche (gohsh) – ADJ – lacking social grace, sensitivity, or acuteness

WORD REVIEW

Acclamation
Autonomous
Bane
Candor
Carp
Cavort
Delineate
Deprecate
Derring-do
Digress
Dissipate
Fracas
Fractious
Gauche
Gerontocracy
Gradation
Lethargic
Olympian
Pristine

4

THE TOILS OF THE PRAIRIE

Jacob and Anna's conversation ended around 10. Tired from the day's activities, Anna excused herself and left to get ready for bed. Anna had learned how to dress and undress in the dark so as not to disturb her sleeping roommate. Exhausted, Anna quickly drifted off to sleep.

Jacob was also drained from the day's adventures, but unlike his other siblings he didn't head off to bed. In his story he had only told Anna what had happened with Samson, but had consciously left out any information about what he had learned from the bank. Jacob had gone into town to discuss their parents' finances and their will. What he had learned was not promising. When discussing the ***bequests*** in the will, Jacob discovered most of the family's bank account had already been depleted. During the final months of his illness, Thomas had the foresight to pay off the family debts, a burden he didn't want his children to have to worry about in case he and Charlotte didn't recover. This was partly good news for Jacob and partly bad news. On the one hand, the Watkins children held the land deed with the cabin free and clear. No one could take it away from them because of past debts. On the other hand, Thomas had all but emptied the family bank account when he paid off the property. So the children had a house, but

---

Bequest (bih-**kwest**) – N – an arrangement in a will

not much more to live on. While the shelter of the house was nice, it would do the family little good if they had nothing to eat. Their situation wasn't ***dire***—there were far worse things they could face—but it definitely wasn't ideal.

Sitting quietly alone at the table, Jacob pondered the situation. Apart from the amber glow from the smoldering wood in the fireplace, the room was all but dark. Jacob could have lit the lantern for more light, but doing so had the possibility of waking his sister. The last thing he wanted was to arouse her suspicions. Now wasn't the time to tell her about the situation. Worrying Anna would do nothing except make his task of finding a solution that much more difficult. There he sat for the next several hours, thinking by the soft, warm light.

At a quarter after one Jacob arouse from his contemplations. His body was stiff from the inactivity. He hadn't yet devised some great solution for the problem, but he was on his way. The children would have to find a means to be self-sufficient. They didn't have the money to purchase the supplies for a great harvest, but they could plant what they needed to survive on. Anna could work in the fields, and Jacob could get a job in town to help cover the expenses. He had his father's gun so he could hunt for meat, and they still had Dolly for milk. Not liking the idea of having to live off charity, Jacob hoped that they would be able to return the milk cow soon. However, at the present it was quite clear that they still needed her. If Jacob could find a job soon, then maybe they could purchase a couple of chickens and have fresh eggs again. Millions of unknowns circled in Jacob's head when he finally got up to go to bed.

Dire (**dahy**-uhr) – ADJ – causing or involving great fear or suffering; dreadful; terrible

It was possible for the small family to survive in Wyoming on their own; he just wasn't sure how they would do it. One thing that was very clear was that until their situation improved, there would have to be sacrifices. Luxuries that the family was used to would have to be forgone for the sake of their survival. Until Jacob could get a job and replenish the bank account, the Watkins family would have to live an economical lifestyle. With this in mind, Jacob headed to his bed to get some rest.

After only a few weeks, the two older Watkins adjusted to their new roles in the household. Immediately following Jacob's takeover of the family's finances, he set out to find a job that would help support them. Unfortunately for him, the townspeople themselves weren't well off and no one was able to take him on as fulltime help. Jacob would have to pick up jobs wherever he could. It wouldn't be until harvest time that the farmers in the area would have something extra for him to do. If the Watkins could hold out until August, a mere five months away, then Jacob could probably make enough money to get them back on their feet. The problem was making it until then. The only consistent job Jacob could find was at Mr. Daniels' store. Twice a week Jacob would come in early in the morning to help Mr. Daniels sort through his new deliveries and put the wares away. Jacob took over all the heavy lifting. Sometimes Mr. Daniels would have Jacob do his deliveries. The job didn't pay very much—50 cents every week—but it was something to count on. While Mr. Daniels often commented on how he didn't know how he had gotten along before without Jacob, deep down Jacob knew the man was more than capable of doing all the work himself. Although he never would have said it out loud, Mr. Daniels had given Jacob the job out of the goodness of his heart.

Anna became responsible for tending to the house, and planting the small section of crops that would sustain the family over the following winter. With their mother's garden neglected, the hope of having fresh fruits and vegetables early this spring was nearly destroyed. Anything that was planted at the present would not be ready to eat until some months later. For the rest of the spring and much of the summer, they would have to live off of the small amount of money Jacob made and what their parents had stored over the previous winter. The supplies consisted mostly of canned foods, stored wheat, and some dried meats. It wasn't a lot, but with parsimony Jacob believed the family could survive until the harvest. When Jacob wasn't searching for jobs around town, he was home with Anna taking care of the land. With every day that passed Anna and Jacob became more aware of the ***exacting*** demands of life on their own.

Hope that they would be able to sustain themselves until the fall soon started to dwindle. After two months of life on their own, Jacob saw their situation deteriorating rather than improving. The influx of settlers through their town had dwindled, and Mr. Daniels had to cut back the hours Jacob worked at the grocery store. Half the work meant half the amount of pay. Covering the difference in what Jacob made in town and what the kids needed to live on, they found themselves taking more money out of the savings then they were putting back in. To make matters worse, Wyoming was experiencing an unusual drought. The spring and early summer rains which promised plentiful fall crops just hadn't materialized. Every day

---

Exacting (ig-**zak**-ting) – ADJ – rigid or severe in demands or requirements

Anna took water from their well to nourish what she had planted. It was a hard job that would likely produce only ***marginal*** results. Though the crops would be enough to get them through the fall, there would be nothing left to store for the winter. This problem was not unique to the Watkins. The drought spelled trouble for the whole region, meaning by the fall Jacob would not have the abundance of work he had been promised. Without their own crops and a way to make up the difference for buying food, it would be almost impossible for the young family to last through the following winter. Keenly aware of their situation, Jacob decided to wait a couple more weeks before bringing the reality of their problem to Anna. *If the rain could just come,* thought Jacob, *everything would be all right.*

The rain didn't come, and Jacob's anxiety over their ***pecuniary*** situation continued to grow as their savings dwindled. Money was more than tight, and the food stored from the previous winter was quickly vanishing. Even Charlie had noticed how the size of his meals had gradually gotten smaller. Whenever Anna tried talking to Jacob about the food supply, his replies were always short. "We just need to hold on a little longer," and "Things will turn around soon," became his favorite answers. Jacob knew, however, that soon there wouldn't be any food left.

The Watkins weren't the only ones suffering from the spring drought. All of the townsfolk were growing apprehensive over their fall harvest. Planning for the

---

Marginal	(**mahr**-juh-nl) – ADJ – at the outer or lower limits; minimal for requirements; almost insufficient
Pecuniary	(pi-**kyoo**-nee-er-ee) – ADJ – of or pertaining to money

upcoming winter had become everyone's ***primal*** concern, with few spare thoughts for less important matters. No one in their small village was in a position to extend extra charity to the three recently orphaned children. To temporarily ease their financial burdens, Jacob had toyed with the idea of taking out a loan—nothing substantial—just enough money to purchase a few livestock and grain for the farm. However, every time he thought over that option he always came to the same conclusion. A loan from the bank would ease their present situation, but it would only make matters worse in the long run. Loans had to be paid back, and with no foreseeable means of making money it would be nearly impossible to pay off both the principal and its interest. There would just have to be another way.

Primal (**prahy**-muhl) – ADJ – first; original or of first importance; fundamental

WORD REVIEW

Bequest	Exacting	Pecuniary
Dire	Marginal	Primal

5

500 REASONS TO MOVE

The first of June brought only clear skies and warmer weather instead of the much anticipated spring rains. What clouds that did float in the sky were as white and airy as a lamb's coat. It had been nearly three months since the weather threatened, or promised depending on one's perspective, rain. To be exact, the last dark clouds were on the day of Thomas and Charlotte's funeral, and even then not a drop fell on the Wyoming prairie. Every day brought more sun and less water for the plants. Brown was in fashion.

The last three months had also taken a heavy toll on the Watkins' farm. Jacob and Anna had little time to tend to the outside of the house and the neglect was conspicuous. The white paint on the side of the house, which Charlotte used to recoat every spring, was starting to chip and fade. A brown film of dust covered the front windows because no one had the time to wash them. The roof needed mending, as it had been damaged from the stress of holding up the previous winter's snow. The only positive to the lack of rain was that a heavy rainstorm would have likely caused the weak areas in the roof to leak and neither of the Watkins children had time to fix it. The house wasn't old, but the harsh conditions of Wyoming necessitated constant upkeep. Falling behind in one area only complicated repairs in other sections of the house. The slow deterioration of the little white cottage was outward evidence of the gradual corrosion of Anna and Jacob's ability to handle life on their own out west.

The Watkins' fields were worse off than the house. The slow decline of the property had begun with their parents' illness, and with time the things that didn't get done earlier in the year simply made it harder for the children to reestablish any sort of control. Despite the lack of rainfall, various wild weeds had sprung up all over the pasture. A mixture of brown soil, yellowish grass, and unidentifiable weeds littered the land, creating plenty of ***fodder*** but no salable crops. The entire yard had retrogressed back to the wild, save for Charlotte's small garden which Anna tended faithfully. Everything else could be a mess, but not the garden. Not only was the garden likely to be the only source of fresh fruits and vegetables, but it was also small enough to manage.

Anna loved working in the garden. As everything else fell apart around her, the manicured patch of land represented the old days of structure and order. An ageless beauty, it was a window to a time before and a small glimpse of their former life. The garden's lush green stood in stark contrast to the overwhelming dryness of the rest of the land. Since her parents' death, there hadn't been a day that Anna failed to water her mother's plants. This tiny bit of fresh green earth gave Anna hope, not only of survival out in the brutal West, but the potential for prosperity. Regardless of how tired, lonely, or sad Anna might be on any day, her spirits were always lifted when it came time to work in the garden.

Fodder (**fod**-er) – N – coarse food for livestock

She would come in with a weight on her chest and leave with a melodious ***descant*** in her heart.

Another reason Anna enjoyed working outside so much was because it was the only part of the day that she had a break from her household duties. It was time for herself when she could think and rest. While Anna could have just as easily worked in the garden with Charlie, she always waited until it was his nap time to do her work. Every day she relished her private time away from everything else that was going on.

Anna was sitting in the garden weeding the tomato plants when she heard the familiar thunder of Samson's hooves. Today was the day Jacob worked part-time at Mr. Daniels' store and he had gotten in the habit of riding Samson so he didn't waste his entire day walking back and forth into town. Engrossed in her work, Anna took only a brief glance to acknowledge her brother and then turned merrily back to her tomatoes. Although they were only just beginning to become little green balls, Anna was convinced that this summer's would be the finest crop of tomatoes yet.

This particular day Jacob was in an unusual hurry. Upon his arrival home, he quickly jumped off their horse and hastily went to put Samson in his stable. He was, however, not in too much of a rush that he forgot to double-check the latch on the adventurous horse's door. The barn felt completely empty now as Samson was the only occupant of the Watkins' stable. Like the rest of the townspeople, Mr. Forrester was feeling the stress of the drought and had to sell a couple of his own cows to pay for their feed so Dolly was needed back at the Forrester dairy farm. Mr. Forrester would never have taken Dolly back if

---

Descant (**des**-kant) – N – a song or melody

it hadn't been absolutely necessary. He, however, did not forget the Watkins' children and continued to ***attenuate*** the severity of their situation with a fresh bottle of milk every week. It wasn't a large quantity of milk, and the children had to forgo all butter and cream, but it was enough to keep the small family nourished. As the youngest, Charlie remained the largest benefactor of Mr. Forrester's gift.

Sitting in the dirt, Anna noticed that her golden summer dress was lightly dusted with brown soil. The ground was cool, a nice complement to the sun's warm rays. A ***zephyr*** stirred from the east, softly blowing her blond curls and making her beloved tomato plants dance in the wind. If it hadn't been for Jacob's shadow, Anna wouldn't have noticed him standing in front of her. Inquisitively, she looked up from her work at the dark ***colossus*** looming over her.

"Are you almost finished?" he asked in an excited tone.

"I can be," she responded.

"OK, good," said Jacob. "When you finish, come inside. We have to talk."

"I'll be there…." she tried to answer.

He was gone before she could respond to him. Jacob was energized, and it was a curious sight, to be sure. Anna couldn't help but wonder what on earth had gotten into her older brother as he disappeared from her sight. Only the slam of the front door left a trace as to where he had gone, one she hoped hadn't wakened the younger brother.

Pulling herself off the ground, Anna arose from her dirt throne. She quickly dusted off the loose dirt from her

---

Attenuate (uh-**ten**-yoo-yet) – V – to weaken or reduce in force, intensity, effect, quantity, or value:
Zephyr (**zef**-er) – N – a gentle, mild breeze
Colossus (kuh-**los**-uhs) – N – anything colossal or gigantic

dress and then her hands. A swift glance over her yellow dress revealed that it needed more than a simple brushing to remove the brown hue. Anna collected her tools and went to the barn to put them away. Her movements were purposeful, yet speedy. This was the first time in a very long time that Anna had seen her brother, normally in a somber mood, get excited about anything. She was clueless as to what had happened, but she certainly couldn't wait to find out. If Jacob were in a fine mood, then something good had to have happened. Perhaps Mr. Daniels had offered him a full-time job. *Oh how wonderful,* she thought as her mind reeled with possibilities. *If Jacob is fully employed, our troubles are over. Tonight we will have to celebrate*! She raced into the house to hear what Jacob had to say.

"I have some really exciting news," began Jacob.

Anna smiled to herself for being so clever. *I knew it,* she thought. *He has a new job and everything is going to be OK.* Jacob was sitting at the table. Anna, however, did not immediately join him. Instead she went straight to the cupboard to grab a couple of glasses. After sitting for an hour in the bare sun, Anna had acquired a hefty thirst. She kept up her busy activities: imagining the day's outcome, listening for Jacob's next words, and pouring two glasses of water.

Jacob was less than thrilled with his sister's pokiness. ***Cognizant*** that anyone doing three things at a time was doing one or more of them halfheartedly, he didn't say another word until Anna sat down with the water. What he had to say was important and he needed her undivided attention. Anna hadn't realized he had stopped talking until she sat down.

Cognizant (**kog**-nuh-zuhnt) – ADJ – aware

"I'm listening," said Anna.

"Good," replied Jacob. "You know Joe Stephens?"

"No," answered Anna.

"Yeah, you do," responded Jacob. "Joseph Stephens, the man who always sits in the back of the church babbling? And the people just roll their eyes at him and mutter, 'Oh Joe.'"

"You mean Crazy Joe?" replied Anna.

"Yeah, Crazy Joe," answered Jacob. "Anyway, Crazy Joe was in Mr. Daniels' store today muttering on about some rich fellow from Boston scouting out land for the next railroad. Joe said that the man from Boston was willing to pay top dollar for any property that fell in the area he was looking at."

Jacob's voice grew more excited as he told his tale. Anna, on the other hand, was confused. She had no idea how a ***proffer*** from the man from Boston to buy land had anything to do with good news. Land scouts weren't anything new on the western frontier. As more and more people moved farther toward the West Coast, the property became more valuable. Men from the East would come every once in a while looking for land they could turn into some sort of profit. Most of them were simply ***acquisitive*** and greedy, but had no idea what it took to make a living on the prairie. This man from Boston, Anna had no doubt, was just another one who would come and go. Cognizant of her other chores, Anna hoped Jacob would soon get to his point.

"So was Crazy Joe telling the truth?" asked Anna. "Is there a man from Boston in town?"

"Yep," said Jacob. "And I left work early to go meet

Proffer (**prof**-er) – N – an offer or proposal

Acquisitive (uh-**kwiz**-i-tiv) – ADJ – eager to get wealth

with him."

Jacob's last sentence caught Anna completely off guard. Stunned, she searched for the words to say.

"Why on earth would you leave work to meet with him?" asked Anna.

"To see if our property was in his area of interest," said Jacob, "and to see how much he was willing to pay for it."

If Jacob's first response had thrown Anna off-guard, his second response nearly knocked her over. She couldn't have heard correctly. There was no way on God's green earth her brother could actually be thinking about selling their farm. The possibility was unfathomable. Convinced Jacob had misspoken, Anna asked him again.

"Why did you meet with the Easterner?" Anna said, letting her prejudices show.

Jacob knew the tone in Anna's voice all too well. Annoyed that Anna didn't wait to listen to all the facts before making a judgment, Jacob had to take a deep breath before continuing on with his story. He couldn't ***coerce*** her to have an open mind, but he could respond in such a way that didn't add any more fuel to Anna's already burning flame of stubbornness.

"I went to see what he was offering for the land," responded Jacob, "and to see if he was interested in our property."

Anna was clearly not satisfied with his response. She was outraged by the very idea, and she wanted Jacob to know it. Defiantly she crossed her arms in front of her chest and took several quick breaths to express her disapproval.

Coerce (koh-**urs**) – V – to bring about through the use of force or other forms of compulsion

Ignoring the childish antics of his sister, Jacob continued. She could be so ***impenetrable***, he thought as he looked at her stubborn pose.

"I originally went to see if he would be interested in a portion of our property. This way we could sell off a piece of it and make enough money to get back on our feet," said Jacob. "I wanted to see what options were available to us."

"And?" asked Anna.

"Well, the good news is that our land is exactly in the middle of where his company is thinking about building, so he is willing to double the price that he was originally offering to purchase it," replied Jacob. "He'll pay us $5 an acre. With 100 acres, that is five hundred dollars."

"And the bad news?" inquired Anna.

"The bad news is that he wants all of it," responded Jacob.

As the words came out of Jacob's mouth, he knew they wouldn't be received well. Anna had already expressed her full displeasure with the entire idea. At this point there was no way she would be willing to have a discussion about it. What had started as a really good option to address their financial troubles had turned into another splinter in their relationship. Even though he was the head of the family, he didn't want to assert his ***hegemony*** over this situation. Jacob had been really excited about talking this through with Anna like two adults. They were a family, and what they needed most at that moment was ***cohesion*** not division.

The two siblings sat across from each other in

Impenetrable	(im-**pen**-i-truh-buhl) – ADJ – inaccessible to ideas, influences, etc.
Hegemony	(**hej**-uh-moh-nee) – N – leadership; predominance
Cohesion	(koh-**hee**-zhuhn) – N – unity

silence. While in reality only a matter of inches separated them, they might as well have been on the opposite sides of the earth. The idea of selling the entire farm had ***polarized*** Anna and her brother and it did not appear that they would come to an agreement any time soon. Selfishly Anna wanted to storm out of the room; it would be a clear signal to her brother what she thought of his idea. However, something inside her told her that would be foolish. After all, she thought, what good would it bring? The tension between Anna and Jacob was abundantly clear. Both knew that a brawl between them would only make matters worse, yet neither wanted to ***capitulate*** to the other's terms. Wise for his age, Jacob decided to take steps to de-escalate the conflict. In a calm, but commanding tone, he ***apprised*** Anna of their situation.

"I know this is a difficult topic," he began, "and this is obviously not the right time to discuss it. Why don't we talk about this later?"

"OK," was the only thing Anna could say.

"Anna, I know you might not like the idea," continued Jacob. "But try and put your feelings aside and think about what is best for the family. Right now we are in a financial pickle, and we have to realistically think about our options. Discussing the possibility of moving doesn't mean we will move."

With that, Jacob finished his water, stood up and left Anna alone in the kitchen. Anna remained motionless for some time, her thoughts racing over the past events.

Polarize	(**poh**-luh-rahyz) – V – to divide into sharply opposing factions, political groups, etc.
Capitulate	(kuh-**pich**-uh-leyt) – V – to give up resistance; to surrender to another
Apprise	(uh-**prahyz**) – V – advise; inform

She thought about everything: their parents, the farm, and the implications of what Jacob was saying. Sure life out west was not exactly easy, but it was an investment for a better future. *Wasn't everything worth having difficult to obtain at some point?* she thought. To leave now would be giving up on all that the family had worked for. A formal ***investiture*** of Jacob's proposal seemed antithetical to their parents' wishes. Anna was convinced that Jacob was wrong. At least that is what she told herself.

Jacob, however, understood far more than Anna. Without a strong harvest, he knew that it would only take one harsh Wyoming winter to completely devastate their ration supply. Summer was now upon them, with prospects for bountiful crops not looking good. A decision had to be made, and time wasn't on their side. They could choose to wait out the summer and hope for the best, or look for another alternative. Leaving the farm was the last thing he wanted to do, but he was convinced there weren't any other options. After dinner, he approached Anna once again, this time hoping she would be more open to the topic.

"Have you given any thought to what we talked about earlier?" asked Jacob.

"Yes," replied Anna.

"And?"

"And I still think it is a bad idea."

Hoping to facilitate more of a dialogue this time around, Jacob let Anna continue to speak. Perhaps by listening to her hesitations, Jacob could more accurately address them. Jacob continued to sit quietly and let Anna take the lead on the discussion. His silence signaled that he

---

Investiture (in-**ves**-ti-cher) – N – the act of establishing or ratifying

wanted Anna to speak her mind.

"I just don't think things are so bad that we need to sell the property," continued Anna. "Sure we have had to be more careful with food and money, but we are getting by."

"And when our food and money runs out," prompted Jacob. "What will we do then?"

"Then I can get a job to help out," answered Anna.

"Right now there is barely enough work for me," responded Jacob. "Besides, who would watch Charlie?"

Anna mumbled a quiet response that was not ***intelligible.*** Jacob thought it best to explain the gravity of their situation; now was not the time to ***downplay*** the seriousness of their circumstances.

"Anna, right now we have only 10 dollars in our bank account," Jacob began. "It is enough to get us through the summer, but not enough to hold us through the winter. Your garden, while very nice, is small and will only produce enough fruits and vegetables to supplement a good harvest; which it isn't looking like we will have this year because of the drought."

"You can always hunt to make up the difference in food," responded Anna.

"That's true, but we aren't the only ones suffering here. If everyone here turns to wild game to make up the difference, then there is no guarantee that there will be any animals left. Not to mention all of the settlers who pass our way who only survive off what they kill."

Anna was overwhelmed by what Jacob had to say.

Intelligible	(in-**tel**-i-juh-buhl) – ADJ – capable of being understood; comprehensible; clear
Downplay	(**doun**-pley) – V – to treat or speak of (something) so as to reduce emphasis on its importance, value, or strength

She knew that things were tight, but she had no idea how bad they actually where. Upset, she burst into tears.

"It wasn't supposed to be like this," she sobbed. "Mom and Dad moved us out here for a better life. Moving now would only ruin everything that they worked for. Selling the house would be like killing them all over again."

With tears streaming down her face, Anna excused herself. She now understood what Jacob was saying, but she wasn't ready to accept it. She needed some time. Change was inevitable, but Anna wanted to cling for just a little bit longer to the life the Watkins once had. Jacob understood her ***nostalgia*** for their former happy life and let her go without saying a word. They each had to mourn the loss of their parents and the broken dream of living out west in their own way. He sat at the table for more than an hour as he waited for his sister's return. Anna came back carrying Charlie with her eyes red and swollen from the tears. She understood at that moment what needed to be done.

"Anna, we have to sell," Jacob quietly whispered.

"I know," was her only response.

The following day Jacob returned to town to speak with the Boston businessman. Jacob relayed the family's interest in his offer, but asked again if the man would consider only purchasing part of the land instead of all of it. The man remained steadfast and assured Jacob that he wanted all of it or none of it. It would do him no good to have a property split ***asunder*** into odd bits surrounding the Watkins' house and garden. This left the Watkins no choice; if they sold they would have to move. The question

---

Nostalgia (no-**stal**-juh) – N – a sentimental yearning for the happiness of a former place or time

Asunder (uh-**suhn**-der) – ADV – into separate parts; in or into pieces

that followed was not whether or not to move, but where to move to? The profit from selling the property was enough to establish them just about anywhere they wanted to go. Anna, still clinging to the romantic idea of living out west, suggested they finish the journey to Oregon, the original destination of their parents. For Anna, the western prairie still held so much potential. If they couldn't stay in Wyoming, then perhaps all they needed to do was move a little bit farther west. Sympathetic to Anna's desire to stay in the western frontier, Jacob had given serious consideration to finishing out the Oregon Trail. However, after thinking about it logically he realized that the same problems they faced in Wyoming were also in Oregon. The western frontier was for the adventurous, not for a young family. The strong 17-year-old knew he could make it on his own, but not with two younger siblings. He was simply not capable of braving the harsh elements of little food, cold winters, rapid diseases, and Indian attacks while trying to care for both his younger sister and brother. Given the Watkins' current situation, further western expansion offered more danger than it did rewards. The family of three needed the reliability of the east, not the ***dubiousness*** of the West. Jacob suggested they travel to New York.

Like Oregon, New York was also not a practical option for the Watkins given its distance from Wyoming. It would take months for them to make the journey. Jacob had only thought about New York because of its reputation for being a place of new beginnings. Since it was the birthplace of their mother, the children had often heard stories of the various travelers who would come to New York from everywhere just to live in the United States. Thousands of

Dubiousness (**doo**-bee-uhs-ness) – N – unreliability; doubtfulness

people every year, from all across the world, came there to start over. Even their great-great grandfather, Jonathan Huntington, had emigrated from England via New York. From their mother's stories, New York sounded like exactly the place the children needed. The United States, however, had changed and the opportunities that once were specific to New York could now be found all across the country. There was no need to travel the entire way back East to enjoy the luxuries of the Eastern coast. By 1854, for the traveler seeking a new life, New York was no longer ***inimitable***; similar opportunities could be found in many places. All Anna and Jacob needed to do was decide what they were looking for and then they could decide where they needed to go.

"There needs to be possibilities for work," Jacob began. "This money is nice, but it won't last forever."

"The journey can't be too long," suggested Anna. "It is going to be rough enough with Charlie."

"But it has to be long enough to get us to a modern city," retorted Jacob, "one that offers some sort of schooling for you and Charlie."

Education was another main reason Jacob felt it best to move back East. While she was well, Charlotte Watkins had made the education of her children her top priority. The daughter of an affluent family, she had obtained nothing but the best education New York could offer. While seemingly impractical on the western prairie, Charlotte had insisted that her children were instructed in classical literature. It wasn't enough for them just to learn to read and write; they needed to become well-rounded

---

Inimitable (ih-**nim**-i-tuh-buhl) – ADJ – incapable of being imitated or copied; surpassing imitation; matchless

adults. For Charlotte, education was the direct ***channel*** to achieve maturity. Jacob knew his mother would want them to continue to learn. Anna, on the other hand, was less than thrilled about the thought of more school. While her mother was alive she had followed Charlotte's lessons dutifully. Her efforts were born out of respect for her mother and not a love of learning. All the same, she knew that perhaps she could learn a few more things.

It didn't take long for the discussion to lead both of the Watkins children to the same conclusion. They needed a city in between both Oregon and New York. They needed a blend of both worlds.

"How about St. Louis?" they both suggestion in unison.

St. Louis seemed so perfect, that they both wondered why they hadn't thought of it before. It was a large enough city that it offered them exactly what they were looking for, but it wasn't so far away that they couldn't make it. It was also somewhat familiar and allowed the Watkins to stay connected to their heritage. After all, their parents had met and fallen in love there. The element of familiarity, however far removed it was, was comforting. Going back to a former home didn't seem as scary as moving off to a strange new land. St. Louis would offer Jacob prospects for work and Anna and Charlie opportunities to go to school. It was the perfect place for their relocation. The Watkins family would move back home. It would be a journey from the West to the East, an ***atypical*** excursion for people in 1854, to say the least.

Channel (**chan**-l) – N – a means of access

Atypical (ey-**tip**-i-kuhl) – ADJ – not typical; not conforming to the type; irregular; abnormal

Once the location of their new destination was decided upon, Jacob went to town to finalize the contract with the Boston businessman. The Watkins weren't the only family who had decided to sell, and Jacob had to wait over two hours for the man to finish the paperwork for the other landowners. Most of the other townsfolk were selling to make a profit on land they had bought for nearly nothing. They weren't looking to make a great move; they would buy another homestead only a few miles off or so. None of the other families were in the same situation as were the Watkins. When it finally came time for Jacob to speak with the railroad man, he felt a little reluctant to sell. He sat a long time poring over the paperwork to make sure that he understood exactly what he was about to do. Part of him was excited for the new opportunity the money afforded him and his siblings; part of him felt like he would let his parents down by selling their property. Signing his name to the contract was not an easy thing to do, and he took his time doing it. He knew that once he put down his mark, it would be official. The Watkins' house ***eponymous*** of their family, that he helped his father build, would belong to someone else, who would no doubt tear it down within a matter of months, and the Watkins' farm would be no more. All memories of the past 10 years came flooding back to him—When they found the property, the day they began to build the house, his and his dad's first real hunt, the birth of Charlie... All of it had taken place on the property he was about to sign away. Jacob's thoughts, however, didn't stop with the memories of the past, but drifted toward his projection of the future. He thought about the situation

Eponymous (uh-**pon**-uh-muhs) – ADJ – giving one's name to a place

and how staying there wasn't what was best for him and his siblings. As painful as it was, Jacob knew he couldn't hold onto the dream of the past in order to sacrifice the future. Without another thought he scribbled down his name: *Jacob Thomas Watkins.*

Once the paperwork was signed, the businessman from Boston summoned his ***cohort*** who took the contract from Jacob to put it in their files. He returned with a thick metal case. The case, which looked like it weighed fifty pounds, was securely sealed with a substantial lock. Taking the small golden key that had hung secretly around the man's neck, the businessman opened the lock. The man then proceeded to carefully return the key to its specified place. The whole time the man kept a keen eye on Jacob. The man didn't trust anyone, and Jacob's stares made him uneasy. Although Jacob had been studying the man out of curiosity and not ill intent, the businessman's demeanor and ***disposition*** signaled to Jacob that it would be better if he turned away. So he did. The man with the heavy metal box was the accountant of the firm that had just purchased the Watkins' family farm. He was in charge of tracking all of the money from this business venture. The squirrelly man had a right to be nervous. He alone had access to the moneybox, which held thousands of the company's dollars. Mishandling the company funds would be an ***infraction*** of his contract; he would not only lose his job but could be thrown into jail until he was able to pay back what had been lost. An overly cautious man in

---

Cohort (koh-hawrt) – N – a companion or associate

Disposition (dis-puh-**zish**-uhn) – N – state of mind regarding something; inclination

Infraction (in-**frak**-shuhn) – N – breach; violation; infringement

his own right, as most accountants are, the man never let the box or the key out of his sight.

Once the box was opened, Jacob was able to catch only a glimpse of what was inside. The accountant had the box turned in such a way that only he could see into it. Slowly and vigilantly the man counted out the sum in which Jacob was to be paid. Once he had counted out the correct sum, he counted it again. A fair man, the accountant did not want to make either the mistake of giving Jacob too little or too much of the company's money. It took the accountant three times before he was satisfied that he had the correct amount. There placed before Jacob were five stacks of equal heights. *500 hundred dollars!* Jacob had never seen so much money in his entire life.

"Do you have something you'd like me to put these bills in?" asked the accountant.

"Um, I brought a bag," replied Jacob.

It was obvious by the old brown rucksack that Jacob had no concept of how large the amount he would actually receive was. The accountant looked at the bag and shook his head. There was no way he would let this young man leave his office carrying all the money that he had in a bag. It was just the type of thing that asked for trouble. As the man stood up he motioned to Jacob to remain seated and to wait for him. Taking his money box with him, the accountant went into the other room. He returned shortly with a smaller metal box. This one didn't have a lock, but it closed properly. It was older and worn by use, but the accountant was satisfied that it would help Jacob get the money home safely. After that, the security of the funds would be up to the lad. The accountant placed Jacob's money in the small metal container with the same caution that he had used in pulling it out of his own. As he organized the bills, the man couldn't resist the urge to count the bills one more time. It was clear by the accountant's behavior that attention to details was his ***forte***. When he was done, all of the bills were stacked neatly in a row. The man showed the case to Jacob for his inspection. With everything in order and with Jacob's approval, the accountant handed the box to Jacob. As Jacob placed the sturdy box in his rucksack, the accountant cautioned Jacob about the trickery and ***duplicity*** that large sums of money bring out in others.

"Money has a strange way of making honest men into liars," the accountant began. "God-fearin' men will do unimaginable evils for the chance at riches and gold. Therefore young man, it is in your best interest not to let a single soul know that you have this cash. Don't even tell your closest ***confidant*** how much money you received today. Otherwise you will see things in people you never wanted to see."

"Should I tell my sister?" asked Jacob.

"Only if you can be absolutely sure that she won't tell anyone else," replied the man. "As soon as people find out that you have this money, you'll be hit up for all kinds of favors. A few dollars here and there may not seem like a lot, but before you know it all of this cash will be gone, and you will be in a worse position then you are right now."

Jacob nodded to the man to show that he was paying attention to what he was saying. It wasn't like the

---

Forte	(fawr-**tey**) – N – a strong point, as of a person; that in which one excels
Duplicity	(doo-**plis**-i-tee) – N – deceitfulness in speech or conduct
Confidant	(**kon**-fi-dant) – N – a close friend or associate to whom secrets are confided or with whom private matters and problems are discussed

old accountant to give advice to those his company dealt with. Normally he paid the bills and let those who received payment do what they wanted with the cash. After all, it was their money and it didn't matter to him whether they saved it or spent it all at the saloon. But Jacob was different from the rest of the folks who had crossed his path. The accountant could see that he wasn't selling his land to get rich or looking for a fast way to have some fun. He could tell that this young man was here with a purpose and needed the cash for his family. The last thing the accountant wanted was for the 17-year-old to experience the cold reality of the wickedness of some folks. Before he let Jacob leave, he offered him one last tip.

"Keep your spending money separate from your saving money. This way you know exactly how much you have to purchase the things you need. It will also keep you from waving around a bunch of cash so that others can see how much you really have."

Jacob took the advice to heart and promised the man that he would be careful. He thanked the accountant and left. Originally, Jacob had planned on leaving the businessman's office and going straight to Mr. Daniels' store to purchase supplies for the trip. However, after thinking about it, he thought it best to take the money safely home. That way he could separate the cash into spending and saving money, and not overspend. He also decided it would be better to come back into town with Anna, because she could help him pick out the things that they needed. Jacob was aware of the chasm in their relationship since their parents' deaths, and he wanted desperately to make things normal between them again. Perhaps by including her in the trip planning she could warm back up to him. Their

exodus from Wyoming was going to be long and treacherous; things would go a lot smoother if Jacob and Anna were getting along.

Exodus (**ek**-suh-duhs) – N – a going out; a departure or emigration, usually of a large number of people

WORD REVIEW

Acquisitive
Apprise
Asunder
Attenuate
Atypical
Capitulate
Channel
Coerce
Cognizant
Cohesion
Cohort
Colossus
Confidant
Descant
Disposition
Downplay
Dubiousness
Duplicity
Eponymous
Exodus
Fodder
Forte
Hegemony
Impenetrable
Infraction
Inimitable
Intelligible
Investiture
Nostalgia
Polarize
Proffer
Zephyr

6

A JOURNEY BEGINS

The Watkins' contract with the Boston businessman gave the children a week to vacate the property. Had they asked, the man would have given them more time. However, once the deal was made official, Jacob thought it best for them to get on the road. Any more time would have just made it that much harder to leave.

The signing of the contract was the ***catalyst*** that triggered move. It didn't take the children long to realize that one week would be barely enough time to get everything done that needed to be done. Things had to be packed. Travel plans needed to be made. Decisions came in all sorts of shapes and sizes. Questions circled around how much stuff they could take, and conversely what things would need to be left behind. Some decisions were easy while others were hard; nevertheless, they all had to be made. Not wanting to be blamed for throwing out all of their parents' belongings, Jacob abdicated the responsibility to Anna. After all, she cared a lot more about the stuff than he did.

Jacob then took on the role of organizing the move in general. He told Anna how many trunks they could take, and she would have to fill them. Anything left

---

Catalyst (**kat**-l-ist) – N – something that causes activity between two or more persons or forces without itself being affected

over would either be sold or donated to the church. The agreement seemed to suit everyone well, and apart from some tantrums from Charlie over not being able to keep ALL of his favorite books, the packing process went along smoothly.

More important than what they were taking back East, was the way in which they were going to get there. The Watkins had the funds to pay for a trip to St. Louis, but not the knowledge to get themselves out of their small town. Jacob had already purchased a used wagon from a local farmer, but the family had no experience with making such an expedition. What they needed was a ***docent***, a seasoned traveler who could guide them safely to their destination. Jacob went looking for someone who understood the complexities of traveling with a toddler and could handle each situation with patience. The best candidate was a father-like figure who could protect the young travelers from the harshness of the wild. The man he found was Howard Simpson, better known as "One-eyed Howie."

June, as Jacob soon discovered, was the prime time for travel, only in the opposite direction in which his family was going. Dozens of well-established docents passed through their small Wyoming town heading west, but not too many of them would be making it back East for some time. When it came to finding the right guide for their journey, the pickings were slim. For this time of year, "One-eyed Howie" was the best they were going to get. Jacob was told under no circumstances ever to refer to him as Howard, since no one knew what happened to the last man who did.

Docent (**doh**-suhnt) – N – a person who is a knowledgeable guide

A ***mercenary*** to the core, "One-eyed Howie" got his nickname from the fact that he watched his money so closely that he would sleep with only one eye closed, a fact that remained unsubstantiated because those who traveled with him were too afraid to check. Thus the nickname stuck, rightly so, too, as no one would dare try to double-cross "One-eyed" by not paying him his due. Howie, as Jacob would refer to him, wasn't a particularly large man. Wider than he was tall, the rugged adventurer lacked the stature to present a dominating presence. However, whatever he lacked in size he made up for in attitude. Gruff, blunt, and unrefined, Howie had an ***astringent*** attitude and he never let others push him around. Although Jacob didn't completely trust Howie, given the particulars of the situation, Howie was hired for the job. The companionship and pleasure of Howie's company would cost the Watkins 50 dollars. Half of the fee was to be paid up-front, the other half to be paid on arrival. While Jacob would never openly ***malign*** Howie's character in front of his sister, the young lad did take to heart the cautioning words of the accountant and never disclosed to him the nature of the Watkins' funds or how much they had.

The Watkins' house was energized the night before the move. Anna and Jacob ran back and forth around the entire house checking and double checking that they had remembered everything. The wagon was packed and locked securely in the barn. For the first time in months the Watkins' barn was also alive with activity. Samson was no longer the sole occupant but was joined by a new

---

Mercenary (**mur**-suh-ner-ee) – N – working or acting merely for money or for the reward

Astringent (uh-**strin**-juhnt) – ADJ – stern or severe; austere

Malign (muh-**lahyn**) – V – to speak evil of; slander; defame

horse they had bought for the journey. They named her Delilah. A solid black mare, Delilah was Samson's perfect complement. Jacob had purchased Delilah thinking that two horses would be great for the trip. When Howie found out that Jacob planned on having two well-bred horses pull the wagon, he nearly died laughing. To Howie it was ***blatant*** that the young man had no idea how much strength was needed to pull the load. He advised Jacob to purchase two strong mules in addition to Delilah. The mules, Howie assured the young man, would do the heavy straining and his "prize horses" would serve as their accompaniment. Jacob followed his advice and bought two large male mules whom he named David and Goliath. With the four frisky animals, the Watkins' barn was filled with the sounds of life. Noises of whimpers, squeals, nickers, and neighs reverberated off the wooden walls. The addition of Delilah, David, and Goliath had ***revivified*** the Watkins' barn to its earlier lively, crowded state.

As the trail guide, Howie had produced a shopping list for the Watkins children to purchase before their trip. This list of supplies included food, water, tools, and other odds and ends that were needed for an extensive journey across the country. Jacob had purchased the equipment from Mr. Daniels' store. During his time as the grocery store's help, he had seen men and women come in to purchase the exact same supplies he was now responsible for getting. Like all the other settlers, Jacob needed flour, potatoes, bacon, dried meat, dried fruits, beans, cornmeal, and yeast. He had even purchased a few dozen eggs for the

---

Blatant (**bleyt**-nt) – ADJ – brazenly obvious; flagrant

Revivify (ri-**viv**-uh-fahy) – V – to restore to life; give new life to; revive; reanimate

road, which he safely wrapped and packed in the cornmeal barrel, a trick he had learned from an old settler who passed through their town earlier that year. Jacob felt like a king leaving the grocery store with such abundance. That night all the supplies which Jacob had purchased were packed and ready to go, along with a basket of several dozen fresh homemade biscuits Anna had made for the journey. Even the money box was placed in a safe location, securely bolted to the bottom of the wagon, where no outlaw or wild Indian would ever dream of looking. Despite the extensive preparation, Jacob and Anna couldn't sit still, and they weren't alone. At half past 11, Charlie was also wide awake and constantly following the two around or getting into things that had just been put away. With Charlie awake, most of the things had to be done twice.

All the excitement set the house buzzing. Everything was moving, well almost everything. There amid the hustle and bustle, in the middle of the living room lay Howie fast asleep on his coat as a makeshift bed. His pudgy, ***flaccid*** body spread out on the floor was a comical sight. Years of traveling and less than ideal sleeping conditions had taught him to sleep anywhere. In his coma-like state, Howie was completely oblivious to his surroundings. The Watkins children on the other hand were not completely oblivious to Howie's presence. Howie had made his bed directly in the middle of the walkway and Jacob and Anna were constantly stepping over him to get across the house. Not only was Howie's presence seen, but it could also be heard. The overweight man snored terribly. Snoring wasn't new for the Watkins—their father had been known on occasion also to snore, but he NEVER snored like Howie.

Flaccid (**flak**-sid) – ADJ – soft and limp

When Howie took deep breaths in and out, it sounded like a thunderstorm. Once or twice, Anna was sure that the man made the whole house shake. Two anguished teenagers, one energized toddler, and a sleeping monster made the house feel incredibly small. For the first time since they decided to move, Anna was thankful to be leaving the farmhouse. At a quarter to one, despite all the anticipation and the snoring concerto, Jacob, Anna, and Charlie were able to fall asleep as well.

Five o'clock in the morning was marked by the sound of a far-off rooster's crow, waking the slumbering party of travelers. Every day the neighbor's rooster crowed, but today it sounded different. Today the crow didn't simply signal the start of a new day, but the beginning of a new adventure, a new life even. It was a ***portent*** of things that were yet to come.

"We ought to get going," sniped Howie to the children.

Howie had been the first to fall asleep and the first to wake up. By the time the rooster had crowed he had already dressed, eaten, and prepared the horses. He might have been gruff, but he was well experienced with the goings-on of cross-country travel. Howie had learned that daylight burned quick, and to get a good day's travel in, time couldn't be wasted.

"What about breakfast?" a half-awake Anna protested.

"I packed ya'll each a bacon sandwich for the road," replied Howie.

As Howie answered Anna's question he tossed a bag full of wrapped bacon sandwiches into her lap. The

---

Portent (**pawr**-tent) – N – an indication or omen of something about to happen, especially something momentous

sandwiches were freshly made with bacon he had cooked that morning. Even through the paper bag, Anna could feel the original warmth of the cooking. Bacon was a luxury that the Watkins had gone without for some time and the smell of the sandwiches made Anna's stomach growl. She quickly opened up the sandwich bag to get her breakfast. As she was in the process of taking her first bite, Howie snatched her sandwich and the bag away from her.

"Hey!" cried a shocked Anna.

"For the road means for the road," snarled Howie. "We can't be waiting around for the princess to take her time having breakfast."

Howie took the sandwich bag and went out, slamming the front door behind him. At that moment it was obvious that Howie was not to be messed with. He clearly had more ***misanthropy*** in him than humanitarianism. Anna made a mental note to listen carefully next time and to always try and stay out of his way. She quickly got up to get Charlie ready to leave. She knew that if Howie had no patience for her, he certainly would not have any for her younger brother.

"Charlie," she whispered softly to the sleeping boy, "It is time to get up." Charlie remained unmoved.

"Charlie," Anna tried again, this time adding a gentle shake. Charlie continued to lie there.

"Charlie, I know you can hear me," continued Anna. "Get up!"

Finally the toddler rolled over and opened his eyes. He stretched his arms and slowly sat up. Charlie wasn't used to getting up that early, and he had gone to bed really late

---

Misanthropy (mis-**an**-thruh-pee) – N – hatred, dislike, or distrust of humankind

the night before. His movements were ***laggard***, signaling to Anna that waiting on him to get up himself was not an option. There was no sense in forcing the small child to get ready for the day since they really didn't need him to be awake to make the journey. Wrapping Charlie tightly in his blankets, Anna picked him up. She decided she would carry him to the wagon. The morning winds on the Wyoming prairie were icy, and Anna wrapped the covers more tightly over her brother. Snuggled in his cocoon, Charlie ***regressed*** to sleep.

Jacob and Howie were already sitting on the driver seat at the front of the wagon. They had finished arranging the horses and mules and were waiting for Anna and Charlie to emerge from the house. Without looking at Howie's face, Anna could feel the disapproving look she was receiving from him. She paid no heed, and went to the back of the wagon to get Charlie settled.

The small traveling party would journey in a typical covered wagon. The wagon itself was nothing special. It was a simple farm wagon that, with the addition of the canvas, a farmer had converted into a Prairie schooner. What made this wagon particularly attractive to Jacob, apart from the price, was that it was just large enough to carry all of the family's belongings. Almost 15 feet long, this schooner served the Watkins needs perfectly. Five big trunks filled the back of the wagon, leaving Anna little space to make a bed for Charlie. The ***spartan*** nature of the

---

Laggard (**lag**-erd) – ADJ – moving, developing, or responding slowly; sluggish

Regress (ri-**gres**) – V – to move backward; go back, to return to a previous state

Spartan (**spahr**-tn) – ADJ – marked by simplicity; avoidance of luxury

simple wagon required Anna to first lay down some pillows for Charlie to sleep on. Like all covered wagons, this one lacked suspension, making the journey along the rough terrain uncomfortable for the riders. Anna didn't want her younger brother to get beaten up from the rocky roads. Once the pallet was made, Anna surrounded Charlie with extra cushions and blankets to make him secure. There the toddler would sleep in his fortress of goose feathers and cloth.

As soon as Charlie was settled, Anna joined Jacob at the front of the wagon. She had hoped that they would be able to walk through the house once more to say their final good-byes, but when he motioned her to join Charlie in the back she understood that wish would have to go unrealized. Saddened, Anna slowly walked to the back of the wagon. She found a place close to Charlie's bed that would be semi-comfortable for their trip.

Anna barely had enough time to get settled before the wagon started to move. The buggy shook from side to side in the rhythm of the horses' trot, tossing Anna along with it. At that moment she knew that it would be a long journey back to St. Louis. Anna had no doubt that they would make it back east in one piece, however, she was pretty sure that piece would be black and blue.

The canvas that covered the wagon was tightly fastened in the back to protect the cargo from the unfriendly elements. Only a small keyhole gap was left open. Through this hole Anna watched her family's cabin get smaller and smaller with the distance. The sun was just beginning to rise as the small caravan departed. Rising just behind the cottage, the sun's golden rays framed the house perfectly. Anna stared at the picture before her as long as she could, searing the image into her memory. Ten years on the prairie had almost ***desensitized*** Anna to its true beauty; however, that day, with the sun shining across the little house, Anna was able to appreciate the western magnificence. Turning away from the gap in the canvas Anna carefully made her way to where Charlie was sleeping. She was tired and saw no point in remaining awake when she wasn't needed. Closing her eyes, she took a deep breath. No matter what the future held, she knew that a part of her would always miss that little farmhouse under the great big Wyoming sky.

Jacob sat up front with Howie, more to keep the old man company than offer his support with the horses. Howie was an expert driver and knew exactly what to do. There on the driver's seat, the crotchety old man was ***transmuted*** into something much more pleasant. Howie did not scoff or yell at the horses to obey his commands, but spoke gently and affectionately to the animals. If asked about it, Howie would say, "The dumb beasts work better when ya talk with 'em like that," but Jacob couldn't help but wonder if there was more to Howie than the image he presented. Perhaps the gentleness Howie showed to the horses represented a ***latent*** quality of softness in the traveler's character that wasn't seen on the surface. Puzzled, Jacob stared at the man who sat next to him, hoping that Howie's actions would help Jacob understand him better.

"What 'r' ya lookin' at?"

"Nothing," answered Jacob quickly. While Howie might have a softer side, Jacob didn't want to push his luck by angering his gruffer side.

Desensitize (dee-**sen**-si-tahyz) – V – to make indifferent, unaware, or the like, in feeling

Transmute (trans-**myoot**) – V – transform

Latent (**leyt**-nt) – ADJ – present but not visible, apparent, or actualized; existing as potential

"Good," replied Howie.

Then came a long pause. Jacob, who hated the thought of going the entire way back to St. Louis in silence decided he would try and get to know Howie a little bit better.

"So," began Jacob, "where are you from and what brought you out west?"

"You want my life story?" asked Howie.

"You could put it that way," replied Jacob.

"It's a long story, kid," responded Howie.

"We've got time," replied Jacob.

"Well, if you insist," said Howie. "I was born. I grew up. Then I decided I wanted some adventure so I moved out west. So here I am traveling with you fine folks. The end."

Jacob took ***umbrage*** at Howie's curt response, which was obvious by the annoyed look on the young lad's face. It would have been more polite of Howie merely to say that he didn't want to talk than to respond the way he just did. *Maybe the whole horse whispering thing was just a fluke,* thought Jacob. *Maybe Howie is just as harsh and rude on the inside as he appears on the outside.* Sure enough, the 40ish-year-old, unshaven, slightly overweight man who smelled faintly of ***bootleg*** whiskey was a mystery. The one thing Jacob could be sure of in that moment was that Howie didn't want to talk about his life story. Not waiting to make the same mistake twice, Jacob didn't dare to pick any other conversation topics. Instead he decided to let Howie start talking. Howie, however, was not one for idle chatter. The two rode the rest of the morning in silence.

Umbrage (**uhm**-brij) – N – offense; annoyance; displeasure

Bootleg (**boot**-leg) – N – alcoholic liquor unlawfully made, sold, or transported, without registration or payment of taxes

WORD REVIEW

Astringent	Flaccid	Portent
Blatant	Laggard	Regress
Bootleg	Latent	Revivify
Catalyst	Malign	Spartan
Desensitize	Mercenary	Transmute
Docent	Misanthropy	Umbrage

7

A BUMPY RIDE

It was well past noon before Howie stopped to water the horses. By that time everyone, except for the old man, was dying for a break. Charlie had been awake for some time and was going stir-crazy in the back. For the last hour or so, Anna had done everything she could to keep the small boy from jumping right out of the wagon. Once the wagon came to a complete stop, she let the child go. Without a moment's hesitation Charlie leapt out of the carriage and started making circles around the horse and wagon. He had never spent that much time cooped up before and he clearly wasn't enjoying this trip. It would take time for the toddler to get used to the extensive amount of traveling in a day. Anna, whose legs had grown stiff from the morning's ride, slowly followed her brother to the open pasture.

Everyone went their separate ways. Charlie ran fast out into the open prairie, exploring everything that he could find. Anna followed Charlie at a safe distance to keep an eye on the little adventurer. Jacob got up to stretch out the soreness in his limbs, and Howie stayed to take care of the animals. After giving them some fresh water, he pulled out pieces of carrots and gave them a small treat. Not wanting to ***protract*** the break, after a short 10 minutes

---

Protract (proh-**trakt**) – V – to draw out or lengthen, especially in time; extend the duration of; prolong

Howie called for the group to reassemble.

"All right," yelled Howie. "It's time to get back on the trail."

"What about lunch?" cried Charlie.

"I was told we have some biscuits in the back that your sister made," replied Howie. "We can eat those on the road."

And with that the small traveling party was ***remanded*** back to their wooden cage. The group had a long way to go and Howie wanted to make the most out of the first day of travel. Today would be the only day that the horses were fully rested and he wanted to take advantage of their energy. Many days of traveling still stretched ahead of them, and the old-timer knew the best way to get the children used to it was through dredging on. It wouldn't do any good to protract the entire trip with a series of unnecessary stops.

It was dusk before the covered wagon pulled to its stop for the evening. Howie had driven the horses slowly but steadily, and with his gentle guiding the group had made it to the edge of Wyoming. Howie had hoped to make it to Platesleaf, a small settlers' town just across the border of Nebraska, but he was content with where they ended up. He didn't mind sleeping under the wide Wyoming skies. Howie instructed the children to get out the supplies for dinner while he unhitched the animals. He sent Jacob to gather wood for the fire, but warned him to stay close to the campsite and not to wonder too far off; he cautioned that dusk was the time in summer when the snakes came out. Most snakes were harmless, but he warned Jacob about the prairie rattlesnake, whose venom was among the most deadly in the area. If bitten, a person needed immediate

---

Remand (ri-**mand**) – V – to send back, remit, or consign again

care. Without the proper treatment, the victim could at minimum lose a limb.

"Most people who get bitten in the wild die," Howie said, "and it's not a pleasant death. There's fever, swelling, and the shakes. Once you get bitten, you're in pain from that moment until the end. So my word of advice is this: Don't get bitten."

There was no drama to the way in which Howie described the results of a snake bite. He told his depressing tale as if he were describing the process of making tea. He ***averred*** as fact that people who got bitten by snakes on the prairie were in a very dangerous situation. Without a doctor in the group or in a nearby town, the bitten person would have no chance of attenuating the effects of the venom or the pain. Howie had it right when he said "Don't get bitten." It was a word of advice that served everyone well to listen to. Jacob was about to leave, but Howie stopped him.

"One more thing," he began. "Most of the time these snakes do ya a favor and let ya know that they are there. When they sense danger they make a distinctive rattling sound. If you hear that sound it means stop what ya're doing and look around. Once you spot the snake, slowly back away. That is no time to panic; quick moments will make them more likely to strike."

Howie then let the anxious Jacob go to get the wood for the fire. In the growing darkness, Jacob's moments were calculated. He was careful not to turn over any big logs, or go into the grass that was too high. He wanted to see exactly where he put his hands. The last thing he wanted was to reach down to pick up a stick and return with a snake instead. From that moment on anything that

---

Aver (uh-**vur**) – V – to state positively as true

sounded remotely like a rattle made Jacob jump. Jacob's extra precaution doubled the time it normally took to get firewood; it was almost completely dark by the time he returned.

In the meantime, Howie and Anna prepared the campground for the small party. Howie was a strong believer in everyone pulling his or her weight on the wagon trail, and even Charlie was given a task to do. The toddler was given a petite twig broom and was told to sweep the campsite. Even the smallest tasks were important assured Howie, and the three-year-old took pride in having his own essential job to do. Once the animals and wagon were secured to the nearby tree, Howie dug the firepit. The Watkins children all worked hard, hoping to ***ingratiate*** themselves with Howie. They were all going to be on the road together for a long time, and they realized the time would go by quicker without tension between the guide and his travelers.

There wasn't enough room in the wagon for everyone to sleep inside; there was only space for two people. Mr. Daniels' store had been sold out of tents, so those who didn't sleep in the wagon would have to sleep either under it, or just under the stars until they were able to find a town that had a tent. It had already been decided that given his age and vulnerability, Charlie would always be able to sleep in the wagon. Howie, as a seasoned trail guide, had absolutely no problem sleeping in the elements and left the decision over sleeping in the wagon to the two older Watkins children. In a normal situation, Anna,

---

Ingratiate (in-**grey**-shee-yet) – V – to establish (oneself) in the favor or good graces of others, especially by deliberate effort

as the girl, would be given preferential treatment and be given the second coveted spot in the wagon. However, on the prairie, formality gave way to survival, and naturally the person who got the better night's rest would be more help the next day on the road. Both Anna and Jacob knew that it would be more beneficial for the group to let Jacob have the sleeping quarters in the wagon. Willing to prove that she was tough and could handle the elements, Anna insisted that Jacob sleep in the wagon with Charlie. Jacob, being the more logical of the two, suggested that they alternate. Thus it was decided that tonight Jacob would get the wagon, and the next night it would be Anna's turn. It was a fair arrangement that left everyone pleased with the compromise. Impressed by her own selflessness, Anna proudly made her bed under the stars.

The ***fervid*** firepit illuminated the small campsite. Under the vast, open, black sky, the four travelers enjoyed a hearty dinner of beans, salted pork, homemade biscuits, and Howie's freshly made coffee. The long day on the road had exhausted everyone, and the hot meal was exactly what they needed to ease the soreness from the road. Howie made more than was needed for the evening meal. Morning would again come early and the group wouldn't have time to have such an elaborate feast for breakfast. Life on the road meant only one hot meal a day; anything else had to be eaten as cold leftovers.

Every day on the road played out similar to the first. The group would rise early in the morning, eat some of the dinner's leftovers for breakfast, travel all day on the road, then stop just before dark to make their campsite and go to bed exhausted. The only exception was that Jacob ended

---

Fervid (**Fur**-vid) – ADJ – burning; glowing; intensely hot

up sleeping under the stars every night, letting Anna have the wagon with Charlie. One night sleeping next to his little brother, who had a ***propensity*** to kick, was enough for him. Anna, who was used to Charlie's nightly antics, happily traded. One night sleeping out in the open stars with bugs and all kinds of animal noises was enough for her. Anna would take a night with Charlie's incessant tossing and turnings to a night with possible snakes any time.

The first couple weeks on the road were the most productive of the journey. Both the travelers and the livestock were at their freshest and could handle extra-long periods of time on the road. In less than a week the small expedition party was able to make it out of Wyoming and halfway through Nebraska. It was a feat that Howie would boast about for years to come. The extraordinary amount of speed was due to a combination of factors. Howie had a special right to brag since the main reason the miniature caravan was doing so well was because of his ***tutelage***. His 26 years of experience as a trail guide meant he knew exactly how long and how fast he could drive the horses and mules. By listening to the animals, Howie could tell when he could push them to go faster or longer, and when they needed to stop. Howie's expertise kept Samson, Delilah, David, and Goliath working at their best. The animals would have followed him anywhere.

Unfortunately Howie wasn't as good with people as he was with the animals. The long days on the roads took their toll on everyone in the traveling party, and the time spent together on the harsh prairie heightened the latent

---

Propensity (pruh-**pen**-si-tee) – N – a natural inclination or tendency

Tutelage (**toot**-l-ij) – N – instruction; teaching; guidance tension in the group. Because of the bumpiness of the trail, settlers didn't typically ride in the wagon. Most groups walked alongside the horses, and only the sick or elderly endured the roughness of a wagon ride. However, in this particular traveling party, one small member was almost instantaneously relegated to the back of the wagon—Charlie. He was perfectly capable of walking alongside the wagon with the others, but he wouldn't. However, when he was put inside the wagon to ride, he complained. No matter what he was doing at any given moment, he would beg to do the opposite. Howie wasn't about to let a three-year-old dictate the pace of the journey. The old man was able to stand only one day of the little tyrant's antics before he commanded that Charlie stay in the back of the wagon no matter what. When Anna protested, Howie relegated her to the back to join him. Anna didn't have to stay back there, and Howie insisted she was free to leave the moment she stopped allowing her younger brother to manipulate her. Angry at Howie's condescendence, Anna sat defiantly in the back with Charlie for five days. Finally her sore backside got the better of her, and she slinked out of the back to walk alongside the wagon.

"So ya finally decided to join the other adults," was the only thing Howie said.

Sore at him, Anna refused to respond to Howie for the rest of the day. Jacob chose to remain neutral in the battle that was waging on between Charlie, Anna, and Howie. While normally Jacob would have stood up for his younger siblings, he had to admit that this time Howie was right. Charlie was acting wild, and Anna was spoiling him by catering to his every whim. It took the time on the trail to notice it, but Jacob realized that since their parents' illness, Anna had done nothing but coddle Charlie. The results had been disastrous. Charlie was a bright little boy and he had quickly learned that Anna's softness meant he could do whatever he wanted. Charlie didn't take Howie's ***rebuke*** well, but Jacob knew that a stern hand was exactly what the youngster needed. *What better place to learn the importance of obedience,* Jacob thought, *than on the trail when the consequences of not listening could be fatal.* Out here Charlie's obstinacy was not just annoying; it was potentially life-threatening. Yet to Anna, Jacob's neutrality made it appear that he was siding with a stranger over his family. Thus by the first week of the journey the lines were drawn and a cold war waged between the two sides of the conflict. Anna and Charlie stood at one end of the battlefield and Jacob and Howie stood on the other. The strain felt by both sides only served to widen the chasm. If left unchecked these ***antebellum*** tensions would transform into an all-out prairie war; something had to be done to lessen the growing conflicts among the group. Otherwise the small traveling party would have their own civil war.

Rebuke (ri-**byook**) – N – sharp, stern disapproval; reproof; reprimand

Antebellum (an-tee-**bel**-uhm) – ADJ – of or during the period before a war, especially the American Civil War

WORD REVIEW

Antebellum	Ingratiate	Rebuke
Aver	Propensity	Remand
Fervid	Protract	Tutelage

8

INTO GULF'S CANYON

They had been on the trail for nearly two weeks before the group of travelers had a chance to take a break from the road, and from each other. By the end of those two weeks they had reached the far border of Nebraska and Howie knew of a reasonably large town where they could spend a couple of days resting from their journey. The town, called Gulf's Canyon, was named after a canyon on the far eastside of town that was as large as a gulf of an ocean. There in Gulf's Canyon the fatigued travelers could get some hot meals and sleep in real beds. Howie wasn't one who would typically indulge in such luxuries for the sake of giving into idle fancies; his main reason for stopping was for restocking their supplies and having the horses reshod. The trail was rocky and without taking care of the animals pulling the wagon, the wagon wouldn't get very far. However, even the tough old man realized that for the good of the whole group, a couple days of rest was greatly needed; so he suggested that they stop. Anna and Charlie immediately agreed. Anna was dying for a hot bath and clean sheets to sleep on, and Charlie could not wait to get out of the back of the wagon. Jacob was the only one who protested. He wanted to get to St. Louis as quickly as possible and to settle into their new city. He argued that they didn't have the time or the money to act like ***spendthrifts***. Eating hot meals,

---

Spendthrift (**spend**-thrift) – N – a person who spends possessions or money extravagantly or wastefully; prodigal

sleeping in hotel beds, and staying in town could be expensive and they needed to be careful with how they spent their money. They could go into town to get supplies and have the horses re-shod, insisted Jacob, but they should continue to sleep outside and eat as inexpensively as possible. As the eldest child, and the keeper of the money, Jacob had the final say. Anna could argue with him as much as she wanted, but it was pointless. Despite the wealth that they both knew they had, Jacob was resolved to act like a ***skinflint***. Even Howie thought Jacob was acting miserly, but it wasn't his business so he kept his mouth shut. He would tend to caring for the horses and gathering supplies, and he would let the siblings work things out as they may. Therefore, a somewhat disappointed group made their way into town.

What they didn't know as they were heading into the city was that very soon Jacob would change his mind concerning the hotel, but not for the luxury of staying in a clean bed. It had been over a year since Howie was last in Gulf's Canyon, and within that short amount of time the town had undergone a great ***cataclysm*** of changes. Sheriff Willfox, a man who helped build the town, had passed away early last spring, right after the last night Howie was there. Willfox had been a model of decency and had run the town strictly by law and order. The streets were safe for women and children; the worst crime in the city was the occasional petty theft from the country store by a rebellious youngster. Even then Sheriff Willfox made sure that the youngster, who often took the goods because of some form of ***klepto-***

Skinflint (**skin**-flint) – N – miser
Cataclysm (**kat**-uh-kliz-uhm) – N – any violent upheaval, especially one of a social or political nature

mania rather than economic necessity, would never do it again. One night in jail with Sheriff Willfox was enough to turn any sinner into the ideal saint. Although stern when it came to the law, Sheriff Willfox was a kind man who loved his town. Everything he did, he did for the good of the community and his efforts paid off. Under his tutelage Gulf's Canyon prospered and remained an idyllic location for young families to come and start their new lives on the western prairie.

What had taken Sheriff Willfox and the other founders nearly twenty years to build was all but destroyed in a matter of months. The Sheriff, who was a devout religious man, had fought hard to keep all forms of debase temptations out of Gulf's Canyon. On the top of his list of carnal enticements were alcohol and gambling. Therefore, since the inception of the town, there was a law prohibiting the building and proprietorship of saloons and casinos. Many investors who had heard of the success of Gulf's Canyon came from miles looking to build the town's first saloon or casino, but everyone was turned away. If the town were going to prosper, insisted Sheriff Willfox, it would do so from the purity of an honest day's work and not from such ***raffish*** establishments as dance-halls and gambling dens. On this matter, Sheriff Willfox remained firm until the day he died.

Unfortunately for the town, the old sheriff was one of the few men left in town who held that view. Once Sheriff Willfox died, his beliefs went with him. Gulf's Canyon town's leadership waited a month to vote on the matter

---

Kleptomania (klep-tuh-**mey**-nee-uh) – N – an irresistible impulse to steal, stemming from emotional disturbance rather than economic need

Raffish (**raf**-ish) – ADJ – gaudily vulgar or cheap; tawdry

out of respect for the departed sheriff, but the law banning saloons and casinos was quickly overturned by a large majority. Under normal circumstances, contrary to fervent beliefs of the departed sheriff, the addition of a saloon or casino would not have dramatically altered the atmosphere of the town. In their proper place, both businesses had the opportunity to enrich the diversity and the culture of any thriving city. As places of entertainment and sport, saloons and casinos attracted tourists and their money. Opening up the city to them had the possibility of enhancing the livelihood of the city and its inhabitants.

Where the town leadership went wrong was in the person they decided to let build such structures. Maxamillion Cartwright III, who everyone just called Big Max, had beguiled the small government into letting him be the first to open Gulf's Canyon to a new world of possibilities. Big Max was a sly-talking businessman who knew exactly what needed to be said to the simple-minded farmers to get their ***sanction*** for his projects. The cunning entrepreneur sold the vision of a new Gulf's Canyon, one that was modern and attractive. Sheriff Willfox's rules had kept the town in the Stone Age, Big Max had argued, but he would bring it into the 19th Century. It didn't take long for the same government of Gulf's Canyon to turn over the future of the city to Big Max. Not only was the out-of-towner given permission to build his dream saloon and casino, but he also was soon given the title of mayor. The men of Gulf's Canyon were all in agreement that a big timer from back East was better equipped to run a city than a lot of corn famers. Truthfully, the corn farmers didn't

---

Sanction (**sangk**-shuhn) – N – authoritative permission or approval, as for an action

want the responsibility of running the city, and in Big Max they found a way to quietly hand over their responsibility under the guise of doing what was best for the city. All they had to do was sit back and watch the town prosper.

The men of Gulf's Canyon ended up watching the rapid decline of the decency of their town. Big Max was a businessman ***solicitous*** of wealth and saw in Gulf's Canyon a golden ticket. As one of the few "modern" cities on the trail out west, the city had the distinct advantage of having no competition. If settlers going west wanted to stop and resupply their wagons, they had to stop at Gulf's Canyon. While many wagon caravans had a large number of families, they were also often made up of numerous single men who were looking to start a new life out west. These men were Big Max's target audience. Big Max would offer the rowdy bunches that passed through the town cheap entertainment. Gulf's Canyon would be Big Max's gold mine. Once he officially came into power, the first thing Big Max did was replace the old corn farmers of the town council with a new group of men like-minded to himself. This newly-positioned ***junta*** made it possible for him to get whatever laws he wanted passed to make the town friendlier to his new changes. By the time anyone thought to protest these improvements, there was barely a trace of Sheriff's Willfox's Gulf's Canyon. A small group of farmers did manage to bring their concerns to Big Max, but they were quickly persuaded, with the assistance of the guns from Big Max's posse, that the newfound changes were for the best. Most of the townsfolk chose to remain silent and

---

Solicitous (suh-**lis**-i-tuhs) – ADJ – anxiously desirous

Junta (**hoon**-tuh) – N – a small group ruling a country, especially immediately after a coup d'état and before a legally constituted government has been instituted

let the new mayor do what he wanted. Some people moved out of town, but the majority, due to financial limitations, remained.

The initial changes made to the town actually did improve Gulf's Canyon. With the relaxation of the outdated rules, the community was able to enjoy their first saloon-restaurant and casino house. Both organizations were friendly to families and would close at a decent hour so as not to be a public nuance. The new entertainment enticed travelers to stay an extra day or two in Gulf's Canyon, and thus a tourism economy opened up. Big Max was so sure of the town's potential for property that he made his saloon, casino, and hotel twice the size that they needed to be. The buildings were dressed with the finest of everything money could buy; everything was new and ***sumptuous***. In less than a couple months Big Max had delivered on his promise of bringing Gulf's Canyon out of the Stone Age and into the modern era. The only problem was that Big Max was an entrepreneur, but not a millionaire. While he might have been the one to have the new buildings constructed, he certainly wasn't the one who paid for it. Big Max had acquired the funds from back East, and had wagered a great deal on the success of his new enterprises. Although Big Max had been right about Gulf's Canyon's potential, he had been wrong on the amount of time it would take to start seeing profits. The sad truth was that Big Max had taken out an exorbitant loan that he wouldn't be able to pay back, at least not in the near future. It was a fact which Big Max became aware of shortly after the first couple of months following the grand opening of his buildings. Big

---

Sumptuous (**suhmp**-choo-uhs) – ADJ – entailing great expense, as from choice materials, fine work, etc.; costly

Max hadn't acquired the loan through a typical bank, and he knew all too well of the costly ***retribution*** he'd have to pay if he didn't make his loan payments on time. Desperate for a solution, Big Max decided to open the town up to those who would otherwise be unwelcome. For a price, Gulf's Canyon could be a sanctuary to any fellow looking to avoid the law. Gulf's Canyon had no sheriff and had a weak mayor who would look the other way for a fee. Needless to say, this attracted not only the tourists looking to have a good time, but all kinds of less-than-reputable characters. It didn't take long for Big Max to sell out the town to anyone who was willing to pay for it. Gulf's Canyon became the center of lawlessness and debauchery. While it was reasonably safe to go out during the day, no decent person would be caught anywhere outside after dark. Soon Gulf's Canyon was completely ***stigmatized*** as being unsafe.

However, Howie had not heard of any of this, and led the unsuspecting group directly into the town's center. From the outskirts everything looked just as it had when he was last there, but as soon as they arrived into town it was evident things had dramatically changed. The once pristine main street was littered with trash. Women adorned themselves in the wildest fashions of Europe and the men appeared to be anything but gentlemanly. Furthermore there were no children anywhere. The scene that played out before the travelers was far from the one Howie was used to seeing in Gulf's Canyon, a town he remembered as so clean it made a person who just took a bath feel dirty, a place where the men and women dressed

Retribution (re-truh-**byoo**-shuhn) – N – requital according to merits or deserts, especially for evil

Stigmatize (**stig**-muh-tahyz) – V – to set some mark of disgrace or infamy upon

in the plain attire of farmers, and where everywhere one looked there were families with not just one child, but many. Immediately Howie knew that something was amiss. He drove the wagon to the back of the general store and parked it next to few other wagons brave enough to wait there. Not wanting to alarm his young crew, he suggested that the children go to the next store and grab something to eat while he inquired about getting the horses reshod. Jacob suggested that he would go with the old trail guide, but Howie was insistent that the young man stay with his siblings and that they remain in the restaurant until he returned. Reluctantly Jacob agreed to remain with Anna and Charlie. Howie watched as the children walked into a simply adorned restaurant called Aunt Betty's Place. By the look of the rest of the town, Aunt Betty's Place was a lone reminder of Sheriff's Willfox's town. Tired from the road, the Watkins sat down to enjoy their first stove-cooked meal in a long time.

Howie had only told the children part of the truth. He was indeed going to look for information about taking care of the horses, but he wanted a lot more information than just that. Having passed through the town numerous times during his travels, Howie had become good friends with the old sheriff. While Howie personally found some of the ***tenets*** of Sheriff Willfox's regime to be a little extreme, Howie liked the man. Seeing Gulf's Canyon in the state that it was, Howie knew that something was seriously wrong. The old traveler went straight to the jailhouse hoping to find news of his friend, the sheriff. When Howie found the

---

Tenet (**ten**-it) – N – any opinion, principle, doctrine, dogma, etc., especially one held as true by members of a profession, group, or movement

jailhouse closed, an oddity for a Tuesday afternoon, he went next door to the barber's shop. There he found an older gentleman sitting on a bench reading a newspaper. Howie knocked on the door frame to get the man's attention.

"Can I help you?" the barber asked halfheartedly.

"Are you free for a shave?" asked Howie.

Puzzled by the question, the old barber looked at Howie then glanced around the rest of his shop. Seeing as there was obviously no one else there, the man looked back at Howie.

"I believe I am free," he replied.

Howie walked into the small barbershop and sat down in the barber's chair. The half bald barber motioned to Howie that he would be with him in a moment. The man proceeded to put down his newspaper and went to gather the supplies that he needed. Howie was not a man who ***preened*** himself fancy, and had probably only sat in a barber's chair twice in his entire life. Normally, when he needed a haircut he would do it himself, and he found that trying to stay shaved on the road was more of a hassle than it was worth. His thick salt-and-pepper beard was a testament that the man hadn't shaved once all year. Howie had another purpose other than grooming for going to the barber; he was there to gather information. Barbershops are often the places for people to congregate, and if there is one person in town who knows everything about what is going on in that town it is the barber. Howie knew that he couldn't simply walk into the man's shop to interrogate him. Howie needed to blend in; he needed

---

Preen (preen) – V – to dress (oneself) carefully or smartly; primp

acculturation into the fashion of the townspeople. Thus he sat in the man's chair and waited for the right time to ask his questions. The elderly barber stood next to Howie stirring up the milky white foam that he would apply to Howie's face. Once the foam was good and frothy the barber turned toward Howie. Just before he put the first dab on the trail guide's face, he stopped. Standing next to Howie, the distracted barber got his first good look at the bushel of hair that adorned the man's face; white foam alone would not be enough to make Howie look presentable, the barber needed something more. Carefully the barber set down his cup of foam, rolled up his sleeves, and pulled out a large pair of ***serrated*** scissors to chop through the rough beard. The pair of scissors were discolored from age, and looked as though any minute it would come apart. Noticing the inquisitive look on his patron's face, the barber smiled and made a joke.

"They may be old," remarked the barber, "but they work, just like me."

"I'm not scared, boss," replied Howie with a smile. "Do your worst."

The old barber liked Howie's attitude and took his last comment as a sort of challenge. When Howie had first walked into the door, the old man couldn't have cared less about the stranger, but now, especially after really seeing the state of Howie's facial hair, the barber wanted to do his best work. The barber was determined to turn the grizzly bear that sat before him into a respectable-looking

---

Acculturation	(uh-kuhl-chuh-**rey**-shuhn) – N – the process of adopting the cultural traits or social patterns of another group
Serrated	(ser-**ey**-tid) – ADJ – having a notched edge or saw-like teeth, especially for cutting

gentleman. The barber began to hack away at the forest of hair on the man's face.

"You want a haircut?" asked the barber.

Although the old man had asked a question, Howie could tell from the man's ***inflection*** that it was meant more as a command. The barber believed Howie NEEDED a haircut and only inserted the word WANT to be polite. This made Howie laugh.

"Sure, old-timer," Howie said jovially. "Why not?"

This answer pleased the barber, and all traces of distance in his demeanor melted away. He soon warmed up to the rugged mountain man and began to chat away.

"You're not from around here, are ya?" questioned the barber.

"Na, I'm just passing through," responded Howie. "I'm comin' from Greater Wyoming on my way back East. I stopped in Gulf's Canyon because I got some horses that are in some bad need of new shoes."

Howie didn't like to give away a lot of personal information to strangers, but he knew that gathering information was a ***quid pro quo*** game. If Howie wanted news about the town he needed to give the barber something. At the barbershop money wasn't the only form of currency.

"Ah, I see," responded the barber. "If you ask any in town they'll tell you to go to Dave; his shop is located by the general store. Dave's work is OK and he's cheap, but when newcomers are in town he tends to forget to *lock* up his stable at night. Things have been known to disappear out of strangers' wagons, if you catch my drift."

Inflection (in-**flek**-shuhn) – N – modulation of the voice; change in pitch or tone of voice

Quid pro quo (**kwid** proh **kwoh**) – N – one thing in return for another

"I understand," replied Howie.

"So it's better for you, and safer for your stuff, to go visit Tim. He's on the outskirts of town near the old church. He's more expensive, but he does a good job. Best of all, he's honest and will look after your stuff like it was his."

Howie had no way of truly knowing whether or not the barber was being honest with him. It was possible that the old barber worked with this Tim to attract naïve travelers into a scam. It could be that Dave was the honest one, and Tim stole from the wagons of strangers. However, this conclusion seemed a little outlandish to Howie. To him the old barber appeared honest and was ***presumably*** telling the truth.

"Couldn't the travelers who had their stuff *lost* take their complaints to the sheriff?" asked Howie.

Howie asked his question in such a way that would give him information about Sheriff Willfox but ***circumvented*** giving away the information that he had previously known the sheriff or the town. The trail guide firmly believed it was more advantageous for him and his traveling party to seem ignorant of the town's goings-on. If Howie played his cards right he could avoid making his group a target of any unwanted attention.

"They wouldn't have to if Sheriff Willfox was still around," responded the barber. "He never in a million years would let a person like Dave, with his questionable reputation, run a business in this town. But things are so

---

Presumably (pri-**zoo**-muh-blee) – ADV – by assuming reasonably; probably

Circumvent (sur-kuhm-**vent**) – V – to avoid (defeat, failure, unpleasantness, etc.) by artfulness or deception; avoid by anticipating or outwitting

different now after his death; the poor sheriff wouldn't even recognize this place. Big Max has made sure of that."

Howie seriously wanted to ask the old barber who Big Max was, and how he came to be in charge but the man had worked fast and both the haircut and the shave were now finished. Of course Howie could have stayed longer and continued his conversation with the man, but he didn't want to run the risk of seeming too inquisitive, for doing so would destroy his perceived ***nescience***. He would just have to get the rest of the information elsewhere.

The barber handed Howie a mirror to review the man's handiwork. At first glance Howie was taken aback by the reflection he saw. It had been some time since he had seen his whole face. Howie looked younger without the scraggly beard and unkempt hair. The barber had taken off more than just several inches of hair from Howie's head. Somehow he had erased the look of the hard years on the road. Howie appeared a little bit softer and approachable. The man who stared back at him in the mirror was not the man Howie was used to seeing. His wild hair had been an unattractive ***excrescence*** to his appearance.

"I think this is your best work yet old-timer," said Howie, as he returned the mirror to the barber.

"I do believe I made a new man out of you," the barber replied with a smile.

"I believe you did," was all Howie could say in response.

"Since you're new in town, here's some advice that you might find helpful. If anyone offers to do something for you, politely decline. They are usually up to no good," cautioned the old man. "You also want to stay at Nina's

---

Nescience (**nesh**-ee-uh-ns) – N – lack of knowledge; ignorance
Excrescence (ik-**skres**-uh-ns) – N – a disfiguring addition

Hotel. It's right in the center of town. The clientele isn't usually the best, but ol' Nina is honest and she'll make sure nothing happens to you and your crew."

Howie paid the man and tipped him an extra 10 cents for a job well done. This pleased the barber who thanked Howie generously. Having gotten the information that he had sought, Howie got up to go check on the children. It had been a little over an hour since he had left them, and he knew they would be just about finished with their meal by now. As Howie walked out the door, the barber called to him in a deep, ***sonorous*** voice.

"And if you have any children with you, make sure that they don't go out alone," hollered the old barber. "Children are such easy targets of mischief."

"Thanks for the advice," said Howie.

The barber's last comment encouraged Howie to make his way quickly to his young crew. Just because the kids had a tendency to get on his nerves didn't mean he wanted anything bad to happen to them. He realized at that moment, when the thought occurred to him that the Watkins might be in danger, that he had grown somewhat fond of the brood. Having been on the road together every day, Howie had learned quite a bit about his traveling party. He heard about the illness of their parents and the fact that they were no longer able to keep their farm. As the leader, Howie felt responsible for the well-being of his horde, and he knew that it was his duty to keep them safe. After all, he thought to himself, misfortunes seemed to ***abound*** one after the other for the Watkins. Howie walked in record

---

Sonorous (suh-**nawr**-uhs) – ADJ – rich and full in sound

Abound (uh-**bound**) – V – to occur or exist in great quantities or numbers

speed back to Aunt Betty's small diner.

On his return journey Howie was now able to adequately comprehend the strange feeling that he had felt when he first strolled into town. Unwittingly he had sensed the overall ***ascendancy*** of Big Max's changes. From the looks of the people, the air of the town, and the uneasiness in his spirit, Howie had discerned corruptness of the new Gulf's Canyon. The old trail guide knew from personal experience there were a lot of wicked men in the world, and he wasn't about to let anything bad happen on his watch.

Howie bounded up the stairs of the dinner and quickly peered in the window to catch sight of his small traveling party. There in the back sat three happy faces, each eating a large piece of homemade apple pie. The Watkins sat by themselves, but from the window Howie could see Aunt Betty herself keeping her eye on the children. Upon seeing everyone safe, Howie was able to let out the breath he had been holding in since he left the barber's shop. He quickly gathered his composure to limit any traces of anxiety from his face or body language. Nothing would be more likely to cause panic in the small group than ***conspicuous*** fear by the leader. Under no circumstances could Howie let on that being in this town made him feel uneasy, nor could he let the children think that he actually worried about them.

Howie entered the diner to receive a sharp look from Aunt Betty. The meaning of her stare was all too clear—*How dare you leave children alone in a place like this?*

Ascendancy (uh-**sen**-duhn-see) – N – governing or controlling influence; domination

Conspicuous (kuhn-**spik**-yoo-uhs) – ADJ – easily seen or noticed; readily visible or observable

Howie forced an apologetic smile, possibly his first ever, and made his way over to the table where the kids were enjoying their dessert.

The ***interstice*** of Howie's excursion went almost completely unnoticed by the Watkins. Aunt Betty had taken such good care of them that not once since they sat down did they want for anything. Utterly oblivious to the goings-on around them, the three youngsters were able to enjoy their meal free from any and all cares. So engrossed were the trio in their pie that they almost didn't notice the figure that stood hovering over them. Had Anna not just finished her piece she might not have even looked up.

"Howie?" a puzzled Anna asked.

Taken aback by Anna's questioning expression, Howie had forgotten how considerably different he looked without his beard and with a new haircut. She thought he looked younger, handsomer, and most importantly, gentler, all words that Anna never thought she would use in her life to describe Howie. But there the rugged outdoorsman stood, so clean-shaven that he could almost pass off as a gentleman. Howie decided not to go into the story about the barber and his new look, but instead jumped right in to make plans for their stay in Gulf's Canyon, a visit that he intended to make as short as possible.

"I found out where we can get the animals taken care of," began Howie. "It will take two days, so I think it's best that we stay in a hotel."

The words *stay in a hotel* made Anna want to squeal for joy. Thoughts of hot baths, comfortable beds, and no bugs came flooding back into her mind. Howie sensed

Interstice (in-**tur**-stis) – N – an interval of time

Jacob's hesitation and cut him off before he could protest.

"Now I know things are a bit difficult fer ya, financially speaking and all," said Howie. "So the hotel bill is on me. I know I could really use a good night's rest."

Howie's offer to pay for the hotel was more stunning than his new appearance. The man who was notorious for only caring about money was willing to pay for their hotel room. It seemed unbelievable. Yet Howie remained ***inexorable*** on this promise; he would take care of the bill. The trail guide was indeed a mystery. It had only taken the first week on the road together for Jacob to change his initial impression of the man who stood before them. Jacob had been wrong not to trust Howie—the man was so fair that he would count out exact change when he paid for things—but he had not been wrong about Howie's gruff nature. Howie looked out for himself and expected others to do the same. Like his softness to the horses, Howie's proposal complicated Jacob's assessment of the man's character. The old rider turned out to be more difficult to dissect than he had first appeared. "One-eyed Howie" proved that first impressions are often wrong. Spending time with someone was indeed the only real way to know that person's character.

Aunt Betty offered Howie a piece of apple pie, but he politely refused, not because he thought that Betty wanted something from him, but because he was growing anxious to get the horses, mules, and wagon to Tim's stable. Howie wasn't so worried about the Watkins' personal belongings—he was after all clueless about their small fortune hidden under the wagon—the old trail guide was concerned about the two beautiful horses. Given Gulf's Canyon's new reputation, Howie didn't want to test how long it would take

---

Inexorable (in-**ek**-ser-uh-buhl) – ADJ – unyielding; unalterable

for someone to notice the prize horses and attempt to take them off the Watkins' hands. The children finished quickly, and as soon as they paid their bill they were free to go. Aunt Betty herself had been their waitress, cook, and then cashier, which ensured her ability to make sure the pie was *on the house.* Anna and Jacob thanked the kind woman. Charlie didn't say anything but instead ran up to her and gave her a great big hug. Aunt Betty was surprised by the youngster's actions. She wasn't used to getting hugs from strangers, especially ones that hug at knee height, but the affection which the toddler showed her made her smile.

It was less than a two-minute walk from the diner to the back of the general store, but those two minutes seemed to last forever. Howie did not idly waste the time, but spent it concocting a plan of action if the horses were missing. On their way out from Aunt Betty's, the small traveling party got their first taste of the rough and tumble nature of the newly renovated Gulf's Canyon. Standing between Aunt Betty's diner and the path to the back of the general store were two men arguing. The men were loud and making quite a scene in the public square. At first Howie thought they would go around the two men, but he soon realized that wouldn't be a good idea. The men were angry, and although it was only the middle of the afternoon, both men were soaked. While at that moment the two men were harmless, the situation was volatile; any minute it could turn dangerous.

"You no-good lying cheat," yelled out the first man. "You stole my wallet!"

"I did nuthin' of the sort, you yellow coward," cried out the second man.

"You're a bilk," retorted the first.

"Bosh!" screamed the second.

There they stood in the middle of their way

shouting ***slanders*** back and forth at each other. The ***calumny*** of defamation continued as they continued arguing. The Watkins had never seen two men standing in the middle of a town square having such an argument. Howie, who had been in a few drunken brawls himself, was unmoved by the scene in front of them. He was more surprised by the onlookers, namely that there weren't any. Normally such a loud confrontation would cause people to stop and stare, but here no one paid any attention to the men's argument. They all went on with their business, as if the theatre were an everyday occurrence. Howie quickly put his hands on the children's shoulders and directed them away from the two men. He was ***steadfast***, determined to get them out of the way of danger.

As they reached the back of the general store, Howie was relieved for the second time that day to see everything in its place. The two horses and two mules were exactly where he had left them. The children wanted to check into the hotel, but Howie insisted that they all stay together as a group. First, they would take the animals to the stable; then they would go to the hotel. Logistically it wasn't the most sensible plan, but it was the safest. Normally the children would question Howie's logic, but not this time. Something in his voice

---

Slander	(**slan**-der) – N – a malicious, false, and defamatory statement or report
Calumny	(**kal**-uhm-nee) – N – the act of uttering calumnies; slander; defamation
Steadfast	(**sted**-fast) – ADJ – fixed in direction; steadily directed

made it ***translucently*** apparent that now was the time to trust the old trail guide. So they all went together.

As Howie had expected, Tim would need a couple of days to tend to the animals. Like the barber, Tim was older and had lived in Gulf's Canyon long before Big Max and his wild crew came to town. Tim was of the Sheriff Willfox generation, and had been a personal friend of the departed lawman. This information put Howie's mind at ease. Tim could be trusted and their belongings would be safe.

"I lock the barn every night," said Tim. "But if a thief really wanted in, he could get in. My dogs sleep in the barn to help keep things safe, but even still if you have something of particular value, it would be best to take it with you."

Jacob knew immediately that meant he needed to take the money box with them. The young man went into Tim's stable where they had parked the wagon. Jacob crawled under the wagon and carefully removed the Watkins' hidden treasure. Not wanting to bring attention to the valuables, Jacob cautiously wrapped the box in a beautiful quilt. He then tucked the quilt under his arm, with the box inside of it, and walked out of the barn.

"I checked the wagon," Jacob began. "And there really isn't anything there of much monetary value. I did, However, find Mama's homemade quilt. It's not worth much to a stranger, but it would be irreplaceable for us."

"Their mama's passed on," added Howie to explain Jacob's sentiment.

"Very well then," said Tim. "Come back on Thursday; the animals will be ready by then."

Translucent (trans-**loo**-suhnt) – ADJ – easily understandable; lucid

It was a long trek from Tim's house on the outskirts of town back to the center. The sun stood high in the sky casting down its burning rays. They made the walk in silence, each one lost in his or her own thoughts. Charlie was due for a nap, Anna wanted to take a bath, Jacob was perplexed by the sudden change in Howie, and Howie was on a constant lookout for danger. Once they were settled in their hotel, Howie pulled Jacob aside to explain the situation of Gulf's Canyon. Howie knew that it would be easier to keep an eye on Anna and Charlie with Jacob's help. Jacob understood and promised to keep things quiet. By sharing the responsibility to care for the younger members of the group, Howie expressed his approval of the young man. Jacob hadn't realized how important it was to him that Howie believed he could handle a job like this until Howie showed confidence in him. The strange circumstances of Gulf's Canyon, and the danger that lurked on the streets had somehow brought the two divergent men to an understanding. Howie respected Jacob as a man, and Jacob respected Howie for his years of experience. Together they took on the burden of leaving Gulf's Canyon in the same condition as, or better than, when they came in.

WORD REVIEW

Abound
Acculturation
Ascendancy
Calumny
Cataclysm
Circumvent
Conspicuous
Excrescence
Inexorable
Inflection
Interstice
Junta
Kleptomania
Nescience
Preen
Presumably
Quid Pro Quo
Raffish
Retribution
Sanction
Serrated
Skinflint
Slander
Solicitous
Sonorous
Spendthrift
Steadfast
Stigmatize
Sumptuous
Tenet
Translucent

9

AMBUSH AT THE WATERING HOLE

Thursday was slow in coming, and the small traveling party from Wyoming spent most of their time waiting inside the hotel. They left their room occasionally to grab something to eat at Aunt Betty's, but then promptly returned to the hotel. Their room in the hotel was clean, but small. It was large enough for four people to sleep comfortable in it, but the room wasn't designed to be an all-inclusive living quarters. Although he was the smallest of the party, Charlie had the hardest time sitting cooped up in the hotel room. While he was happy to be out of the back of the wagon, the little boy couldn't understand why he couldn't run around the town.

Howie knew that it was safer for the group to remain ***discrete***, holed up in the hotel, and isolated from the rest of the town. If no one realized that they were in Gulf's Canyon, then they could slip in and out of the town unnoticed. Without any real law enforcement, staying out of the spotlight seemed the best way to protect themselves from any mishaps. However, with two teenagers, a middle-aged man, and a toddler spending every waking hour together, the hotel room quickly felt cramped. Ironically, the travelers who previously couldn't wait to spend a couple of days in a real town were itching to get back on the road.

Discrete (dih-**skreet**) – ADJ – apart or detached from others; separate

Because Tim wouldn't be done with the wagon and horses until the evening on Thursday, the group wasn't going to leave until the following morning. The hotel room might have been cramped during the day, but everyone in the party agreed that sleeping on the beds at night made it almost worth it. It just didn't make sense for them to leave Gulf's Canyon only to get one or two hours on the road before they had to stop and sleep. It was decided they would get up early on Friday morning, have breakfast at Aunt Betty's, then hit the road.

Howie had hoped to be able to leave the wagon and the animals at Tim's until they left on Friday morning, but after speaking with the older gentleman Howie found out that it would be impossible. Tim was leaving himself in the wee hours on Friday. Unless Howie wanted to get his wagon before four in the morning, he would have to retrieve it Thursday night. Howie knew the children would never be ready to go before six, so he made arrangements to have the animals and wagon stored in the hotel stable. This made Howie a bit nervous because he wasn't sure how secure the stable would be. To minimize the risk of drawing attention to their caravan, Howie decided he would move the animals and wagon into the stable under the cover of darkness. He knew that thieves wouldn't look to steal something they didn't know was there. Howie and Jacob would slip out after the others had gone to bed and secretly move their wagon into the hotel stable.

On any other night, slipping in and out of town would have been rather simple. Usually once the sun set, Gulf's Canyon's nightlife would remain exclusive to the saloons and casinos. Most people who were up at that time of the evening were too drunk or engrossed in other activities to worry about what was going on in the streets. But on this particular night Big Max, a self-made ***impresario***, had organized an evening of outside entertainment for the town. On a whim, the mayor decided to throw a big festival to honor himself. There were music, dancing, dramas with ***intermezzos***, drinking, and games. If the group had spent any time outside of their room they would have realized that Thursday evening was the worst night to try to do anything under the cover of darkness, for lamp stands and candles filled the streets. The outdoor festivities may have made it harder for Howie and Jacob to do their job, but it couldn't stop them from doing it. Everything had already been organized for the swap, and Tim was waiting for them to come and retrieve their belongings.

When Howie and Jacob left the hotel room, the town square was alive with action. Every lamp that the town owned was lit, illuminating the entire surroundings. Noises of joviality filled the air as music, laughter, chatter, and singing mixed together to form a melody of gaiety. Cigarette smoke, perfume, and whiskey choked the fresh oxygen out of the environs. The streets were crowded with people. Leaving the hotel, Jacob and Howie had to push their way through the crowd to make their way out of town. That night, Gulf's Canyon was one giant party.

Jacob and Howie were several miles outside of the town square before the last of the festival sounds finally faded away. They had been among the crowd for less than ten minutes but they carried the smells of the party with

---

Impresario (im-pruh-**sahr**-ee-oh) – N – a person who organizes or manages public entertainments, especially operas, ballets, or concerts

Intermezzo (in-ter-**met**-soh) – N – a short dramatic, musical, or other entertainment of light character, introduced between the acts of a drama or opera

them. A rather large lady, who had already had too much to drink, had spilled part of her beer on Jacob. He was disgusted not only by the smell of beer-soaked clothes, but by the woman's improper behavior. It was simply uncivilized for a woman to ***comport*** herself in such a way.

Luckily by the time Howie and Jacob returned from Tim's, the outside party had mostly died down, or at least had moved back indoors. The lights in the casino were still ablaze and the sound of ***effluent*** music could be heard all the way to Nina's hotel. A dozen or so people had remained outside, but they all seemed too preoccupied with their own activities to notice Howie and Jacob with their cargo. The two men were tired and hurried to complete their work. In the hotel stable, Howie did his best to secure the animals and wagon. Someone is going to have to work hard to steal this stuff, Howie thought.

"All right, Howie," said Jacob. "I think that's as good as it is going to get. Let's go inside."

"I just don't feel good about leaving it here," replied Howie. "Somethin' just doesn't feel right."

"You've tied up the horses the best you could," responded Jacob, "There just isn't anything else you can do. It will either be here in the morning or it won't."

"That's not good enough for me," answered Howie. "I think I'll spend the night here."

Jacob tried to talk the old trail guide out of spending the last night in Gulf's Canyon sleeping in a barn, but the old man would hear nothing of it. Howie was too stubborn to let the rascals of the town get the better of him. It was his job to see that the Watkins and

---

Comport (kuhm-**pawrt**) – V – to behave
Effluent (**ef**-loo-uhnt) – ADJ – flowing out or forth

their belongings got to Missouri safely, and he was going to do it. Finally Jacob gave up and went inside alone. Howie situated himself in the back of the wagon with his trusty pistol lying across his chest.

Howie had been right to stay behind that night, for despite all of their efforts for secrecy, a ***faction*** of Big Max's gang had caught a glimpse of the beautiful horses. They had watched the two men enter the barn with their precious cargo, and waited outside for them to leave. These men had every intention of taking not only the horses, but anything of value in the Watkins' wagon. The band of robbers was frustrated by the return of only one man from the barn. They waited a half hour longer for Howie to leave, too, but he never did. Howie's resolve to stay behind and look after the wagon thwarted their plans for a middle-of-the-night heist. The men had to find another way to obtain the goods. The simplest plan would have been to take the horses regardless of Howie's presence for there were five men and they could have easily taken on one lone trail guide. The problem was the inevitable brawl that would come from attacking the man guarding the wagon. It was bound to draw attention, and that was something the men couldn't afford to do. As the hotel owner, Nina paid Big Max a hefty sum of money every month for protection from that kind of thing, and any of Max's men were caught robbing her barn, chaos would break out. Deliberately stealing from Nina's hotel was outright ***insurrection***, and Big Max didn't take kindly to insurgents in his group. The

---

Faction (**fak**-shuhn) – N – a group or clique within a larger group, party, government, organization

Insurrection (in-suh-**rek**-shuhn) – N – an act or instance of rising in revolt, rebellion, or resistance against civil authority or an established government

men would be publicly tarred and feathered, for sure. They would have to wait for another opportunity to fulfill their wicked desire.

Following Howie's orders, Jacob made sure Anna and Charlie were awake and ready to go by a quarter to six. From a distance the gang of thieves watched every move the group made. With the light of the morning sun, they had missed their opportunity to loot Nina's barn. They just couldn't risk getting caught in town, but they weren't ready to give up entirely.

When the travelers entered the diner, their breakfast was waiting for them at their usual table. Aunt Betty had been expecting them, and she wanted to give them a farewell breakfast that would start their second half of their journey off right. She offered a spread of scrambled eggs, homemade bread, freshly churned butter, smoked bacon, and coffee. The president himself didn't start his days off with a better breakfast. Unfortunately they didn't have the time to really sit down and enjoy their breakfast. They still had days of travel before them, and the family was ready to get back on the road.

With everyone rested, including the livestock, Howie decided once again to make the most of the morning hours. He drove the horses fast and hard and was able to get the animals to maintain a steady trot for prolonged periods of time. Sadly, the old trail guide was unaware that the more distance he put between himself and the town, the closer he brought his small company to danger. The robbers knew the Nebraska prairie far better than he did, and had decided to set a trap for the wagon several miles outside of Gulf's Canyon. There was only one watering hole, a river ten miles from the city on the route from Gulf's Canyon to the next evening resting spot. The thieves knew any good trail guide would stop there to give their animals a break. The men stationed themselves in the distance and waited for the unsuspecting group to arrive. There they would ambush them, and take what they wanted while the travelers were under ***duress.***

Big Max's men were correct in thinking Howie would stop the wagon at this particular riverbed. It was summertime, and the sun's brutal rays required that the group stop whenever there was water so the animals could have a drink. There was no way for Howie to have ***prescience*** of the trap that was waiting for them. By then the wagon was several hours outside of Gulf's Canyon, and Howie believed them to be free from danger. He had spent so much energy concentrating on getting out of the city that he had let his guard down once they were gone. It was an understandable, but unfortunate mistake. Howie even left his pistol sitting on the wagon bench when he stopped to water the animals. Jacob, Charlie, and Anna took the small break to stretch their already tired legs.

As soon as the group stepped away from the wagon, the small gang of robbers left their hiding places, and closed in around them. Five men lurked in the distance ready to pounce at their leader's command. A tall man in brown cowboy boots raised his hand and signaled to the others the time to strike. In one synchronized motion, the thieves jumped out of their hiding places and surrounded the unwary victims. The tall man stepped in closer with his shiny pistol and addressed the group.

Duress (doo-**res**) – N – compulsion by threat or force

Prescience (**presh**-uhns) – N – knowledge of things before they exist or happen; foreknowledge; foresight

"Stick 'em up," he barked.

The leader of the band of robbers offered this ***platitude*** with a smile. He then motioned for the other members to round up the trail guide and the three youngsters so they could keep a better eye on them.

"We won't be long," the man continued. "We just want your horses and your valuables, and then we'll be on our way. If nobody moves, then nobody gets hurt."

The men quickly went to work searching the wagon for any goods that might be of value to them. It didn't take long for them to discover one trunk full of Charlotte Watkins' fine silverware. They were antiques which had once belonged to Charlotte's grandmother. After her marriage to Thomas, Charlotte's father had allowed her to take the silver with her, a fact the man concealed from his wife Isabella. The silverware held more sentimental value than monetary, but the ***philistine*** robbers couldn't tell the difference. They believed they had found real treasure.

"Hey, boss," called out one of the robbers. "There's real silver back here."

"Then grab it," replied the tall leader.

"There's a whole trunk full of it," responded the robber. "It's too heavy to take by itself."

Annoyed with the incompetence of his companion, the tall man moved to the back of the wagon to take a look for himself. His pistol, however, remained fixed on the captives. After seeing the trunk of silver, the tall man agreed that it was too much for them to carry on their own. His solution was to take the whole wagon.

Platitude (**plat**-i-tood) – N – a flat, dull, or trite remark, especially one uttered as if it were fresh or profound

Philistine (**fil**-uh-steen) – ADJ – lacking in, hostile, or smugly indifferent to culture

"Well it looks like we'll be relieving you of all your stuff," said the tall man. "We don't want to leave you empty-handed on the prairie—it can be such a dangerous place, you know. I think we can leave you the mules."

The tall robber signaled to the other man to take the horses from Howie, but leave the mules behind. Along with their own horses, the robbers hitched Samson and Delilah to the wagon.

The leader's sarcastic remarks only further enraged Jacob, who was having a hard enough time remaining silent as it was. With his mocking words, the robber was a like a ***picador***, prodding Jacob to attack. Although not prone to outright acts of brawn, his anger made him ***intrepid***. The courageous 17-year-old wasn't about to stand by idly while these slimy men took away all their belongings. The Watkins had gone through too much to let philistines benefit from all their hard work. Jacob stood and carefully watched the leader, looking for his moment to strike. The men were almost finished hitching up the horses before Jacob got his moment. The tall bandit had kept his eye and his gun on the group the whole time; that is, until the job was just about completed. One of his clumsy partners working with the horses dropped something that made a loud noise. Automatically the leader turned his head to see what had happened. Jacob knew this momentary distraction would likely be the only chance that he got. The young man prepared to spring into action, his gaze fixated on the bandit's gun. *If I can get the gun,* thought Jacob, *I can gain some leverage in this situation.*

Howie, who had already formulated a plan on

Picador (**pik**-uh-dawr) – N – one of the mounted assistants to a matador, who opens the bullfight by enraging the bull and weakening its shoulder muscles with a lance

Intrepid (in-**trep**-id) – ADJ – resolutely fearless; dauntless

how to overtake the men later, could see that Jacob was instead planning to attempt a daring rescue right now. Howie had ***empathy*** for Jacob—he knew how hard it was to sit there and do nothing—but the old tracker also knew that going against five men with guns did not offer good odds. Howie wanted to let the men complete their robbery and be on their way. Howie knew of an Indian tribe that lived in the nearby prairies. The trail guide and the Indians had often traded with one another, and over the years they had become friends. Howie knew with their expert tracking skills, it wouldn't take long for them to recover the belongings. With more men and the power of a surprise, the traveling party could easily overcome these adversaries. Unfortunately, there was no good way for Howie to explain all of this to his irritated companion. In Jacob's mind it was now or never, and he certainly wasn't about to choose never. Howie tried to stop him, but it was too late; as soon as the leader turned his head, Jacob pounced.

Jacob ran directly into the leader and reached for his gun. The force of the collision had been strong, but not strong enough to knock the tall man off his balance. It took the startled man only a couple of seconds to regain his composure. The two men struggled, Jacob using all of his might to pry the gun out of the bandit's hand, and the bandit doing all he could to shake the teenager off of him. The wrestling match was fought with great intensity, with each man gaining and then losing ground. Finally Jacob saw an opportunity to gain the upper hand. With one hand he grabbed the pistol and with the other one he threw a

---

Empathy (**em**-puh-thee) – N – the intellectual identification with or vicarious experiencing of the feelings, thoughts, or attitudes of another

great big punch right into the nose of the tall robber. The force of Jacob's punch threw the bandit to the ground with blood tricking down his nostrils. Jacob arose from the match victorious.

Jacob's victory, however, would be short-lived. The tussle between him and the bandits' leader had caught the attention of the other men, and one of the robbers aimed his pistol directly at Jacob. All the man needed was a clear shot to take, and Jacob's victory afforded the man this opportunity. Howie, who had been watching not only the brawl but also the reactions of the other men, spotted the gun. Without hesitation, the old trail guide ran to push Jacob out of the ***trajectory*** of the man's bullet. Howie shoved Jacob with all his might and the impact threw Jacob to the ground. Jacob lost his grip on the gun, and the pistol went flying. Howie had succeeded in getting Jacob out of danger, but he hadn't been fast enough to save himself. As soon as the old man hit the ground he felt an intense burning sensation on the left side of his chest. Howie looked down at his shirt to see a red blotch get larger and larger; Howie had taken the bullet.

The tall leader picked himself off the ground, dusted the dirt from his pants, and retrieved the gun from the place where it had landed. His face, already ***turgid*** where Jacob had punched him, was filled with malice. Once he retrieved his gun, the bandit deliberately walked slowly over to Jacob. Howie's thrust had been hard, and had knocked the wind out of the teenager. He remained on the ground trying to catch his breath. With the sunlight

---

Trajectory (truh-**jek**-tuh-ree) – N – the curve described by a projectile, rocket, or the like in its flight

Turgid (**tur**-jud) – ADJ – swollen; distended

to his backside, the tall man appeared inhumanly large as he stood towering over Jacob. The bandit stared at the now defeated young man. In an effort to remind Jacob of the mistake of punching him, the bandit took his hand and dramatically wiped the blood from under his nose, and then, with a smile, pointed his gun directly at Jacob's face. Standing in the sunlight the man looked more like an evil ***chimera*** than a person. Time froze as Jacob stared down the barrel of the outlaw's gun.

"What do you men think?" asked the leader with a wicked smile. "Should we kill him now, or leave him for the wild animals to eat?"

"Kill him" cried two of the other men.

"Na, leave him," cried the other two. "We got what we came here for."

The group was ***bipartite***—half of the men wanted the leader to pull the trigger, while the other half didn't want the blood of the young man on their hands. It was one thing to be a robber; it was another to be a murderer. The robbery had already become more complicated with the injury of the old trail guide; they didn't want to make it worse with the deliberate killing of an unarmed child.

The tall leader looked at his companions and just laughed.

"Well, it's a good thing this isn't a democracy," the bandit said with a smirk.

With his evil smile still intact, the outlaw cocked his gun.

"NOOO!" screamed Anna.

Chimera (ki-**meer**-uh) – N – a horrible or unreal creature of the imagination; a vain or idle fancy

Bipartite (bahy-**pahr**-tahyt) – ADJ – divided into or consisting of two parts

The young girl had been paralyzed with fear. The whole fight with Jacob attacking the outlaw, Howie getting shot, and now the man aiming a gun at Jacob was too much for the fifteen-year-old. She held Charlie close and turned her head away from the gruesome scene. She began to sob. A thousand emotions bubbled up inside of her; she was scared, angry, sad, and remorseful for being so spiteful to Jacob over the last several months. She knew that once that man pulled the trigger, she would never be able to make things right with her brother again. Anna felt ashamed for letting her ***egomania*** come between herself and her family. Had she the chance to do it over again, there were so many things she wanted to change. With only a matter of seconds left, Anna did the only thing she knew to do. She apologized.

"I'm sorry Jacob," she cried out. "I'm so sorry for how I have been acting since Mom and Dad's death."

"It's OK, Anna," called back Jacob, trying to keep his young sister calm. "I forgive you. I am sorry, too."

Anna was grateful for her brother's ***magnanimous*** words, but she was afraid that their reconciliation came too late for them to repair their relationship. Any second the robber would pull the trigger and put a bullet in Jacob just as the other thief had done to Howie. Dreading the next sound, she pulled Charlie closer and held her eyes fast. But instead of a gunshot, Anna heard laughing; confused she opened her eyes and turned toward Jacob.

There stood the menacing outlaw chuckling with

Egomania (ee-goh-**mey**-nee-uh) – N – obsessive love for oneself and regard for one's own needs

Magnanimous (mag-**nan**-uh-muhs) – ADJ – generous in forgiving an insult or injury; free from petty resentfulness or vindictiveness

cruel laughter. The man had lowered his gun and it rested safely in the holster on his hip. The reason for the man's unexpected decision was ***indeterminate***. The outlaw did not offer any explanation or ***apologia*** for his actions, but instead turned away from Jacob and called out to the other members of his group.

"Y'll done yet?" asked the leader in an impatient tone. "It's high time we let these fine people get back on the road."

The man stopped for a minute and surveyed the scene that lay before him. He saw Anna and Charlie huddled up together, he glanced over at Jacob still shaking from his brush with death, and then he looked at Howie lying on the ground.

"Someone better get that man to a doctor," the leader said with a wicked smirk. "Otherwise it might be too late."

The band of robbers congregated near the wagon and quickly rode away from the terrorized group. As promised, the thieves took only the horses and wagon and left the mules for the small traveling party. As soon as the dastardly gang was a safe distance way, Anna instantly ran toward Jacob.

"Are you OK?" she asked frantically.

By then Jacob had the opportunity to regain both his breath and his composure.

"I'm fine," he cried out. "Go check on Howie. Is he still alive?"

Howie was motionless on the ground, and from that distance Anna couldn't tell whether or not he was breathing. She left Jacob's side to examine just how bad a condition their

---

Indeterminate (in-di-**tur**-muh-nit) – ADJ – not clear; vague
Apologia (ap-uh-**loh**-jee-uh) – N – a defense or justification of a belief, idea, actions, etc.

trail guide was in. As Anna approached Howie, a sense of fear overcame her. *What if he is dead?* She thought to herself. With as much courage as she could mount, Anna faced the gruesome sight before her. Howie's skin was colorless, paler than snow. The whiteness of his face was exaggerated by the deep red stain on his shirt. Anna shuddered. At first glance Anna was sure that Howie was gone; his body appeared lifeless. Just when she was about to turn to tell Jacob the tragic news, she caught sight of something. There, ever so subtly, was the gentle up and down movement of his chest. Howie, at least for now, was alive.

"He's alive!" Anna screamed with excitement.

"We'd better get him to a doctor fast," responded Jacob.

"Should we go back to Gulf's Canyon?" asked Anna.

"I'm pretty sure those men were from Gulf's Canyon," replied Jacob. "They knew we were coming. Who's to say if we went back, the leader wouldn't change his mind and decide to finish us all off. If something happens to Howie, then the outlaws are liable for murder. As the only witnesses, it could be pretty tempting for them to get rid of us."

"What are we going to do then?" asked Anna.

"The only thing we can do," answered Jacob. "We have to keep heading east. Pray that we come across a town, or someone with medical experience. Otherwise we're going to have to get that bullet out ourselves."

Jacob had no prior medical experience, but it was clear that they needed to do their best to stop the bleeding. Jacob gathered any article of clothing that wasn't vital, and used it to bandage Howie's wound. The seventeen-year-old then removed Howie's belt from his waist and fastened it around his chest. It wasn't a perfect compression, but it would have to do. As Jacob aided the old trail guide, he was as careful as he could be not to make anything worse.

Once he was bandaged, Jacob and Anna lifted the man onto the back of one of the mules. It took a couple of tries for the two teenagers to hoist the 200 pound man up, but they were eventually able to do so. Time was of the essence; Jacob knew the faster they got Howie some help, the better his chance of survival. Jacob instructed Anna to ride with Charlie on the back of the other mule, and he would ride with Howie. There wasn't a choice; they needed to ride as fast as the animals could take them.

Anna held Charlie close as she pushed the mule to run faster and faster. Charlie was small, and liked to wiggle, but she wasn't about to let him slip off the galloping mule. Jacob led the way, obtaining remarkable speed for a mule carrying two men. It would have made more sense for Anna to ride with Howie, if speed hadn't been a factor; but as it was, Anna didn't have the strength to hold on to Howie and guide the mule. They rode and rode, searching for any trace of human life. They found none. Soon dusk was upon them and there was not enough light to guide their way. Without a guide or direction, it was too dangerous for them to carry on. They had to stop for the night. Fortunately Jacob's improvised bandage had stopped Howie's bleeding. The trail guide was still unconscious, but his condition remained stable. However, there was no way of knowing if he would make it through the night.

Although by then they had already slept several nights under the open skies, that night would be different. Without their wagon, they had no supplies. There were no ***incendiary*** devices to make fire, no food for dinner, and no weapons to protect themselves. They were completely

---

Incendiary (in-**sen**-dee-er-ee) – ADJ – used or adapted for setting property on fire

exposed on the western prairie. On top of everything, they had no guide, at least no conscious guide, who could tell them if they had picked a safe area to sleep. In the darkness, there could be anything waiting for them.

Anna helped Jacob move Howie off the back of the mule and gently lay him down on the ground. That night it didn't feel like summer. The Nebraska wind was cold, and without the sun's warm rays, the outside temperature began to quickly drop. Charlie stood next to Howie, his teeth chattering from the evening's cool front. They had no blankets, extra clothing, or fire to ***modulate*** the wind's icy effects. All they had was each other: Jacob, Anna, and Charlie, huddled together next to Howie in an effort to keep warm. Fatigued and frightened, the three Watkins children passed out from exhaustion.

Drum, drum, drum went the noise that woke Anna from her drowsy slumber, her head pounding from the lack of sleep and food. It was still dark and she had trouble focusing her eyes. Anna looked around for the origin of the noise, but saw and heard nothing. Tired, she laid her head down to fall back asleep. *Drum, drum, drum.* This time the noise was louder and clearer. Anna quickly sat up. *Drum, drum, drum. There it is again,* thought Anna. She turned and shook Jacob. Jacob started to say something, but Anna put her hand over his mouth.

"Shhh," she said in a whisper. "Listen."

Drum, drum, drum. There was no mistake now; something or someone was approaching. Anna and Jacob scanned the area to see what was going on. This time it wasn't just darkness. Dozens of tall torches were

---

Modulate (**moj**-uh-leyt) – V – to regulate by or adjust to a certain measure or proportion; soften; tone down

headed straight for the sleeping travelers. As the lights drew closer, the noise got louder, until it was so close that Anna couldn't tell if the drumming noise was coming from the lights or her own heart. The sound then picked up speed...
d*rummmmmmmmmmmmm, drummmmmmmmmm, drummm-mmmmm.* And then...it just stopped. Curious, Anna and Jacob looked at one another and then back at the direction of the floating torches.

When they returned their gaze toward the lights, they saw a frightening sight. A ferocious, ***leonine*** figure approached them. The shadows from the torches made the form appear gigantic. Terrified, their eyes remained fixated on the shape that drew closer. It wasn't a huge lion that neared, but a man wearing the skin of a mountain lion as a headdress. Anna wasn't sure which one was more petrifying—a real lion or a man that had killed a lion and then wore it as a trophy. The man was tall, strong, and dark-skinned. Apart from his headdress, he wore clothes that were unfamiliar. His face was painted, and his stare was stern. Even though they had never before seen anything like the figure that stood before them, there was no doubt in their minds that they were staring ***vis-à-vis*** with an Indian.

On their first trail ride to Wyoming, Anna and Jacob had heard stories of American Indians. They had been told of their wild ways and their hate for the pale-faced man. Some ***xenophobic*** settlers characterized the Indians as preferring to be left on their own and dangerous

---

Leonine (**lee**-uh-nahyn) – ADJ – resembling or suggestive of a lion

Vis-à-Vis (vee-zuh-**vee**) – ADV – face to face

Xenophobic (**zen**-uh-fohb-ik) – ADJ – fearing or hating foreigners or strange customs

savages when disturbed. Later the Watkins had learned that most Indians looked at the influx of western settlers as an opportunity for mutual growth and learning. The Watkins children had never met a real Indian before, but could only hope that the man who stood before them would be welcoming.

The lion-man was soon joined by a number of other men dressed in a similar fashion. Apart from the elaborate headdress of their leader, these men were also adorned in the same strange clothing and painted faces. Given the prominence of his headdress and the space the other men gave him, the first man was clearly the Indian's chief. There were more than a dozen men surrounding the small campsite. The once dark area was now fully illuminated by the brightness of their torchlight. For a moment the two groups just stared at one another, neither saying a word.

Silently the chief made the first move, and approached the terrified group. He walked straight to the children, and then turned toward Howie. The man bent down, gently put his hand to Howie's throat, then stood up and walked back toward his men. Two other men appeared from behind the circle of Indians bringing forth blankets, while others took their torches and started a fire. The men with the blankets prepared a place on the ground and placed Howie's motionless body on it. They motioned for the children to move back, and handed them a thick animal hide to cover up with. The Watkins thankfully took the gift and moved out of the men's way. Mystified, they watched and waited as the Indians did their work.

Once Howie was laid next to the fire and his makeshift bandages removed, an ancient-looking Indian came out of the crowd. His body was frail and hunched over. He walked slowly but with determination. With great sense of respect, the other men moved quickly out of his way. This old Indian carried with him a handful of supplies including bowls and herbs. The Indian poured water into his bowl and gently began to make a concoction. This mixture served two purposes: the first to cleanse Howie's wound, and the second to ***mitigate*** his future pain. After the wound was clean, the Indian took his time examining Howie. The trail guide had been fortunate. Not only had the bullet missed his heart, as the robber had shot him too high in the chest, but also the bullet had gone through him and was not lodged his body. This meant the old Indian only needed to properly dress his wounds.

As the children watched the Indians care for Howie, a younger Indian approached them. He carried something in his hand; it was large and it looked heavy. Still unsure of the Indians intentions, the advances of the younger Indian caused the Watkins' apprehension. What had appeared as a weapon from the distance turned about to be a basket full of food. The young Indian set down a huge basket of a variety of different things the children could eat. While they didn't recognize everything in the basket, among the items were flat bread, some meat, and corn. Starving, the children helped themselves to as much food as they could stomach. The young Indian seemed pleased by the children's appetite.

Life certainly held many surprises. There they were, in the middle of the Nebraskan prairie eating an Indian dinner while an Indian medicine man completed his pains-taking ***lucubration*** on their heroic trail guide.

Mitigate (**mit**-i-geyt) – V – to lessen in force or intensity, as wrath, grief, harshness, or pain; moderate

Lucubration (loo-kyoo-**brey**-shuhn) – N – laborious work, study, thought, etc., especially at night

WORD REVIEW

Apologia
Bipartite
Chimera
Comport
Discrete
Duress
Effluent
Egomania
Empathy
Faction
Impresario
Incendiary
Indeterminate
Insurrection
Intermezzo
Intrepid
Leonine
Lucubration
Magnanimous
Mitigate
Modulate
Philistine
Picador
Platitude
Prescience
Trajectory
Turgid
Vis-à-Vis
Xenophobic

10

REVENGE AT THE RIVERBEND

Anna awoke with a pounding headache and a stiff body from the previous day's travels. The last thing she could remember was falling asleep huddled next to Jacob and Charlie. Anticipating the inevitable sensation of being cold, she slowly stirred from her resting place. Sleeping outside without a blanket was one of her least favorite arrangements. However, the sensation never came, because as Anna finally opened her eyes she saw that she wasn't outside in the cold, but was cozily nestled inside a tent. Not only was she sufficiently covered with buffalo skin blankets, but in the corner of the room was a type of ***brazier*** spewing heat. The warmth radiating from the little box could be felt from where she was lying.

The teenager was so comfortable curled up in the warmth that she closed her eyes and tried to go back to sleep. She would have succeeded in that endeavor if curiosity and hunger pains had not gotten the best of her. Questions like, *"Where am I, and how did I get here?"* circled in her thoughts. For the groggy girl, the previous day was all a blur. Anna had to really concentrate to remember what had happened in the prior 24 hours. Suddenly images came flooding back to her. She remembered the high-jacking, riding through the

---

Brazier (**brey**-zher) – N – a metal receptacle for holding live coals or other fuel, as for heating a room

prairie looking for help, stopping for the night....and then everything came clear. *The Indians!*

Anna quickly sat up and looked around. Sure enough, she was sleeping in an Indian tepee. The thought made her both fearful and excited at the same time. Apart from their brief encounter last night, Anna had never before met a real-life Indian. She only knew the stories. Anna had no idea how to behave in this foreign culture. The ***archetype*** of the Indian warrior that she had learned from storybooks was silent and stoic, leaving little information about their everyday culture. Anna could only learn by observing and doing. For someone who always had a plan, the thought of ad-libbing was terrifying. She was fearful of doing, or saying, the wrong things. Villagers often called Indians savages, and Anna had no desire to find out the reason why.

Anna anticipated finding Jacob and Charlie also asleep in the tepee, but when she surveyed the tent she realized she was all alone. She had no idea what time it was, but the inside of the tent was rather dark. *Perhaps they slept in another tent,* Anna thought. Struck by the desire to make sure her brothers were OK, Anna forced herself out of bed. She decided she would go find Jacob and Charlie, and then.... go back to bed. As she stood up, her stomach made a loud noise. Her desire for food ***eclipsed*** her desire for sleep. Maybe she would also find something to eat.

Anna opened the tepee door, only to be blinded by a very bright light. It was not night as she originally thought,

---

Archetype (**ahr**-ki-tahyp) – N – the original pattern or model or first form; prototype

Eclipse (ih-**klips**) – V – to make less important by comparison; surpass

but well into the afternoon. The tepee was thick and had deceived Anna into thinking it was still dark night outside. The sun sat high in the sky and people were out and about. Apparently Anna was the only one who was still in bed.

The stunned teenager left her resting place and walked out into the sun. She half expected to be met by a thousand stares, but no one seemed to pay any attention to her. The Indians were busy completing their daily duties; they had no time to gawk at the pale-faced girl. The Indian campsite was large, with many different tepees; all set in an ***elliptical*** border around the main campfire. Anna felt like she was in a maze, and wondered if she would ever find the other members of her family. *In a sea of dark-skinned Indians, how hard could it be to find two white boys?* Anna thought.

Although it was harder than she originally thought, Anna did eventually find her brothers. Jacob was in the middle of the campsite speaking with the chief from the previous night. The tall Indian was no longer wearing his lion-skin headdress, but Anna recognized him all the same. He had an air of dignity about him. The chief both looked and carried himself as a leader. Even Jacob carried himself a little bit differently when he sat and talked with the chief.

Charlie wasn't too far from Jacob, and sat in a circle of Indian children. They were playing some sort of game. It hadn't taken the toddler long to adapt to his new surroundings. He sat there laughing and smiling as they played. Despite the difference in their skin-tone, Charlie even looked like the other children. The little Indian boys were dressed only in their pants and were barefoot. For the toddler who felt confined by the stiff clothing of shirts and

---

Elliptical (ih-**lip**-ti-kuhl) – ADJ – having the form of an ellipse

shoes, he thought it was perfect. It didn't take him long to be running around in only his pants, too. Charlie was happy and free. Though clearly from two different cultures, the use of play to interact was ***homologous*** for the children.

Seeing that Charlie was safe, Anna made her way over to Jacob and the chief. The two men were having a discussion. Anna hesitated walking up to them directly, because she didn't want to interrupt their conversation. Instead she waited by her brother's side for a good time to speak. The men were discussing the robbery and the recent decline of Gulf's Canyon. The chief had explained to Jacob that the ***ethos*** of the town quickly changed after the death of the sheriff, and the new regime had caused quite a bit of trouble for the area. Big Max and his gang hadn't been much of a problem for his tribe, since the men were too afraid of the Indians to interfere with them. In reality, the chief's people posed no threat to Big Max or his posse, but the Indians thought it best to let the men keep thinking that they did. The chief liked the peace that their dangerous reputation afforded them.

It took Anna a few minutes to realize that it was a little bit strange that her brother could have a conversation with an Indian chief without any communication problems. The thought only dawned on her when the chief turned to one of the other men beside him and spoke in a tongue that she couldn't understand. Anna soon discovered that the chief had learned English some ten years back, when an American had spent some time living among the villagers.

Homologous (huh-**mol**-uh-guhs) – ADJ – having the same or a similar relation; corresponding, as in relative position or structure

Ethos (**ee**-thos) – N – the character or disposition of a community, group, person, etc.

This man was a trapper and wanted to learn the ways of the chief's tribe. He had come long before the influx of settlers to the West, and had stayed over a year with the tribe. The chief reflected fondly on the time the white man had spent with them. It had been a ***symbiotic*** relationship: the white man had learned the ways of the Indians, and the Indians had gained a better understanding of the white man. The man had taught the chief English, and the ways of trade. He had even helped modernize some of the Indian's way of life, and as a gift had given them the brazier that was in the children's tepee.

"We didn't make all of the changes Howard suggested," said the chief. "We like our simple way of life, but some things like medicine and the heating box were helpful to my people."

Anna and Jacob were shocked at what the man had just said, and exchanged glances of surprise.

"Did you just say, 'Howie?'" inquired Anna.

"Certainly," replied the chief, "One-eyed Howard has been a friend of the Kuawns for many years. We are the reason he is called 'One-eyed.'"

"And why is he called 'One-eyed'?" asked Jacob. "Is it because he's so greedy with his money?"

The Kuawns' chief laughed at this suggestion as he remembered the many examples of ***largess*** Howard had generously demonstrated to the Indians over many years. The man the chief knew was anything but greedy. Such defamation of Howie was so preposterous that the chief continued to laugh for a solid minute. Anna and Jacob,

---

Symbiosis (sim-bee-**oh**-sis) – N – any interdependent or mutually beneficial relationship between two persons, groups, etc.

Largess (lahr-**jes**) – N – generous bestowal of gifts

who obviously didn't understand what was so funny, could only exchange inquisitive glances.

"Whoever told you that," chuckled the chief, "can't tell a beautiful lady from a horse's behind."

"Then how did Howie get his nickname?" probed Anna.

"He got it on his first hunt with us," began the chief. "Howard had never used a bow and arrow before and the old goat wanted to try without having any instruction. He said he didn't need any. 'I can shoot a gun, I can shoot an arrow,' he said."

The Watkins children laughed at the old chief's impersonation of their trail guide. The Indian had played the part perfectly and even included Howie's voice inflections and hand gestures. The chief had all the subtle ***minutiae*** of Howie's mannerisms correct. He then continued with his story.

"Anyway, Howard had in his sights the most beautiful buck I had ever seen. He was in the best position of the hunting party; all he needed to do was aim correctly. He would have, too, if he had not aimed with one of his eyes closed. The arrow landed right in the tree next to the buck."

"And the buck?" asked Anna.

"He was startled, but unharmed. He ran away before anyone else had a chance to shoot him. Howard's nickname is a reminder of what his stubbornness can cause."

The chief continued to tell the children stories of Howie's ***intermittent*** visits over the years to the Kuawns. The stories ranged from more hunting trips and long

---

Minutiae (mi-**noo**-shee-uh) – N – precise details; small or trifling matters

Intermittent (in-ter-**mit**-nt) – ADJ – stopping or ceasing for a time; alternately ceasing and beginning again

treks in the winter snow to Howie's feeble attempts to learn basket weaving. Anna's favorite of the Kuawn chief's stories was the time Howie dodged his ***conscription*** into the Mexican-American War by dressing up as one of the Indian women. Many draft dodgers were suspected of hiding out in the friendly Indian tribes. When the army came looking for Howie at the Kuawns, they were boldly greeted by the man in female Indian clothing. Because of the gracious hospitality of the Kuawns, the men stayed longer than anyone had expected. Howie had to stay in disguise for almost a week. He ate, worked, and experienced all aspects of life as a Kuawn woman. After seven days dressed as a woman, Howie even became a ***couture*** of Indian fashion, able to give advice on how to make their clothes more comfortable. Howie was so good at pretending to be one of the women that he received a marriage proposal from the lieutenant. Howie politely refused, claiming he was already spoken for by another young Indian in the tribe.

"I didn't really understand why the men had come to take Howard away," explained the chief. "But I knew that Howard was trying to elude his responsibilities. I naturally couldn't give him away—he was a friend after all—but I certainly didn't make it easy for him to get away with his deception."

The chief didn't go into details of what he meant by his last statement, but Anna and Jacob could just imagine. They hadn't known the Kuawns' chief for very long, but they could tell from his stories that he had

---

Conscription (kuhn-**skrip**-shuhn) – N – compulsory enrollment of persons for military or naval service; draft

Couture (koo-**toor**) – N – a fashion designer

quite a sense of humor. They only wished they had met the chief under better circumstances so they could see his interactions with Howie.

Their story time was interrupted by the arrival of the old medicine man. The elder ***genuflected*** lightly in deference to the chief and then began to speak. His words were soft and inaudible to the Watkins. They assumed that he was speaking of the welfare concerning their wounded friend. Anna could only guess at the man's age, as there was nothing definitive about him to guide her assessment. All she knew was that he was old. His face had more wrinkles than she had ever seen before, and his checks were delicately sunken in. His eyes were as dark as coal, and were only half opened. The skin from his forehead drooped down. He never smiled. Anna would have been afraid of him if he hadn't had such a calming presence. It was hard for her to describe, but there was something about this Indian elder that made her think that Howie was in good hands. The older man finished speaking with the chief, kneeled again, and went back the same way he had come.

"Askuwehetea has just informed me that we can go visit Howard," began the chief. "Our friend lost a lot of blood yesterday, but he made it through the night, which is good. He's awake now. Would you like to see him?"

The children were overjoyed at the news that Howie was safe and awake. They could barely contain their excitement when they answered the chief's question.

"Yes," shouted Jacob and Anna together. "Thank you, Chief!"

"Please, call me Hiamovi," replied the Indian.

Genuflect (**jen**-yoo-flekt) – V – to bend the knee or touch one knee to the floor in reverence or worship

"Thank you, Hiamovi."

The children followed Hiamovi toward the tepee Askuwehetea had entered only seconds before. Howie's tepee was similar to the one the Watkins had slept in last night. It was warm, cozy, and dark. The old trail guide's cot was in the middle. Although Howie was wrapped in blankets, the children could see pieces of his bandages on his chest. The medicine man had dressed Howie's wounds well. The chief was the first to approach Howie's bed and Howie slowly turned his head toward him.

"How ya doing, Hami?" asked Howie with a smile.

The chief chuckled and responded.

"You know I don't like it when you call me Hami, Howard," said the chief.

"And you know that I hate to be called Howard," smiled Howie.

"Then I guess we're even," answered the chief.

"I guess so," said Howie.

Howie's visitors could see the pain on the trail guide's face as he lay there in bed. It had been a rough night for the prairie man, and his body was feeling the effects of it that morning. Yet Howie had an ***impregnable*** spirit, and he wasn't about to let a little thing like a gunshot wound keep him from enjoying his time with old friends.

"You know, I'd been planning on coming to see you," said Howie. "I just didn't realize I'd be here so soon."

"I would have shot you myself if I had known it would get you here faster," teased the chief.

Impregnable (im-**preg**-nuh-buhl) – ADJ – strong enough to resist or withstand attack; not to be taken by force, unconquerable

"Speaking of which," began Howie, "how did you find me?"

This was the exact question which had been on the Watkins children's minds the entire time. They were also curious about how the Indians had come upon them the previous evening. They knew that it couldn't have been an accident that the Indians found them; they had come prepared with the medicine man, food, and blankets for the group. The Indian rescue party had definitely been an act of ***premeditation*** rather than spontaneity.

"Yesterday I went out with a hunting party," began the chief. "We had been out all day and had made it to the northern end of our land where there is a river. It had been a long, hard day of hunting, and we stopped to get a drink and take a rest. While we were resting, I heard some voices on the other side of the river. The noises were muffled, so a couple of my men and I went in closer to get a better look. What we found on the other side of the river was a group of men arguing. They were standing by a wagon that had two beautiful horses."

"Samson and Delilah!" Anna cried out, interrupting the chief's story.

As soon as the words came out of her mouth, Anna blushed. She was ***mortified*** that she had just rudely interrupted the chief. She was pretty sure that other people had been put to death for less than that.

"Sorry," she sheepishly apologized.

"It's OK," responded the chief with a smile. "As I was saying, the men were arguing about a job that had

---

Premeditation (pri-med-i-**tey**-shuhn) – N – sufficient forethought to impute deliberation and intent to commit the act

Mortify (**mawr**-tuh-fahy) – V – to humiliate or shame, as by injury to one's pride or self-respect

gone wrong. One of the men seemed really worried about getting into trouble for shooting a man and then leaving him to die. The robber paced back and forth saying that he didn't want the man's blood on his hands. The men continued to argue back and forth about what to do about the man they had shot and the children they had left him with."

Hiamovi told the group that he stood there listening to the argument for a few minutes. It wasn't the first time that he had seen such men hiding out on this tribe's land, and he had decided to do the same thing he had always done—let the white man be. Whatever was going on there was not his or his people's issue. Policing all bandits was not a ***soluble*** problem and the Kuawns' chief did not want to get his people involved.

"I was just about to turn to leave when the tall man from the group stirred from where he was sitting and walked directly up to the man who had been causing all the commotion. At first the tall man didn't say anything, but pulled a gun out of his holster and pointed it directly at the other man's face. He then threatened to shoot that man with the gun of his victim. At first I didn't understand what the tall man meant, but then I took a closer look at the gun. I realized that I had seen that gun a thousand times before. It was yours, Howard. I knew at that moment that you needed our help. I gathered up my hunting party and we returned to camp. Once we were back, I summoned a rescue party and we went out looking for you."

Everyone was fascinated by the chief's story. It had been more than luck that his hunting party had taken a

---

Soluble (**sol**-yuh-buhl) – ADJ – easily solved or explained

rest at the exact place their robbers had been arguing; it had been a ***stupendous*** blessing.

"Those crooks have my gun," Howie said with indignation. "I hate that."

It seemed funny to Anna that Howie was more upset that the robbers had his gun than that they had shot him. Rallied by the chief's story, Howie attempted to sit up and get out of bed. He wasn't sure what he was going to do, but Howie certainly wasn't going to lie in bed while the robbers were in the area. Unfortunately, Howie didn't realize how weak he actually was, and his attempt to get out of bed only made him dizzy. The old trail guide quickly laid himself back down. Somewhat embarrassed by his weakness, Howie attempted to regain some of his rough attitude with the tone of his voice.

"As soon as I can get out of the bed," he huffed, "I'm going to teach those crooks a lesson."

"Yes, my friend," replied the chief, "but now you should get some rest."

Howie nodded and closed his eyes. Seeing that he needed his sleep, the chief motioned to the children that it was time to go. Howie was improving and they could come and visit him later. Although Askuwehetea was older than the chief, his position in the tribe was lower. Therefore as Chief Hiamovi stood to leave, the old medicine man gently bowed out of respect. This small action by Askuwehetea was a small visual representation of the class ***stratification*** in the Kuawns' tribe. Following

---

Stupendous (stoo-**pen**-duhs) – ADJ – causing amazement; astounding; marvelous

Stratification (strat-uh-fi-**key**-shuhn) – N – the hierarchical or vertical division of society according to rank, caste, or class

the lead of the medicine man, Jacob and Anna bowed humbly before the chief as well. Hiamovi was pleased by the children's respect but told them that in the future it was unnecessary. They were the Kuawns' guests, and a guest always had a place of highest respect.

After hearing Chief Hiamovi's tale of how he came across the robbers, Jacob was full of questions. He wondered if the men were still close to the Indian's campsite, and if so, whether they could go retrieve their belongings. There weren't many things in the wagon that Jacob was sad about losing, but the loss of the money box was huge; without it, the Watkins didn't have a hope of starting over. Not only would they be orphans, but they would be penniless, homeless orphans. As he was almost 18, Jacob could likely get a job, but his earnings alone wouldn't be enough to provide for all of them. Anna and Charlie would have to go to an orphanage just to be clothed and fed. Having his family split up was not an option for Jacob. While he knew that he couldn't get the wagon back alone, Jacob was certain that with the help of the Indians, justice could be served ***retroactively*** to the crooks, just days after their crime. As soon as they were a few feet from Howie's tent, Jacob bravely asked the chief of the Kuawns for help.

"Hiamovi," Jacob began with a soft voice.

"Yes?" inquired the chief.

Jacob gathered his courage and began again; this time his tone was strong and confident.

"Hiamovi," said Jacob. "I know that it isn't the way of your people to get involved in the affairs of others.

Retroactive (re-troh-**ak**-tiv) – ADJ – operative with respect to past occurrences

However, this band of robbers took everything that my siblings and I own. They took our wagon, our money, our belongings, and our horses. Without those things we couldn't even hope to survive. They threatened our lives and shot Howie..."

Anger began to fill Jacob's tone as he spoke of the robbery. His voice no longer reflected his timidity before the chief, but his indignation about the opprobrious acts of the wicked men. He had a right to plead his case and Jacob felt justified in doing so. The young man could have gone on forever if the chief hadn't stopped him there.

"And you want to know if we could help you get justice?" the chief asked.

"Yes," answered Jacob, somewhat startled by the chief's intuition.

"And it is possible that they are already far away with all your belongings without any hope of your getting them back," continued the chief.

"Well, umm," replied Jacob.

"And if they aren't, going there will risk not only your lives again but also the lives of my men?" inquired the chief.

"Now that you put it that way..." answered Jacob.

"Of course we'll do it, my boy," the chief said with a smile. "My people and I would be honored to help you and Howie find justice from these men. I have had a pair of my best trackers keep watch on them since finding them in the woods; they are still there hiding out. We will ride at nightfall for a surprise attack. After tonight they will think twice before robbing again. After all, frogs taste better in the summertime."

Jacob was confused by the apparent ***non sequitur*** but quickly learned it was a phrase of good luck. Hiamovi had listed all the reasons Jacob's desire was impractical and dangerous, yet the chief had already taken steps to honor it. The stunned young man could only say a hesitated thank you. The ***verisimilitude*** of the chief's irritation at the beginning of the conversation made Jacob question whether he might have angered Hiamovi. However, the smile on the chief's face now told him that Hiamovi's harsh words were not a ***censure***, but rather a joke. It was only after Jacob replayed the whole conversation again in his mind that he really understood that the Kuawns had intended all along to help the Watkins retrieve their belongings. *No wonder Howie and Hiamovi are such good friends,* thought Jacob. *They are both impossible to read.*

"Come, children," said the chief. "Let us go get something to eat."

For Anna, who had slept through breakfast, the chief couldn't have said anything better. She quickly followed the chief toward the middle of camp where the women were preparing the midday meal. Jacob, who was lost his in thoughts, just stood there. Halfway to the camp's center, Anna turned to say something to her brother, but he wasn't beside her. She looked back to see him still in the spot near Howie's tepee. Not wanting to walk all the way back, she hollered at him.

"Jacob! Come on. Let's eat," cried Anna.

Non Sequitur (non **sek**-wi-ter) – N – an inference or a conclusion that does not follow from the premises

Verisimilitude (ver-uh-si-**mil**-i-tood) – N – the appearance or semblance of truth; likelihood; probability

Censure (**sen**-sher) – N – strong or vehement expression of disapproval

Anna had shouted so loud, that everyone else turned around to see what the small white girl wanted. When they realized that nothing was wrong, they went back to work, wondering how such a loud noise could come out of one so small. Yet Anna's call had brought Jacob back to reality and he hurried to join her and the others for the noon-time meal. Charlie was also there, still dressed like the other Indian boys, and ran to meet Anna. The toddler was having a wonderful time playing Indian, and he couldn't wait to tell his sister all about it. Together with the Kuawns, the Watkins enjoyed a feast of buffalo meat, freshly made flat bread, corn, and beans. After their meal, Chief Hiamovi suggested that the children take a rest. Later that night they would ride to the isolated camp of the bandit ***pariahs*** and carry out their ambush.

"I need you fully rested tonight, Jacob," said the chief. "We will leave at dusk."

"What about me?" asked Anna. "They stole from me, too. I want to be there when they get what's coming to them."

"Anna," shushed Jacob.

"I know, small one," replied the chief with a smile, "but a surprise attack is no place for a young lady. It is better for everyone if you stay here and look after your little brother. He will soon grow tired of playing with strangers and will need you."

Anna knew the chief was only using Charlie as an excuse to keep her off the hunt, but she didn't want to argue with him. Deep down she knew he was right. She didn't want to distract her brother or the chief by having them worry about her or Charlie getting hurt. They had a very important job and more than anything she wanted

---

Pariah (puh-**rahy**-uh) – N – an outcast

them to be successful. However, just because Anna didn't want to distract the men from their job, didn't mean she was planning on sitting out of the action. Anna decided that she would follow the small hunting party and watch from the sidelines. *If no one knows I am there,* thought Anna, *no one can worry about me getting hurt.* Anna, of course, knew the opposite was true, too. If no one knew she was there no one could help her if she got hurt. However this small detail didn't interest the young girl. She was confident she could stay out of trouble. Until then she decided to follow the chief's advice to get some sleep.

The rhythmic sound of beating drums awoke Anna from her deep slumber. At once, she knew what the sound meant—the men were getting ready for war. Well, maybe not war, but they were certainly preparing to give the outlaws a real reason for their Indian ***paranoia.*** Anna jumped out of bed, trying carefully not to awaken the toddler sleeping next to her, and snuck out of the tepee. Quietly, Anna slipped out of her tent and hid behind a stack of wood just to her left. There she was well hidden and had the perfect view of the assembling warriors.

Somewhere around 20 to 30 men stood gathered around the chief in the middle of the camp. Their faces were all adorned with war paint. Once again Hiamovi was wearing his lion-skinned headdress. Jacob was standing among the Indian men. He, too, was dressed for war. Chief Hiamovi was confident his men would successfully ***surmount*** the robbers in the planned attack. The men carried bows, arrows, knives, and various other weapons. The chief with

---

Paranoia (par-uh-**noi**-uh) – N – baseless or excessive suspicion of the motives of others

Surmount (ser-**mount**) – V – to prevail over

his headdress and the men with their weapons were a terrifying sight. If Anna didn't know that the purpose of this group was to help her family out, she would have been petrified. At that moment she was very thankful that they had made friends with the Kuawns instead of enemies. This time the men didn't carry any torches; they wanted the utmost surprise when they launched their attack. Slowly and steadily, the chief led his party into the woods. They would make it to the outlaws' camp just as the night became completely dark.

Anna waited until the party of men was out of sight before she moved from her hiding place behind the wood pile. Just as she began to move, Anna felt a tug on the back of her dress. Frightened, she turned around to face the person who had caught her. No one was there, at least not at her eye level anyway. Anna looked down to see the 32-inch Charlie clutching the gathers of her skirt. Anna was relieved and annoyed all at the same time. She had only two options: she could either go back with Charlie into the tepee to wait for the group to return, or she could take the little monster with her and thus put both of their lives in danger. Neither option appealed to Anna, but she wasn't about to miss all the action. Anna rationalized Charlie's presence; at least by having him with her she was being less disobedient to the chief than if she left him alone in the tepee. However, Anna knew that she was acting in the ***penumbra***, the shadowy place between being somewhat disobedient and being completely disobedient. Anna was concerned about possible danger, but she wasn't worried about the effects an Indian ambush

---

Penumbra (pi-**nuhm**-bruh) – N – a shadowy, indefinite, or marginal area

would have on little Charlie's ***psyche.*** The poor child had gone through so much over the past few months, with the death of their parents, the move back east, the robbery, and the shooting of Howie, that he was no longer a ***tabula rasa.*** *It might even do the little guy some good,* thought Anna, *to see the good guys win.*

Anna picked up Charlie and whispered to him to keep quiet. Together they made their way to a row of unattended horses. Anna hoisted her younger brother up onto a horse and then untied the reins from the post. Time was of the essence as Anna and Charlie made their surreptitious exit. Anna moved with caution, hoping not to attract any attention. The last thing she wanted was a nosy Indian woman to catch her and Charlie and send them back to their tepee. Luckily for the two, no one in the campsite noticed the *borrowed* horse, or its two stowaway passengers. Once Anna was out of the campsite, she quickened the horse's speed. Following the faint sound of the drums, Anna kept just enough distance between herself and the warriors.

The warriors drumming quieted, and Anna realized they would soon be approaching the campsite of the thieves. She watched as the Chief's men began to take their positions. Staying out of the way of the action, Anna hid herself, Charlie, and the horse directly behind some trees. The chief had been right in his temporal estimate. By the time the large group of men reached the outlaws' campsite, it was completely dark. The darkness was a friend and not an enemy to the Indians. They knew the terrain by

---

Psyche (**sahy**-kee) – N – the human mind or soul

Tabula Rasa (**tab**-yuh-luh **rah**-suh) – N – a mind not yet affected by experiences, impressions, etc.

heart, and the absence of light gave them the advantage. The men surrounded the camp, each with their weapon and drum. The weapons, Anna would soon find out, were there just as a precaution. Hiamovi was a ***vulpine*** chief and knew how to cunningly win the battle without shooting a single arrow. Years of defending his territory from other tribes and hostiles had given him the experience he needed for that night. The robbers' hiding place was not ***tenable*** against the attack of crafty Indian chief.

Once the Indians were in position, he signaled his command. Suddenly the roaring sound of Indian war drums began to play. They grew louder and louder as the warriors began to yell their frightful cry. The robbers, who had been fast asleep, awoke to the terrifying noise. Disoriented from the ruckus, the robbers quickly began to scatter into the woods, right into the traps the Indians had laid for them. One by one the Indians seized the men, until there was only one left in the camp. The tall leader had not run away like his cowardly companions, but had decided to stick his ground. The only semi-intelligent member of the group, he had run toward the campfire for light instead of into the darkness of the woods. There he stood with Howie's gun shaking in his hands.

The chief seized this opportunity to show himself to the man. Walking out of the darkness, the lion-skinned man was a fearsome sight. The chief was unarmed, and intrepidly walked directly toward the man. The foolish leader believed this to be his chance to shoot an imprudent Indian who dared to approach him unarmed. The tall man

---

Vulpine	(**vuhl**-pahyn) – ADJ – cunning or crafty
Tenable	(**ten**-uh-buhl) – ADJ – capable of being held, maintained, or defended, as against attack or dispute

smiled and unsteadily raised his gun to the chief's chest. The chief's advance had served as a distraction to the robber, who was unaware of the encroachment of Hiamovi's men. As the outlaw aimed his gun at the chief he suddenly felt the cold prick of an Indian's arrow at the back of his neck. The man knew instantly that he had lost. The robber slowly dropped the gun to the ground and raised his hands over his head.

The Indians had won the bloodless battle in less than five minutes. All of the robbers had been rounded up to face judgment for their crimes. The Watkins' wagon was still intact and their horses, while frightened by the Indian's drumming, appeared to be unharmed.

Excited by the outcome, Anna quietly slipped out from behind the tree with Charlie, and did her best to race back to camp before anyone knew that the two of them had been missing.

WORD REVIEW

Archetype
Brazier
Censure
Conscription
Couture
Eclipse
Elliptical
Ethos
Genuflect
Homologous
Impregnable
Intermittent
Largess
Minutiae
Mortify
Non Sequitur
Paranoia
Pariah
Penumbra
Premeditation
Psyche
Retroactive
Soluble
Stratification
Stupendous
Surmount
Symbiosis
Tabula Rasa
Tenable
Verisimilitude
Vulpine

11

RIVERBOAT JUSTICE

The rowdy gang of Indians came riding back to camp loudly celebrating their victory over the band of robbers. Chief Hiamovi was at the front of the column, sitting on the driver's seat of the wagon, beaming with pride from the brilliant execution of his plan. Hiamovi was like the Indian's ***Nestor***, a strong leader driven by his wisdom and bravery. He had long since won the respect of his people, and they had sworn allegiance to him. Hiamovi's men had unquestionably followed his orders, and things couldn't have gone better for the Indian war party. The rest of the group followed the wagon, playing their victory songs on their drums and crying wildly in their native tongue. Marching solemnly behind them were their captives. Jacob had the honor of watching over the band of robbers, a job he did smugly with the barrel of Howie's gun.

Anna and Charlie had returned the horse just in time to see the celebratory entrance of the men. The entire camp buzzed from the noise of the shouts and drums. Women and children emerged out of their tepees to join the merriment of the victors. Hiamovi rode the wagon directly to the middle of the camp, dismounted, and in a rich voice called out to his people. Anna had no idea what he had said, but she knew it must have been profound.

Nestor (**nes**-ter) – N – the oldest and wisest of the Greeks in the Trojan War and a king of Pylos

The men and women responded with elation. The crowd cheered their leader as if he had won the most important battle of the Kuawns' existence. The men continued to play their drums, the women brought out firewood, and the children began to dance. It was a ***multifarious*** celebration and the adults and children alike enjoyed every element of the varied events.

Charlie ran to join his Indian friends in their triumphal dance. He didn't know the steps, and he certainly didn't feel the rhythm, but he hopped around in merriment. Anna joined the festivities with more caution, hoping not to bring too much attention to herself. The crowd was large and she felt confident she could join the party without arousing suspicion. Her plan unfortunately failed. As soon as she was close to the campfire Chief Hiamovi made his way toward her.

"Are you enjoying the festivities?" he asked.

"Yes, very much so," shyly replied Anna.

"And did you enjoy the battle from your spot behind the trees?" inquired the chief.

Anna's eyes darted back and forth, unsure of how the chief could know that. She then ***ostensibly*** tried to act surprised by the chief's question; by giving him a look that said, I have no idea what you mean. It was a look they both knew was false.

"I thought so," responded the chief. "Keep in mind, small one, the next time you decide to disobey an order, do it alone. It is foolish to put yourself in danger, but it is reckless to endanger the life of a little one. Things turned

---

Multifarious (muhl-tuh-**fair**-ee-uhs) – ADJ – having many different parts, elements, forms, etc.

Ostensible (o-**sten**-suh-buhl) – ADJ – outwardly appearing as such; professed; pretended

out all right this time, but just imagine if the robbers hadn't gone quietly. I am not so sure Charlie could survive a gunshot wound the way our friend, Howard, did."

The chief looked at Anna with seriousness. He had decided not to ***reprimand*** the young girl for her insubordination, nor did he plan on telling Jacob about her outing. The chief did, however, want Anna to understand the danger she had put herself and her younger brother in. Chief Hiamovi knew he wouldn't be doing the fifteen-year-old any favors by ignoring the truth.

"I see great potential in you, my child," continued the chief, "but before you can become great, you must first learn to control that which now controls you. Emotions and passions can greatly enrich your life, but the ***siren*** call of adventure can lure you to danger. If you can learn to channel your rushing river of feelings with a sense of controlled calmness, then you can use them to accomplish so many different things. With some time and maturity, I have no doubt that in your own right you will be a great warrior too."

"Thank you sir," Anna softly replied.

Having said what he wanted to say, the familiar jovial smile returned to the chief's face.

"Good, now go enjoy the festivities," remarked the chief. "After all, we did just safely bring back your horses and belongings. I'd say you, of all people, should have something to celebrate."

Chief Hiamovi patted Anna on the head and went off to join his people in the singing and dancing. He was a

---

Reprimand	(**rep**-ruh-mand) – V – to reprove or rebuke severely, especially in a formal way
Siren	(**sahy**-ruhn) – ADJ – seductive or tempting, especially dangerously or harmfully

good chief who loved his tribe. He ruled above his people as a demigod; but lived by the ***manifesto*** that a leader rules best by being one of the people. It was only by living, working, fighting, and celebrating among his tribe that Hiamovi could truly know what was best for them. So the chief danced with his people.

Anna would soon join the dancing, too, but first she stood next to the big bonfire thinking about what the chief had said to her. Chief Hiamovi's words had ***resonance***, and they continued to play over and over again in her head. No one had ever said anything like that to her, and although she didn't fully comprehend the chief's meaning, she knew she someday would. As for that day, she took his speech as a sort of challenge to her—a challenge not to let her emotions get the best of her, and to think through her actions more carefully. For the spirited teenager, it wouldn't be an easy challenge to succeed at, but deep down she knew that she would be better for trying. At fifteen, Anna Watkins still had a long way to go to develop into the person she had the potential of becoming; but every journey has a starting point. That night, by the light of stars and campfire, surrounded by scores of merry Indians, Anna decided to start her own voyage.

"Anna, dance with me" a tired but enthusiastic Charlie called out.

"OK, Charlie," Anna replied with a smile.

The time for deep thinking was over. Now it was time for dancing! Happily, Anna ran to join the circle of

---

Manifesto (man-uh-**fes**-toh) – N – a public declaration of intentions, opinions, objectives, or motives, as one issued by a government, sovereign, or organization

Resonance (**rez**-uh-nuhns) – N – the prolongation of sound by reflection; reverberation

Indians celebrating the victorious retrieval of the Watkins' belongings.

The Indian celebration continued well into the early morning hours. Charlie had made it until midnight, but shortly after he collapsed onto a pile of wool blankets sitting next to the chief's tepee. Around two in the morning, Anna could barely keep her eyes open. She wanted desperately to go to bed, but she didn't want to be rude. After all, the men had gone to battle for her and her family, and Anna and Jacob were the guests of honor. She had no way of knowing if leaving the party early was a minor, ***venial*** offense, or a great disrespect to her Indian hosts. As for her older brother, Jacob didn't seem to mind the late hours in the least. The young man was having a wonderful time. He would go from dancing, to talking with the Indian girls, to mingling with the other Indian warriors. Anna knew she would find no help from him in getting an excuse to go to bed early. She would have used Charlie as an excuse to leave the party, but a nice, older Indian lady had long since put him to bed.

Anna's next hope was the chief. She knew if she could get his blessing to let her leave, then no one would question her. Anna looked everywhere for the Kuawns' leader, but among the throngs of people even the chief was hard to find. Finally she spotted him on the other side of the bonfire. He was surrounded by his men and women, laughing, drinking, and having a magnificent time. Anna hated the thought of interrupting the merry group, but she knew that she wouldn't be able to last much longer. She

---

Venial (**vee**-nee-uhl) – ADJ – able to be forgiven or pardoned; not seriously wrong, as a sin

just had to speak with the chief. Anna took a ***rectilinear*** path toward Hiamovi to reach him as quickly as possible.

As Anna made her way through the crowd, she accidently bumped into a very old-looking woman. Anna had thought the medicine man was old, but compared to this woman, Askuwehetea was in the prime of his life. Anna's gentle nudge had almost pushed the frail woman to the ground. Embarrassed, Anna apologized. The old woman stared at Anna with a crazy look and mumbled something in the Kuawns' tongue. Not knowing how to respond, Anna gave the woman a shy smile. The woman smiled back with a toothless grin. This smile only made the woman look crazier. Facing the woman, Anna had a better chance to look at the Indian who stood before her. At first glance she appeared similar to the other Indians, but under a closer examination, Anna realized there was something different about this woman. Her clothing was more elaborate, decorated with feathers, jewelry, and other odds and ends. Anna couldn't be sure, but by the adornment of the old lady, Anna guessed she was a Kuawn ***sibyl***, someone who might be able to tell Anna what would happen in their future.

"One so young shouldn't be in such a rush," spoke the crazy old lady.

"I'm sorry," answered Anna. "I didn't mean to push you; I was just trying to get to the chief."

"And what is so important that you need to see the chief during this celebration?"

"I wanted to ask if it would be all right if I went to bed."

"No one is allowed to leave the victory celebration until all the spirits of the earth have been thanked."

Rectilinear (rek-tl-**in**-ee-er) – ADJ – forming a straight line
Sibyl (**sib**-uhl) – N – a female prophet

"Oh," said Anna. "And how many spirits of the earth are there?"

"2,352," replied the old woman.

Anna shuddered to ask her next questions, but she knew she had to.

"And how many have we already thanked?" inquired Anna.

"1,478" answered the Indian.

"Well, in that case I'd better get back to dancing," replied a disappointed Anna.

Not wanting to disrespect the Kuawns' ***piety***, Anna turned back to retake her spot next to the bonfire. As Anna turned to leave, the old woman broke out in uncontrollable laughter. Anna thought it was very rude that the woman would laugh at her misfortune and was starting to very much dislike the insane-looking lady. She was half-tempted to disregard what she said and go to bed anyway. However, the old woman was not laughing at Anna's misfortune, but rather at Anna's gullibility. The old Indian prophetess called back to Anna and explained that the party was a ***secular*** celebration and had nothing to do with the Kuawns' religious beliefs. Anna could go to bed whenever she wanted and didn't have to speak with the chief. Everyone would understand. Anna thanked the old woman and headed back toward her tepee. On her way to the tent, Anna thought about the Kuawns. Anna could usually determine the ***etymology*** of words she

---

Piety	(**pahy**-i-tee) – N – reverence for god or devout fulfillment of religious obligations
Secular	(**sek**-yuh-ler) – ADJ – of or pertaining to worldly things or to things that are not regarded as religious, spiritual, or sacred
Etymology	(et-uh-**mol**-o-gy) – N – the derivation of a word

didn't know, but the origin of the word "Kuawn" left her dumbfounded. Although she had no idea what *Kuawn* actually meant, unless it meant joker, it would have to be a ***misnomer.*** *That would be a better name,* Anna thought, *because the Kuawns seemed to love playing jokes on their guests.*

No one arose early the next morning, and the campsite was as silent as a grave until the afternoon. The silence of the Indian camp was enjoyed by everyone but the five frightened men who sat as prisoners in the Kuawns' camp. Tied together around a wooden stake, and carefully guarded by stern-looking Indian warriors, not one of the robbers had dared to speak since their arrival at the campsite. Even the quick-tongued leader kept his mouth shut for fear of losing his scalp. As the quiet morning dragged on, the five men from Gulf's Canyon had plenty of time to contemplate their fate. With each passing hour, the fear of the Kuawns' retribution grew stronger.

At one that afternoon, the chief called a meeting of his tribal wise men to discuss the future of the five prisoners. Chief Hiamovi had no desire to keep the men in his camp longer than necessary, and wanted to be quickly rid of the troublemakers. It was exhausting work keeping round the clock watch on the prisoners, and the chief wanted life to return to normal for his people. The men sat in the chief's tent for more than three hours. They took a break for a meal and then returned to their discussion. Hiamovi was not in the habit of allowing outsiders in private meetings of the Kuawns' leadership. However, this situation was special and he decided to make an exception to his rule. After a second break,

---

Misnomer (mis-**noh**-mer) – N – a misapplied or inappropriate name or designation

chief Hiamovi invited Jacob, Anna, and Howie into the meeting. Howie, who had made dramatic improvements in his health, was carried into the meeting on his coat. There, for one time only, the chief ***enfranchised*** the three and allowed their voices to be heard concerning the matter of the robbers. It was nightfall before the group was able to reach a decision. The extended length of time was due to the ***dimorphic*** nature of the group with half of the assembly seeking to administer the justice themselves, while the other half wanted to hand over the bandits to the local law enforcement jurisdiction. Since the crime had technically been committed in Gulf's Canyon's jurisdiction, the men would have to be returned there to receive their punishment. Given the lawless nature of that community, Chief Hiamovi felt that it would be a waste of their time to return them. At Gulf's Canyon the men would receive only a stern warning and then go free. That wasn't justice, and could encourage others to come looking for trouble in the Indian camp.

Once it was decided to keep this matter among the tribe, the next decision that had to be made was the appropriate punishment for the five men. Again the group was split. Half of the assemblage thought it was fair to administer ***stringent*** punishment, and the other half wanted something more lenient. The discussion went back and forth for two hours before Hiamovi decided to put a stop to it. The wise leader stood up and addressed his group.

Enfranchise	(en-**fran**-chahyz) – V – to grant a franchise to; admit to citizenship, especially to the right of voting
Dimorphic	(dahy-**mawr**-fik) – ADJ – having two forms
Stringent	(**strin**-juhnt) – ADJ – rigorously binding or exacting; strict; severe

"Who are we to decide what is right and fair?" began the chief. "Our judgment will always be biased. Therefore we must do our best to combat those biases by choosing an action that is somewhere between what we want to do, and what we know we should do."

As Chief Hiamovi spoke, the entire group was silent. His words rang out loud and clear. Hiamovi spoke with confidence and conviction. He had heard the arguments from both sides, and as the leader, he knew the time for talking was over. He was ready to make the final decision.

"We want justice, but we should also give mercy," continued the leader. "It is over these two things that you have argued the better part of the evening. How can we find a balance between these two? By giving the men exactly what they deserve and nothing more. I now know what needs to be done. Thank you for your time."

With that, Hiamovi ended the meeting and sent his wise men away. The Indians respectfully bowed before their leader and left. Soon the only people left in the tent, other than the chief, were Howie and the two Watkins children. These three anxiously waited to hear the decision the chief had made about the ***punitive*** actions toward the prisoners.

"We shall do to the men the exact thing which they did to you," said the chief. "We cannot indulge in vengeance for that would offend justice."

Then the chief turned and addressed Howie.

"It is not my place to decide what should be done with the one who shot you, my friend," continued the chief.

Punitive (**pyoo**-ni-tiv) – ADJ – serving for, concerned with, or inflicting punishment

"That is a decision that only you can make. You can think it over and make your choice in the morning. Judgment for the robbers begins tomorrow morning at dawn."

Howie nodded with understanding, but said nothing in response. The chief then smiled at him and the children. It had been a long day of discourse and Hiamovi was ready for some time to himself. The chief summoned two of his men to take Howie back to the medicine man's tepee. Hiamovi thanked the children for joining the gathering and sent them on their way. Before they left, he assured them that everything would be OK.

The next morning as the sun was just beginning to rise, the Indian campsite was once again alive with the sound of drum music. On this morning, the music was not jovial as it had been on the night of the celebration, but it was full of somber ***staccato*** notes that made up a poignant melody. As the crowd began to gather in the center of the campsite, the five condemned men were brought into the middle of the group. Chief Hiamovi stood high on a wooden platform and spoke loudly to the crowd. The chief's speech was entirely in the Kuawns' native tongue. The music and the strange cries of the Indian chief made the robbers shudder with fear. They had no way of knowing what the large man in the mountain lion-skinned headdress was saying, but they were certain it concerned their future.

Chief Hiamovi spoke to the tribe as a whole that morning to read out the sentence he and the council of elders had decided the night before. Only a small group of Indians would actually accompany him in carrying out the robbers' punishment, but the chief wanted the entire

---

Staccato (stuh-**kah**-toh) – ADJ – composed of or characterized by abruptly disconnected elements

tribe to know what was happening that day. Once the chief finished speaking, he gathered Jacob, Anna, and Howie along with some of his strongest warriors. In total, the group numbered about 20. Hiamovi, atop his prized horse, led the way out of the camp to the site he had picked to carry out the men's judgment.

The leader led the group straight into the middle of a ***necropolis***, the resting home of many of their revered ancestors. The sun's morning rays danced through the thick trees onto the ancient burial markings, casting an eerie glow to the area. The solemnity of the Indians, the gloom of the burial grounds, and the haunting sounds of the drumbeats worked together to terrify the five robbers. They knew that in a place like this, their judgment wouldn't be favorable. However, the burial grounds were not Hiamovi's destination. He had only taken his party through there to give the men a good scare. Despite the seriousness of his composure, the chief laughed inwardly at the cowardliness of his captives.

The chief led his party to a large river. The water flowed freely and was almost rushing down its path. On one side of the river bank sat a large wooden vessel which no longer had its ***halyard*** or other necessary rigging. A bare boat with no sail, no oars, or anything to give it any direction, the craft was only good for floating. Hiamovi motioned to his men to bring the captives to the boat. The robbers were then placed into the boat with their hands still tied behind their backs. The chief then called out for Howie. With the help of two strong Indian men, the old

---

Necropolis (nuh-**krop**-uh-lis) – N – a historic or prehistoric burial ground

Halyard (hal-yerd) – N – any of various lines or tackles for hoisting a spar, sail, flag, etc., into position for use

trail guide emerged from the back of the group. The men aided him to the chief's horse, and the chief handed his friend back his gun. The eyes of the robbers grew wide. This was the first time they had seen the man they had left for dead. With his gun in his hand, Howie stood up straight and turned toward the helpless men in the boat. He signaled for his Indian helpers to stay by the chief. Now was his time for retribution and he wanted to face his enemies with pride.

Still in pain from his gunshot wound, the old trail guide slowly made his way toward the vessel. His face was stern and his eyes locked onto the men who robbed the children and almost took his life. Howie was angry, not only for his own pain but also for all the pain he was sure these men had put others through. Men like the ones who sat before him made life difficult for the good people such as the Watkins who were trying to make the world a better place. These men were scum, and didn't deserve mercy.

Howie raised his gun and pointed it at the leader. He knew that it wasn't the leader who shot him, but if it hadn't been for that tall man none of it would have happened. The trail guide had the opportunity to take out the mastermind, leaving his followers to scatter. All it would take was one quick pull of his trigger to end the saga that had brought them to the river bank that morning. No one would blame Howie for doing it either. There was no doubt in the old trail guide's mind that his wagon hadn't been the first victim of this gang, and Howie wasn't the first man they had shot.

Howie had the opportunity, the justification, and the ability to take his shot, but something kept his hand from pulling the trigger. Maybe it was because there were impressionable children present and vengeance wasn't the precedent he wanted to set for them. Maybe it was because

Howie didn't want to stoop to the robbers' level by shooting an unarmed man. Holding his gun to the defenseless leader made Howie feel like a ***hypocrite*** since he considered himself an honorable man. Whatever the reason, Howie decided not to shoot. He lowered his gun and spoke to the wicked men who sat before him.

"Y'all don't deserve mercy," Howie began. "But I'm gonna give it to you anyway. But mark my words, if I ever hear of y'all robbing and shooting innocent people again, I will hunt you down personally and shoot every last one of ya."

Chief Hiamovi had watched Howie's actions very closely, and as it became clear to him that Howie was not going to shoot, he made his way slowly toward the river bank.

"You made the right decision, my friend," the chief said quietly.

Several other Indian warriors followed the chief's example and made their way to the river bank. There they began to push the boat full of robbers into the river. The water at the river bank was shallow and ***eutrophic***, and the collection of algae on the shore gave the water a green tint. Chief Hiamovi didn't know how far the river would take the outlaws, but part of him hoped it would carry them all

---

Hypocrite (**hip**-uh-krit) – N – a person who pretends to have virtues, moral or religious beliefs, principles, etc., that he or she does not actually possess, especially a person whose actions belie stated beliefs

Eutrophic (yoo-**trof**-ik) – ADJ – characterized by an abundant accumulation of nutrients that support a dense growth of algae and other organisms, the decay of which depletes the shallow waters of oxygen in summer

the way to the ***estuary*** many miles away at the outlet to the ocean. The chief believed a sea voyage would do the men some good. At the very least he wanted them far away from Howie, the Watkins, and his people. The harsh prairie life had enough problems without the complications of having to hunt down and punish such lawless men.

The water wasn't strong enough to carry the boat from the shoreline, so the group of Indian warriors moved to the side of the boat where each grabbed a part of the boat's ***bilge*** and began to walk the vessel into the middle of the river. When they were a little more than waist-deep into the river, the men let go of the boat. The water's strong currents did the rest of the work, and the voyage of the five outlaws began. The Indian warriors waited to make sure the water carried the boat a good distance before they returned to shore. Hiamovi then instructed the same men to follow the boat until it was off the Indians' land. Whatever happened to the men once they reached the end of the Kuawns' property was no concern to the chief. They were stranded in a strange land just as they had stranded the Watkins. Chief Hiamovi felt pleased with the punishment. Apart from the small group that followed the boat, the rest of the party turned to head back to camp.

Once the party had returned to the camp, Askuwehetea came running—if one could call the hurried walk of an ancient man running—to meet them. He was horrified that his patient, after only a couple of days in bed, had been

---

Estuary (**es**-choo-er-ee) – N – that part of the mouth or lower course of a river in which the river's current meets the sea's tide

Bilge (bilj) – N – either of the rounded areas that form the transition between the bottom and the sides on the exterior of a hull

allowed on such an outing. The old medicine man located Howie and began to scold him. Despite the time Howie had spent with the Kuawns, he was only partially fluent in their native tongue. He didn't understand everything that the old man said, but he could tell by Askuwehetea's tone that the old man wasn't happy with him. Howie had survived a gunshot wound to the chest, but now he wondered if the frenzied manner of his doctor might put him back into a sickbed with an ***iatrogenic*** headache. Dutifully Howie obeyed Askuwehetea's orders and returned to his tepee. Jacob and Anna wanted to follow Howie into the tent to speak with him, but the chief stopped them. Now wasn't the time to get in Askuwehetea's way. He suggested that they tend to other matters, such as checking their belongings, and come back to see Howie later that day.

With all the excitement from the past several days, Anna and Jacob had completely forgotten to check the wagon to see if everything was still there. There were 500 good reasons for the children to inspect their wagon. They thanked the chief for his suggestion and made their way to the place their wagon was being kept.

Apart from the mud collected from the robbers' ride through the forest, the outside of the Watkins' wagon remained roughly in the same shape as the last time they had seen it. The children only hoped that the inside contents would be the same. Together, Jacob and Anna climbed into the back of the wagon and began the search through their belongings. The exploration was multifarious: not only did they want to make sure their stuff was unharmed, but also they wanted to find out if anything was missing. The

---

Iatrogenic (ahy-a-truh-**jen**-ik) – ADJ – caused by the diagnosis, manner, or treatment of a physician

Watkins could live without most things in the wagon, but it would be really hard for them to start over without their money—finding it was the ***preeminent*** task.

The first place Jacob checked was under the wagon in his secret hiding place, but as he had feared, the morning they left Gulf's Canyon he had forgotten to put it back there. They had been in such a rush that morning to get out of the city that he had simply thrown it in the back of the wagon still hidden in the ***millefleur*** quilt their mother had made. Jacob had planned on putting it back in its hiding place on their first water break. Unfortunately that was the water break that they had been robbed. Anna found the quilt in the back of the wagon, but it, too, was empty. Panicked, the children opened up trunk after trunk looking for the lost money box, but it wasn't anywhere to be found. The Watkins searched for over two hours in the back of the wagon without any luck. The robbers must have found the money and done something with it. It was possible it was hidden somewhere back in the forest, but there was no way of being sure. With the robbers on their way to the Gulf of Mexico, there was no one the Watkins could ask. The poor children felt so stupid for not checking the wagon first. Had they only known the money was missing before they sent sailing the only people who knew of its whereabouts! Dejected, they returned back to camp.

Howie must have sweet-talked Askuwehetea into letting him out of his tent prison, because when the Watkins returned to the center of the camp the old trail guide was

---

Preeminent (pree-**em**-uh-nuhnt) – ADJ – eminent above or before others; superior; surpassing

Millefleur (meel-**flur**) – ADJ – having a background sprinkled with representations of flowers

sitting next to the chief in the open air. The two men were exchanging stories and having a wonderful time enjoying each other's company. They smiled at the children and waved them over to join their conversation.

The children had no desire to join the men, but rather wanted to go hide in their tepee. They were embarrassed and didn't want to face the men who had done so much to help them. They were also a little bit scared to tell Howie that they no longer had the money to pay him. Sheepishly they walked over and joined the conversation.

"Hey, kiddos," said Howie without his familiar gruff ***locution***. "What have you two been up too?"

"They've been going through the wagon to make sure everything was OK," replied the chief on the children's behalf.

"And?" asked Howie. "Is everything as it should be?"

"Oh, ya…" stumbled Jacob. "Well, almost."

"Everything is there except 500 dollars," blurted out Anna.

"You kids had that kind of cash on you?" asked Howie, shocked. "Why didn't you say something before? We could have taken better care to make sure it was safe."

"I know," began Jacob. "It's just that I thought the fewer people who knew, the better. It was all we had from selling our farm and we couldn't afford to lose it."

"Say no more, kid" Howie responded gently. "You did what you thought was best."

"Now we don't even have enough to pay the rest of your fee," added Anna.

"We don't need to worry about that now," smiled Howie. "There is nothing we can do to change the situation

---

Locution (loh-**kyoo**-shuhn) – N – a particular form of expression; a word, phrase, expression

at the present. Why don't you two come join us and we can figure out the solution to this problem later."

"Is there a solution?" asked Anna with tears forming in her eyes.

"There is always a solution, dear one," responded the chief. "Now come. Worrying about it right now won't bring the money back. We will give it some thought and make a decision about what to do later."

The kind words of Howie and Chief Hiamovi didn't make the problem of the lost money go away, but it certainly helped ease the troubled minds of the two teenagers. Not knowing how the situation would sort itself out, the Watkins decided to try to not let their worries ruin their night. They had faced so many trials over the last few months, and somehow everything always turned out all right. So they hoped that this, too, would sort itself out in the end.

WORD REVIEW

Bilge
Dimorphic
Enfranchise
Estuary
Etymology
Eutrophic
Halyard
Hypocrite
Iatrogenic
Locution
Manifesto
Millefleur
Misnomer
Multifarious
Necropolis
Nestor
Ostensible
Piety
Preeminent
Punitive
Rectilinear
Reprimand
Resonance
Secular
Sibyl
Siren
Staccato
Stringent
Venial

12

A JOYOUS REUNION

Four weeks had passed since that fateful day when the Watkins discovered their moneybox was missing. While the shock of losing every dollar that they owned had since subsided, the burden of being homeless, poor, and orphans weighed heavily on the elder children's shoulders. For the time being, the Watkins remained with the Kuawns. The children repeatedly attempted to speak to Chief Hiamovi about their situation, but he continued to insist that there was a solution and to tell them to simply relax. When pressed on how long they had to wait, the Chief smiled and told them to be patient. Seeing that they didn't have much of a choice, the children reluctantly followed the chief's advice. In the meantime, the Watkins adapted to the Kuawn way of life. Although it had taken almost the entirety of the month, both Jacob and Anna settled into their new routines. Jacob would leave early in the morning with a Kuawn hunting party and Anna would stay behind to help the Indian women tend both the crops and the campsite. Even though neither of the Watkins were complete novices at their particular jobs, after only a few days with the Kuawn tribe, they quickly learned they had a lot to learn. Jacob soon learned how to hunt with a bow and arrow and to track animals with complete silence. Had his father Thomas been alive, he would have been very proud of how well his son adopted the lessons from his Indian mentors. In a similar fashion, Anna watched the Kuawn women very carefully and took every opportunity to incorporate their ***superlative*** farming techniques. Anna was amazed by the way in which the women were able to turn barren soil into a ***fecund*** patch of fresh fruits and vegetables. More than anything, the young lady wished she had the opportunity to apply the Indians' methods to her mother's old garden in Wyoming. Anna was convinced her newfound knowledge was a valuable ***accretion*** to her gardening skills.

Howie's health had also dramatically improved over the last several weeks. In fact, the old medicine man had done such a good job taking care of the rugged trail guide that Howie looked like a new man. The combination of his injury and Askuwehetea's strict diet helped Howie slim down a much needed ten pounds, and the color of Howie's skin went from ruddy to radiant. Howie experienced the odd sensation of being better off after being shot in the chest than he was before. The Watkins could hardly imagine that the clean-shaven, thinner, and friendlier man at the Kuawn campsite was the same man who had started the journey with them a few months before. Howie, however, wasn't the only one who had changed. Since leaving Wyoming it was clear that the Watkins children had also dramatically changed. The last several months had not been easy, but the trials had matured both Anna and Jacob. Even Charlie wasn't immune to the change; the time he spent with the Indians taught him the necessity of obedience and sharing, as the Indian women did not put

---

Superlative (suh-**pur**-luh-tiv) – ADJ – of the highest kind, quality, or order; surpassing all else or others; supreme; extreme

Fecund (**fee**-kuhnd) – ADJ – very productive or creative intellectually

Accretion (uh-**kree**-shuhn) – N – an increase by natural growth or by gradual external addition

up with his selfish ways. For the first time in a long time, Charlie learned the meaning of the word *no.* The trip had been the starting ***matrix*** for everyone's transformations to the more mature people they had become.

August had just arrived on the western prairie when Chief Hiamovi summoned the Watkins children into his tepee one evening. This wasn't an unusual request, as the children had often spent the late summer evenings with both the chief and Howie. Normally the small group would spend hours laughing as they all exchanged stories and reminisced over the day's events. The regularity of the meetings with the chief made it impossible for the children to uncover the ***subtext*** of Hiamovi's invitation for this one specific get-together. However, tonight would determine the Watkins' future.

The sun had just set when Jacob, Anna, and Charlie sat down next to Chief Hiamovi in the middle of his tepee. As his guests arrived, the chief motioned to a ***subservient*** Indian to pour three more glasses. "Let's drink Rattler's Kiss," the chief declared, using the proper ***metonym*** for his favorite black tea and wormwood mixture. As the server prepared the drinks, Anna shuddered.

Matrix	(**mey**-triks) – N – something (such as a situation) in which something else develops
Subtext	(**suhb**-tekst) – N – the underlying or implicit meaning, as of a literary work
Subservient	(suhb-**sur**-vee-uhnt) – ADJ – serving or acting in a subordinate capacity
Metonymy	(mi-**ton**-uh-mee) – N – a figure of speech that consists of the use of the name of one object or concept for that of another to which it is related, or of which it is a part, as "scepter" for "sovereignty," or "the bottle" for "strong drink," or "count heads (or noses)" for "count people"

Rattler's Kiss, a specialty of the Kuawn people served after the evening meal, was an extremely bitter drink. However, everyone drank it and the Watkins were no exceptions. The concoction of herbs was said to have almost a mystical power in helping aid digestion. While it never failed to ease any of the Watkins' stomachaches—which occurred often since the children weren't used to their new Indian diets—the drink was utterly unpleasant to consume. When ask how she liked it, Anna replied that it had a disagreeably acrid taste. Jacob refused to openly comment on his opinion of the drink, but silently he believed Anna had described it accurately. Surprisingly, the only one in the family who enjoyed drinking the tea was Charlie. However, coming from a child who loved eating dirt, his estimation didn't hold much weight with his older siblings. Charlie was gleaming as the Indian served the Watkins their tea; Anna and Jacob could produce only halfhearted fake smiles.

Not long after the children sat down, Howie strolled in. The trail guide might have lost some extra pounds over the last few weeks, but his self-satisfied countenance remained. With his health back, Howie was ready to once again take on the world. Howie wasn't looking for any more encounters with outlaws ***per se***; however, if he happened to run into some in the future, he would be prepared. Confidence was a defining feature of the prairie man. Once Howie sat down and was served his tea, the chief began to speak. Upon opening his mouth, it didn't take the Watkins children long to realize tonight's meeting wouldn't be like the previous ones.

"Summer is drawing to a close," began the chief. "Soon autumn will be upon us."

Per Se (pur **sey**) – ADV – by, of, for, or in itself; intrinsically

The chief's tone was serious, and the children listened intently. Hiamovi's curious opener had caught everyone's attention.

"The animals have begun their migration patterns," continued the chief, "and the time has come for my people to move on."

"What do you mean?" asked Jacob.

"We Kuawns are also pioneers of the West," answered the chief. "However, unlike the White Man, we do not permanently settle in one place. We follow the wild game. When they go, we go."

"And now?" inquired Anna.

"And now it's time to go," responded the chief.

"When will you be leaving?" inquired Jacob

"By the end of the week," answered the chief. "I know this must come as a shock to you, and I'm sorry. My hunters just informed me that the there are no more ***bevies*** of quail to hunt in the forest. The absence of gamebirds is the first sign of the changing seasons. For us to prepare for the upcoming winter we must move now to our other campsite."

Anna and Jacob were stunned by Chief Hiamovi's declaration. Unable to speak, the children listened as the chief continued on.

"I don't want you children to get the wrong impression," began Hiamovi. "Just because my people and I are moving, doesn't mean you three are not welcome to come with us. You have proven yourselves to be of noble character, and the Kuawns would be honored to call you some of our own."

There was no higher praise in either Jacob or Anna's mind than the words which Chief Hiamovi had

---

Bevy (**bev**-ee) – N – a group of birds, as larks or quail

just spoken. Hiamovi was an honorable man, and when he talked he spoke with conviction. His compliment of the Watkins' character was not hollow praise. Along with the chief's kind words, the Watkins were humbled by Hiamovi's offer. Hiamovi's ***dictum***, that the children would be welcomed into the Kuawn tribe, filled the children's hearts with pride. Less than a month ago, the children had been strangers and now the chief was extending an invitation to become a part of his sacred way of life. He was proposing more than just friendship; Hiamovi was offering kinship. The Watkins were given the rare opportunity to join the Kuawns. Joining the Indian family was not a decision to take lightly. Jacob and Anna both knew that if they decided to unify with the Kuawns, there would be no opportunity to ***secede*** from the Indian alliance. Saying yes to Hiamovi required that they permanently adopt the Indians' way of life. Jacob and Charlie would be groomed to become Kuawn hunters, and Anna would be trained to become a sound Kuawn woman. They would learn their language, their culture, and their religion. The Watkins were particularly not looking forward to learning the ***syntax*** of the Kuawn grammar, along with adjusting to the strange customs. While the two elder children understood that Hiamovi would never expect them to relinquish their past, he would require them to revere the Kuawns customs more. Although the Watkins would only be a few hundred miles

---

Dictum (**dik**-tuhm) – N – an authoritative pronouncement; judicial assertion

Secede (si-**seed**) – V – to withdraw formally from an alliance, federation, or association, as from a political union, a religious organization, etc.

Syntax (**sin**-taks) – N – the study of the rules for the formation of grammatical sentences in a language

from either their past life in Wyoming or their potential future life in St. Louis, living among the Kuawns would be like entering a completely different world.

"I understand you two have a lot to talk about," continued Hiamovi after a long pause. "Unfortunately I must ask that you make up your minds rather quickly. There is an abundance of work to be done for our move, and I must inform my elders if they should expect the addition of three new Kuawns. Therefore, I will need your final decision as a ***definitive*** answer by tomorrow evening."

Knowing that the children would want some time to discuss his offer in private, Chief Hiamovi excused the Watkins. Jacob, Anna, and Charlie thanked the chief for his hospitality and his kindness. Confounded by the enormous decision that lay before them, the group left in silence.

Once again the Watkins faced a ***ponderous*** choice, one they would not take lightly. Staying with the Kuawns meant security but it also required substantial sacrifice; continuing their journey to St. Louis allowed the children to retain their familiar way of life, yet it entailed considerable uncertainty. One way or another, the children would be giving up something in return for another. Ultimately the choice came down to what was most important to the Watkins: protection or continuing the legacy of their parents.

As the Watkins departed, they were greeted by the cool winds of the August evening. The night sky was as black as coal, and the normally visible glimmering stars were nowhere to be seen. Traditionally the children would return to their tepee after spending the evening in

---

Definitive (dih-**fin**-i-tiv) – ADJ – having its fixed and final form

Ponderous (**pon**-der-uhs) – ADJ – of great weight; heavy; massive

the chief's tent, but this night Jacob led the family right behind the last row of tepees to a secluded patch of large wildflowers. The cluster of ***lupines*** with pale blue blossoms was so large that it created a quiet place just far enough out of the center of the campsite for the family to talk without being interrupted. While neither Anna nor Charlie had ever been to this spot before, Jacob was a frequent visitor. It was the place he came to be by himself and think—a pastime he often enjoyed since their arrival at the Kuawns.

The private family meeting began with a somber tone. As the eldest, Jacob felt compelled to try and lighten the mood.

"I know that we are all thinking about how tough the decision will be," began Jacob. "However, we should first remember the enormous honor we have been given by having to make this decision."

Understanding what Jacob meant, Anna nodded in agreement.

"It is also important that we make this decision based not only on emotions," continued Jacob, "but on what is best for our family as a whole. Neither choice will be easy; therefore we have to choose the option that is best for us, regardless of what anyone else wants us to do or not do."

All the changes the Watkins had experienced had proved to Jacob his family was ***malleable***, able to adapt to any situation. In his mind, this crossroad was no different. Jacob was convinced that as long as the family made the decision together, either choice could be the right answer.

The Watkins remained in their secret place well

Lupine	(**loo**-pin) – N – plant having tall, dense clusters of blue, pink, or white flowers
Malleable	(**mal**-ee-uh-buhl) – ADJ – adaptable or tractable

into the night. They discussed the pros and cons of staying versus leaving. They considered where they had come from, and what they wanted in the future. They deliberated what their lives would look like if they stayed or went. Together they exhausted every factor they could think of that could influence the decision that had to be made. Jacob and Anna even felt it necessary to include Charlie in the conversation. Although the three-year-old couldn't fully grasp the consequences of the decision, his opinion certainly mattered in the discussion of possibly fundamentally changing the Watkins' culture. The elder children listened intently to Charlie's comments and concerns, and weighed his thoughts along with their own, excluding of course any comments made about *Rattler's Kiss.*

It was midnight when the Watkins reached their decision. The night's sky was as black as ever, with one minor exception. As the children were leaving their hiding place, a shooting star flew across the sky. Anna had only seen such a sight once before in her life and the flying piece of ***interstellar*** dust made her smile. At that moment she tightly closed her eyed and made a silent wish. She wished that her family's future would be as bright as the shining stars. Deep down she knew the star had no magical powers, but she made her wish anyway.

As the Watkins walked back to the center of camp, they were greeted by a familiar voice.

"It's pretty late to be taking a scenic walk in the forest," said the voice.

Startled by the voice, all three of the children

Interstellar (in-ter-**stel**-er) – ADJ – located, taking place, or traveling among the stars especially of the Milky Way galaxy jumped and turned to see who was addressing them. There, sitting outside of his tepee smoking a pipe, was Howie. Howie often sat outside his tepee late at night as he smoked. He found the warm taste of the tobacco and the cool breeze of the night air to be relaxing, providing a ***purgative*** cleansing of the day's problems. Happy to see a friend, the Watkins went to join the trail guide.

"Long night, huh?" asked Howie.

"You can say that again," answered Jacob. "The chief gave us a lot to think about tonight."

"Have you made your decision?" inquired Howie.

"Yes," began Jacob. "The only sensible thing to do is to stay with the Kuawns. We were just on our way to inform the chief."

Jacob went on to explain to Howie that living with the Kuawns was not the Watkins' ideal future, but that the family wasn't really in a position to turn down such a generous offer. Sure it would be difficult to fully adapt to their way of life, but sometimes life was just difficult. Jacob continued to insist that given the fact that the Watkins had no money and no future prospects back East, there was simply no point in continuing on to St. Louis. After all, the Watkins didn't even have the money to pay their trail guide. Howie, being the ***contrarian*** that he was, challenged Jacob's conclusion.

"Is living with the Kuawns really what is best for you and your siblings?" contested Howie. "Would you really be happy here?"

"We could learn to be happy," interjected Anna.

Purgative (**pur**-guh-tiv) – N – cathartic
Contrarian (kuhn-**trair**-ee-uhn) – N – a person who takes an opposing view

"Happiness is staying together as a family. Chief Hiamovi is giving us an option that we are not sure that we would have in St. Louis."

"So if you could guarantee that you could stay together as family," began Howie, "then you would choose to continue to St. Louis."

"If by staying together you mean having the ability to provide for ourselves, then yes," answered Jacob.

Jacob's answer brought a huge smile to Howie's face. Howie understood all too well that the Watkins' decision to become a part of the Kuawns was based solely on their desire to do what was right for their family. While the Watkins had utterly enjoyed the past month they spent with the Indians, internally they longed for something familiar. They were happy to be good friends with the Indians, but deep down they wanted to grow up with their own customs and culture. The Watkins had a ***protean*** quality to adapt to anything, but that didn't mean they wanted to make dramatic changes. Howie had a lot of respect for both Jacob and Anna. It took a lot of character for the teenagers to continually make what they considered the right choice, even when it wasn't the one they wanted to choose. If he ever had children, Howie hoped that they would turn out just like the ones who sat in front of him.

"Why are you smiling?" inquired Anna.

"Because I have an idea that I know will make you happy," answered Howie.

Howie's response puzzled the Watkins. What on earth could he be talking about? They both silently wondered. The old trail guide didn't leave them long

---

Protean (**proh**-tee-uhn) – ADJ – versatile; able to play many kinds of roles

in suspense. He knew what he was about to say would mark a pivotal ***solstice*** in the Watkins' life, and he wanted to share it with them as soon as possible. Over the last couple of months, Howie had developed affection for his traveling companions, and it delighted him to see them happy.

"Well, I have considered retiring for some time," began Howie. "After all, I have spent the better portion of my life on the road, and I was thinking that St. Louis sounded like just as good a place to end up as any other. I've traveled through the city numerous times picking up caravans, and the city has always suited me. And, well, after my nearest brush with death, I realized that I'm getting too old for this type of lifestyle..."

As Howie spoke the Watkins noticed something unfamiliar in Howie's demeanor. It was hard to detect at first, but as the rugged mountain man continued to speak the children noticed that his voice had a rolling, ***undulant*** tone. Although it was very subtle, the wavering quality of his voice said one thing: Howie was nervous. The trail guide cleared his voice and began once again with his thoughts.

"Well, I guess what I'm trying to say," continued Howie, "is that spending these last few months with you made me realize how much I missed out on having a family all these years. Don't get me wrong—I wouldn't take back my experiences for anything, but now it's time to do something different."

"What are you planning on doing?" asked a still confused Anna.

Solstice (**sol**-stis) – N – a turning point

Undulant (**uhn**-juh-luhnt) – ADJ – wavelike in motion or pattern

"Well, when Hami offered to adopt you children into the Kuawn family," answered Howie, "I realized there was nothing I wanted more than to make you three a part of my family. Now I know it's not as exciting as living with the Indians, but I thought we all could go to St. Louis and make a new life there together."

Howie's last words caught the attention of a half-awake Charlie.

"So you want to be our new daddy?" inquired the blunt three-year-old.

"Well, maybe not your dad," answered Howie with a smile. "I was thinking I could be more like an uncle."

"Uncle Howie," responded Anna. "I think I could get used to that."

"Uncle Howie," repeated Charlie, as he ran up to give the old man a huge hug.

"Well, we never had an uncle before," added Jacob with a smile. "Why not?"

Within a matter of minutes the Watkins had ***imputed*** kinship to their former trail guide. Before the trip began, Howie and the children had seemed unlikely to develop a friendship, but adversity had brought the small traveling party together and time had created a familial bond among the group.

The Watkins' adoption of Howie as their new uncle couldn't have been more right. For the first time in months, the Watkins children felt like a complete family. Something which they had lost earlier that spring had been restored. While the addition of Howie could never replace their parents, his presence allowed the Watkins to begin the new life with a fresh start. Howie

Impute (im-**pyoot**) – V – to attribute or ascribe

was appointed to his new role without any pomp or ceremony. It was just a quiet agreement among friends.

Chief Hiamovi couldn't have been happier for the Watkins and his dear friend Howie over the new arrangement. While he admitted that he would miss the children when they left the Kuawns, he understood that their solution was better in the long run. He also made them promise that they would make a point to come back and visit him and his people. It was a pledge the Watkins and Howie wholeheartedly agreed to. Even though the traveling party and the Kuawns were soon to go their separate ways, Chief Hiamovi guaranteed that the group would not leave without the ***panoply*** of an Indian procession. It was a grand gesture of friendship.

"Indian parades are a sight to see," side Hiamovi.

The chief grinned, and then added, "When you leave, you will see the Kuawns in all their glory."

True to his word, on the morning that the Watkins left the Indian camp, Chief Hiamovi organized a spectacle like none other the children had ever seen. There was a grand event with music, dancing, and colors everywhere. Every man, woman, and child was dressed in a vibrant costume and had his or her face painted. Flowers adorned the campsite, and even the ***hibiscus*** blossoms looked like they had put on their best dress. It was extraordinary. The Kuawn parade was more like an elaborate escort than an entertainment procession. The Indians encircled the Watkins' wagon as it slowly rolled out of the campsite. It was their way of sending their friends

---

Panoply (**pan**-uh-plee) – N – a wide-ranging and impressive array or display

Hibiscus (hahy-**bis**-kuhs) – N – also called China rose, a woody plant of the mallow family having large, showy flowers

off on their final leg of their journey with a blessing. They sang songs, played their drums, and called out to the small traveling caravan. The Kuawns continued on their parade until they reached the end of their territory. From the edge they stood and continued to warmly send off their friends. Captivated by the scene, the Watkins continued to enthusiastically wave to their gracious hosts. It was a fitting ending to their time with the Indians.

Charlie had the hardest time saying good-bye. The last month was the first time the toddler had been surrounded by other children his own age for any extended period of time. He had enjoyed every minute of life as an Indian boy. The three-year-old was reluctant to give it all up, and especially disliked having to wear clothes again. He made his older siblings promise that they would return soon, and stood up hollering and waving to his new friends until long after they were all out of his line of sight. As he waved with one hand, with the other, the small child held tightly to an eagle feather his best friend at the camp had given him. This was his little Indian treasure.

Although it had been an ***oblique*** path so far, the single wagon train of settlers was once again on its way to St. Louis, directly this time. Over the last month the Watkins had lost a small fortune, but they had gained a large extended family. All the money in the world couldn't have purchased the love of the Kuawns and Howie or the invaluable experiences the children had had on their journey East. Even though the entire group understood that their path to St. Louis was almost at an end, they knew that their new life was just about to begin.

Oblique (uh-**bleek**) – ADJ – not straight or direct

This time around, the atmosphere of the traveling party was different. The once brusque Howie spoke openly with the children about his past. During the course of several weeks, the Watkins learned of Howie's love of studying English words and language, and how when he was young he dreamed of going to school to study ***lexicography***. Yet, like so many stories of life in the 1800s, personal tragedy and the need for survival circumvented the pursuit of aspirations. The group didn't dwell on the past exclusively, but they spoke often of the future. They discussed the types of jobs Howie and Jacob would find, and the types of schools Anna and Charlie would attend. They envisioned their new house and neighborhood. Often their conversations would span from the early mornings on the trail to the last hours of the night. Life was once again full of hope and excitement. Among other things discussed, the group decided the first place they wanted to visit when they got to St. Louis was the site that had started it all. The group was on the path to St. Peters.

It was late one evening when the small traveling party finally reached their ultimate destination. The city lights sparkled in the night as if they were personally welcoming Howie and the children. The group could hardly believe they had made it. Exhausted from weeks on the road, the group decided to pull into the first hotel they could find. Tomorrow they would explore their new home, but tonight they would rest.

Despite the fatigue of travel, no one could sleep past sunrise. The excitement of finally reaching St. Louis

---

Lexicography (lek-si-**kog**-ruh-fee) – N – the writing, editing, or compiling of dictionaries

was ***prevalent*** throughout the group. No one could wait to get up and see the place they had been dreaming about over the past few months. The arrival in St. Louis marked both the ending of one journey and the beginning of another. It was now time to make a new home.

After speaking with the hotel's manager, Howie and the children decided to explore the city on foot and leave the wagon and animals behind in the stable. A friendly soul who had lived in St. Louis his entire life, the hotel manager had been happy to answer the group's questions about the city and offer suggestions of what places to visit, and what parts of town to avoid. He informed Howie and Jacob that finding a job in St. Louis did not require extensive search or ***byzantine*** cunning, as the current economy was booming. If they looked hard enough, they were sure to find something that fit their fancy.

"Yes, sir" smiled the manager, "St. Louis is the place you want to be!"

It was good news all-around as the group listened to the manager's advice and wrote down places that they needed to go. They learned of the places to live and where Anna and Charlie could go to school. Although some schools in the area ***proscribed*** teaching girls after the age of 12, the manager knew of a private girl's school, Woodland Heights, which had recently opened that allowed women to be educated until they were 18. All the Watkins needed to do to get Anna enrolled in the following school year was go speak to the headmistress. Fortunately for the visitors,

---

Prevalent (**prev**-uh-luhnt) – ADJ – widespread; of wide extent or occurrence; in general use or acceptance

Byzantine (**biz**-uhn-teen) – ADJ – complex or intricate

Proscribe (proh-**skrahyb**) – V – to denounce or condemn (a thing) as dangerous or harmful; prohibit

the school was on the way to another place of interest located just past St. Peters. As they turned to leave, the hotel manager interrupted them.

"Please don't take this the wrong way," began the manager. "I don't mean to be rude, but Woodland Heights is a respectable establishment. If you walk in there looking like that, they won't take you seriously."

Confused by the hotel manager's comments, the group looked around at each other. As it turned out, the traveling party did indeed look like they had spent several months living on the open road. While their time at the Indian camp had been an exciting adventure, they all arrived in town looking like a wild group of outlaws. Howie's long hair and beard had quickly regrown, neither Jacob nor Charlie had received a haircut in months, and Anna's golden curls were locks of chaos. This was the first time the group had been in a real town for some time, and they wanted to make a good impression when they met the headmistress of the school or went out to look for jobs. Luckily for the travelers, the hotel they happened upon had a partial salon in the back and the man they were speaking to was the barber. He smiled at the travelers and motioned that they follow him, which they did gladly. An hour later, looking their finest, the group reemerged energized to tackle the tasks of the day. They looked and felt great.

Howie and the children thanked the manager for his help and bade him good-bye. There were so many things to get done, and they didn't want to waste a minute. Happily they made their way into the heart of the city, all the while absorbing the sights and sounds of their new home. The ***propulsive*** nature of excitement quickened their steps as they wandered the novel territory.

It was around noon when they arrived at the gates of St. Peters. The tall building glistened in the sunlight. Despite the years of wear, the church had aged well and remained as beautiful as their parents had described it. The Watkins felt a strange sense of peace standing in front of this cathedral. It was here that their father had studied, grown up, and had married their mother; and while they didn't know it at that moment, it would be this building that would connect their past to their future. Full of immense tranquility, the children and their adopted uncle quietly walked through the courtyard and made their way into the building.

The church was as exquisite on the inside as it had been on the outside. Adorned with stained-glass windows, a rainbow of colors merrily danced on the mahogany wood pews. Statues of the holy family and the saints cheerfully greeted the guests. Given the time and day, the sanctuary was empty, and the stillness of reverence was captivating.

As the visitors softly approached the front of the building, a velvety voice broke the silence. Curious about the origins of the sound, the group turned to see a finely dressed woman speaking to one of the priests. The woman spoke eloquently. Her commanding tone and her handsome attire suggested that she came from a world of ***plutocracy*** where rich people expected to get their way. Although streaks of gray in her otherwise amber hair betrayed the fact that she was in her fifties, time had been kind to her. The elegant lady had aged well. The

---

Propulsive (pruh-**puhl**-siv) – ADJ – driving or causing to move forward or onward

Plutocracy (ploo-**tok**-ruh-see) – N – the rule or power of wealth or of the wealthy

group wouldn't have given the lady a second thought if they hadn't overheard the last part of her conversation.

"And you said you have no idea where I can find Mr. Watkins," inquired the lady.

"I'm sorry ma'am", replied the priest. "He must have left here before I came."

The lady thanked the man for his help and the priest left. Disappointed, the woman turned to leave. Believing it to be more than coincidence that the woman was asking for a Mr. Watkins at St. Peters, Anna boldly walked up to the aristocrat. Her companions followed behind.

"Excuse me, ma'am," began Anna. "I don't mean to be rude, but are you by chance looking for a Thomas Watkins?"

Taken aback by the approach of the young girl, the lady took a moment to reply.

"Why, yes, I am," responded the shocked woman.

"I'm sorry to have to tell you this," continued Anna. "Mr. Watkins and his wife, Charlotte, passed away earlier this year."

"Oh, there must be some mistake," responded the lady with a sigh of relief. "The Thomas Watkins I am looking for didn't have a wife. He was a priest."

"There is no mistake, ma'am," continued Anna.

"How do you know?" asked the woman.

"My name is Anna Marie Watkins," she responded. "He was my father."

The last words of Anna brought tears to the stranger's eyes. First they were tears of sadness, but they quickly turned into tears of joy.

"It's nice to meet you Anna," replied the woman. "My name is Anna Marie Perkins. Thomas Watkins was my brother."

Anna could hardly believe what she was hearing. Although she had never met her aunt before, Anna instantly recognized familiar features in the woman's coloring, facial structure, and disposition that reminded her of her beloved father. Within seconds of their introduction the two embraced. Wiping the tears from her eyes, Anna quickly introduced their long-lost aunt to her brothers, Jacob and Charlie. Anna Marie hugged the two boys and proudly commented how much they looked like their father, Thomas. Anna Marie asked the children to tell her all about what had happened to their parents, and they retold her the tale of their courtship and marriage, their move to Wyoming, their cottage on the prairie, their parents' illness, and lastly their decision to move back East to start over. Mrs. Perkins, a widow, explained that she understood the pain of loss, and the need to start over. Mr. Perkins had left her a large estate, but the money wasn't enough to ease her loneliness. Having no children of her own, she wanted to come back to St. Louis and try to find the only family that she had ever had, her brother. While she was sad that her brother was gone, she couldn't have been happier to have found his children.

All the commotion had left one member of the group standing quietly on the sidelines. While Howie was excited for the children to have found their long-lost aunt, he couldn't help but feel a sense of sadness at this reunion. The Watkins no longer needed an adopted uncle when they had a blood-related aunt. Not wanting to interrupt the joyous reunion, Howie unobtrusively turned to leave. Realizing that one member of the group was missing, Jacob turned to find Howie. Seeing him walking to the door, Jacob called out in all his might.

"Uncle Howie," screamed Jacob. "Get yourself over here!"

Howie smiled and turned back to the group. Upon his return Jacob quickly introduced the former trail guide to his aunt.

"Aunt Anna Marie," began Jacob. "This is our Uncle Howie. Without him, we wouldn't have survived one day on the trail."

Howie smiled at Anna Marie, and Anna Marie turned and blushed. As the two exchanged proper introductions, it became quite clear to the children that there was something more than a friendly exchange happening between the two adults. There was a spark, and the Watkins couldn't be more excited. Those feelings would soon ***proliferate*** to something much larger. It wouldn't take long before another wedding would take place at St. Peters, and Howie would become the children's official uncle.

Proliferate (pruh-**lif**-uh-reyt) – V – to increase in number or spread rapidly and often excessively

WORD REVIEW

Accretion	Lupine	Propulsive
Bevy	Malleable	Proscribe
Byzantine	Matrix	Protean
Contrarian	Metonymy	Purgative
Definitive	Oblique	Secede
Dictum	Panoply	Solstice
Fecund	Per Se	Subservient
Hibiscus	Plutocracy	Subtext
Impute	Ponderous	Superlative
Interstellar	Prevalent	Syntax
Lexicography	Proliferate	Undulant

GLOSSARY

Abject - (ab-**jekt**) - ADJ - utterly hopeless - page 11 - chapter 1

Abound - (uh-**bound**) - V - to occur or exist in great quantities or numbers - page 132 - chapter 8

Absolve - (ab-**zolv**) - V - to free from guilt - page 20 - chapter 1

Abysmal - (uh-**biz**-muhl) - ADJ - awful - page 12 - chapter 1

Acclamation - (ak-luh-**mey**-shuhn) - N - a loud shout or other demonstration of welcome, goodwill, or approval - page 60 - chapter 3

Accretion - (uh-**kree**-shuhn) - N - an increase by natural growth or by gradual external addition - page 206 - chapter 12

Acculturation - (uh-kuhl-chuh-**rey**-shuhn) - N - the process of adopting the cultural traits or social patterns of another group - page 128 - chapter 8

Acquisitive - (uh-**kwiz**-i-tiv) - ADJ - eager to get wealth - page 80 - chapter 5

Admonish - (ad-**mon**-ish) - V - to scold - page 18 - chapter 1

Aegis - (**ee**-jis) - N - protection - page 22 - chapter 1

Affluence - (**af**-loo-uhns) - N - an abundance of wealth, property, or other material goods - page 20 - chapter 1

Agrarian - (uh-**grair**-ee-uhn) - ADJ - rural; agricultural - page 13 - chapter 1

Ambrosia - (am-**broh**-zhuh) - N - something especially delicious to taste or smell - page 23 - chapter 1

Amorphous - (uh-**mawr**-fuhs) - ADJ - lacking definite form; having no specific shape; formless - page 13 - chapter 1

Antebellum - (an-tee-**bel**-uhm) - ADJ - of or during the period before a war, especially the American Civil War - page 116 - chapter 7

Apologia - (ap-uh-**loh**-jee-uh) - N - a defense or justification of a belief, idea, actions, etc. - page 154 - chapter 9

Apprise - (uh-**prahyz**) - V - advise; inform - page 83 - chapter 5

Arcadia - (ahr-**key**-dee-uh) - N - any real or imaginary place offering peace and simplicity - page 22 - chapter 1

Archetype - (**ahr**-ki-tahyp) - N - the original pattern or model or first form; prototype - page 164 - chapter 10

Ascendancy - (uh-**sen**-duhn-see) - N - governing or controlling influence; domination - page 133 - chapter 8

Astringent - (uh-**strin**-juhnt) - ADJ - stern or severe; austere - page 99 - chapter 6

Asunder - (uh-**suhn**-der) - ADV - into separate parts; in or into pieces - page 86 - chapter 5

Attenuate - (uh-**ten**-yoo-yet) - V - to weaken or reduce in force, intensity, effect, quantity, or value - page 78 - chapter 5

Atypical - (ey-**tip**-i-kuhl) - ADJ - not typical; not conforming to the type; irregular; abnormal - page 89 - chapter 5

Autonomous - (aw-**ton**-uh-muhs) - ADJ - not subject to control from outside - page 55 - chapter 3

Aver - (uh-**vur**) - V - to state positively as true - page 111 - chapter 7

Bane - (beyn) - N - a person or thing that ruins or spoils - page 62 - chapter 3

Battery - (**bat**-uh-ree) - N - any large group or series of related things - page 50 - chapter 2

Behemoth - (bih-**hee**-muhth) - N - any creature or thing of monstrous size or power - page 44 - chapter 2

Belligerence - (buh-**lij**-er-uhns) - N - a warlike or aggressively hostile nature, condition, or attitude - page 45 - chapter 2

Benediction - (ben-i-**dik**-shuhn) - N - an utterance of good wishes - page 17 - chapter 1

Benefactor - (**ben**-uh-fak-ter) - N - a person who confers a benefit; kindly helper - page 41 - chapter 2

Bequest - (bih-**kwest**) - N - an arrangement in a will - page 67 - chapter 4

Bevy - (**bev**-ee) - N - a group of birds, as larks or quail - page 209 - chapter 12

Bilge - (bilj) - N - either of the rounded areas that form the transition between the bottom and the sides on the exterior of a hull - page 199 - chapter 11

Bipartite - (bahy-**pahr**-tahyt) - ADJ - divided into or consisting of two parts - page 152 - chapter 9

Blatant - (**bleyt**-nt) - ADJ - brazenly obvious; flagrant - page 100 - chapter 6

Bootleg - (**boot**-leg) - N - alcoholic liquor unlawfully made, sold, or transported, without registration or payment of taxes - page 107 - chapter 6

Brazier - (**brey**-zher) - N - a metal receptacle for holding live coals or other fuel, as for heating a room - page 163 - chapter 10

Bristle - (**bris**-uhl) - V - to be visibly roused or stirred (usually followed by up) - page 45 - chapter 2

Byzantine - (**biz**-uhn-teen) - ADJ - complex or intricate - page 221 - chapter 12

Calumny - (**kal**-uhm-nee) - N - the act of uttering calumnies; slander; defamation - page 137 - chapter 8

Candor - (**kan**-der) - N - the state or quality of being frank, open, and sincere in speech or expression - page 63 - chapter 3

Capitulate - (kuh-**pich**-uh-leyt) - V - to give up resistance; to surrender to another - page 83 - chapter 5

Carp - (kahrp) - N - to find fault or complain querulously or unreasonably - page 63 - chapter 3

Cataclysm - (**kat**-uh-kliz-uhm) - N - any violent upheaval, especially one of a social or political nature - page 120 - chapter 8

Catalyst - (**kat**-l-ist) - N - something that causes activity between two or more persons or forces without itself being affected - page 97 - chapter 6

Cavort - (kuh-**vawrt**) - V - to prance or caper about - page 59 - chapter 3

Censure - (**sen**-sher) - N - strong or vehement expression of disapproval - page 177 - chapter 10

Channel - (**chan**-l) - N - a means of access - page 89 - chapter 5

Chimera - (ki-**meer**-uh) - N - a horrible or unreal creature of the imagination; a vain or idle fancy - page 152 - chapter 9

Circumnavigate - (sur-kuhm-**nav**-i-geyt) - V - to go or maneuver around - page 46 - chapter 2

Circumspect - (**sur**-kuhm-spekt) - ADJ - watchful; cautious - page 21 - chapter 1

Circumvent - (sur-kuhm-**vent**) - V - to avoid (defeat, failure, unpleasantness, etc.) by artfulness or deception; avoid by anticipating or outwitting - page 130 - chapter 8

Coerce - (koh-**urs**) - V - to bring about through the use of force or other forms of compulsion - page 81 - chapter 5

Cognizant - (**kog**-nuh-zuhnt) - ADJ - aware - page 79 - chapter 5

Cohesion - (koh-**hee**-zhuhn) - N - unity - page 82 - chapter 5

Cohort - (**koh**-hawrt) - N - a companion or associate - page 91 - chapter 5

Colossus - (kuh-**los**-uhs) - N - anything colossal or gigantic - page 78 - chapter 5

Compelling - (kuhm-**pel**-ing) - ADJ - having a powerful and irresistible effect; requiring acute admiration, attention, or respect - page 23 - chapter 1

Comport - (kuhm-**pawrt**) - V - to behave - page 144 - chapter 9

Concert - (**kon**-surt) - N - agreement of two or more individuals in a design or plan; combined action - page 25 - chapter 1

Confidant - (**kon**-fi-dant) - N - a close friend or associate to whom secrets are confided or with whom private matters and problems are discussed - page 93 - chapter 5

Connubial - (kuh-**noo**-bee-uhl) - ADJ - of marriage or wedlock - page 23 - chapter 1

Conscription - (kuhn-**skrip**-shuhn) - N - compulsory enrollment of persons for military or naval service; draft - page 169 - chapter 10

Conspicuous - (kuhn-**spik**-yoo-uhs) - ADJ - easily seen or noticed; readily visible or observable - page 133 - chapter 8

Contrarian - (kuhn-**trair**-ee-uhn) - N - a person who takes an opposing view - page 214 - chapter 12

Cornucopia - (kawr-nuh-**koh**-pee-uh) - N - an abundance of something good - page 42 - chapter 2

Corroborate - (kuh-**rob**-uh-reyt) - V - to make more certain; confirm - page 16 - chapter 1

Countermand - (**koun**-ter-mand) - V - to revoke or cancel - page 14 - chapter 1

Couture - (koo-**toor**) - N - a fashion designer - page 169 - chapter 10

Croesus - (**kree**-suhs) - N - a very rich man - page 17 - chapter 1

Curmudgeon - (ker-**muhj**-uhn) - N - a bad-tempered, difficult, cantankerous person - page 24 - chapter 1

Cyclopean - (sahy-kluh-**pee**-uhn) - ADJ - gigantic; vast - page 27 - chapter 1

Decalogue - (**dek**-uh-lawg) - N - Ten Commandments (Exodus. 20:2–17) - page 14 - chapter 1

Declaim - (dih-**kleym**) - V - to speak aloud in an oratorical manner; make a formal speech - page 30 - chapter 1

Definitive - (dih-**fin**-i-tiv) - ADJ - having its fixed and final form - page 211 - chapter 12

Delineate - (dih-**lin**-ee-yet) - V - to trace the outline of; sketch or trace in outline; to portray in words - page 62 - chapter 3

Deprecate - (**dep**-ri-keyt) - V - to express earnest disapproval of - page 54 - chapter 3

Derring-do - (der-ing-**doo**) - N - daring deeds; heroic daring - page 60 - chapter 3

Descant - (**des**-kant) - N - a song or melody - page 77 - chapter 5

Desensitize - (dee-**sen**-si-tahyz) - V - to make indifferent, unaware, or the like, in feeling - page 106 - chapter 6

Dictum - (**dik**-tuhm) - N - an authoritative pronouncement; judicial assertion - page 210 - chapter 12

Digress - (dih-**gres**) - V - to deviate or wander away from the main topic - page 57 - chapter 3

Dimorphic - (dahy-**mawr**-fik) - ADJ - having two forms - page 193 - chapter 11

Dipsomaniac - (dip-suh-**mey**-nee-ak) - N - a person with an irresistible craving for alcoholic drink - page 13 - chapter 1

Dire - (**dahy**-uhr) - ADJ - causing or involving great fear or suffering; dreadful; terrible: a dire calamity - page 68 - chapter 4

Discrete - (dih-**skreet**) - ADJ - apart or detached from others; separate - page 141 - chapter 9

Disposition - (dis-puh-**zish**-uhn) - N - state of mind regarding something; inclination - page 91 - chapter 5

Dissipate - (**dis**-uh-peyt) - V - to scatter in various directions; disperse; dispel - page 61 - chapter 3

Docent - (**doh**-suhnt) - N - a person who is a knowledgeable guide - page 98 - chapter 6

Downplay - (**doun**-pley) - V - to treat or speak of (something) so as to reduce emphasis on its importance, value or strength - page 85 - chapter 5

Dragon's Teeth - (**drag**-uhnz teeth) - N - the seeds of conflict - page 32 - chapter 1

Dryad - (**drahy**-uhd) - N - a deity or nymph of the woods - page 17 - chapter 1

Dubiousness - (**doo**-bee-uhs-ness) - N - unreliability; doubtfulness - page 87 - chapter 5

Duplicity - (doo-**plis**-i-tee) - N - deceitfulness in speech or conduct - page 93 - chapter 5

Duress - (doo-**res**) - N - compulsion by threat or force - page 147 - chapter 9

Dystrophy - (**dis**-truh-fee) - N - a condition caused by inadequate nutrition - page 49 - chapter 2

Eclipse - (ih-**klips**) - V - to make less important by comparison; surpass - page 164 - chapter 10

Effluent - (**ef**-loo-uhnt) - ADJ - flowing out or forth - page 144 - chapter 9

Egomania - (ee-goh-**mey**-nee-uh) - N - obsessive love for oneself and regard for one's own needs - page 153 - chapter 9

Elixir - (ih-**lik**-ser) - N - a panacea; cure-all; sovereign remedy - page 33 - chapter 1

Elliptical - (ih-**lip**-ti-kuhl) - ADJ - expressed with extreme or excessive economy - page 165 - chapter 10

Empathy - (**em**-puh-thee) - N - the intellectual identification with or vicarious experiencing of the feelings, thoughts, or attitudes of another - page 150 - chapter 9

Enfranchise - (en-**fran**-chahyz) - V - to grant a franchise to; admit to citizenship, especially to the right of voting - page 193 - chapter 11

Epitaph - (**ep**-i-taf) - N - a commemorative inscription on a tomb or mortuary monument about the person buried at that site - page 30 - chapter 1

Eponymous - (uh-**pon**-uh-muhs) - ADJ - giving one's name to a place - page 90 - chapter 5

Estuary - (**es**-choo-er-ee) - N - that part of the mouth or lower course of a river in which the river's current meets the sea's tide - page 199 - chapter 11

Ethos - (**ee**-thos) - N - the character or disposition of a community, group, person, etc. - page 166 - chapter 10

Etymology - (et-uh-**mol**-o-gy) - N - the derivation of a word - page 191 - chapter 11

Euphonious - (yoo-**foh**-nee-uhs) - ADJ - pleasant in sound; agreeable to the ear - page 44 - chapter 2

Eutrophic - (yoo-**trof**-ik) - ADJ - characterized by an abundant accumulation of nutrients that support a dense growth of algae and other organisms, the decay of which depletes the shallow waters of oxygen in summer - page 198 - chapter 11

Exacting - (ig-**zak**-ting) - ADJ - rigid or severe in demands or requirements - page 70 - chapter 4

Excrescence - (ik-**skres**-uh-ns) - N - a disfiguring addition - page 131 - chapter 8

Exodus - (**ek**-suh-duhs) - N - a going out; a departure or emigration, usually of a large number of people - page 95 - chapter 5

Expostulate - (ik-**spos**-chuh-leyt) - V - to reason earnestly with someone against something that person intends to do or has done - page 25 - chapter 1

Extemporaneous - (ik-stem-puh-**rey**-nee-uhs) - ADJ - impromptu - page 43 - chapter 2

Extramurally - (ek-struh-**myoor**-uhlly) - ADV - outside the boundaries of - page 16 - chapter 1

Extrude - (ik-**strood**) - V - to thrust out; force or press out; expel - page 29 - chapter 1

Faction - (**fak**-shuhn) - N - a group or clique within a larger group, party, government, organization - page 145 - chapter 9

Fecund - (**fee**-kuhnd) - ADJ - very productive or creative intellectually - page 206 - chapter 12

Fervid - (**fur**-vid) - ADJ - burning; glowing; intensely hot - page 113 - chapter 7

Flaccid - (**flak**-sid) - ADJ - soft and limp - page 101 - chapter 6

Flagrant - (**fley**-gruhnt) - ADJ - shockingly noticeable or evident; obvious; glaring - page 49 - chapter 2

Fodder - (**fod**-er) - N - coarse food for livestock - page 76 - chapter 5

Forestall - (fohr-**stawl**) - V - to prevent, hinder, or thwart by action in advance - page 44 - chapter 2

Forlorn - (fawr-**lawrn**) - ADJ - desolate or dreary; unhappy or miserable, as in feeling, condition, or appearance - page 31 - chapter 1

Formative - (**fawr**-muh-tiv) - ADJ - pertaining to formation or development - page 28 - chapter 1

Forte - (fawr-**tey**) - N - a strong point, as of a person; that in which one excels - page 93 - chapter 5

Fracas - (**frey**-kuhs) - N - a noisy, disorderly disturbance or fight; riotous brawl; uproar - page 59 - chapter 3

Fractious - (**frak**-shuhs) - ADJ - refractory or unruly - page 56 - chapter 3

Frenetic - (fruh-**net**-ik) - ADJ - frantic; frenzied - page 50 - chapter 2

Furlong - (**fur**-lawng) - N - a unit of distance that is equal to 220 yards - page 40 - chapter 2

Gall - (gawl) - V - to make sore by rubbing - page 51 - chapter 2

Gauche - (gohsh) - ADJ - lacking social grace, sensitivity, or acuteness - page 64 - chapter 3

Genuflect - (**jen**-yoo-flekt) - V - to bend the knee or touch one knee to the floor in reverence or worship - page 170 - chapter 10

Gerontocracy - (jer-uhn-**tok**-ruh-see) - N - a governing body consisting of old people - page 57 - chapter 3

Gradation - (grey-**dey**-shuhn) - N - any process or change taking place through a series of stages, by degrees, or in a gradual manner - page 58 - chapter 3

Gratuitous - (gruh-**too**-i-tuhs) - ADJ - given, done, bestowed, or obtained without charge or payment; free; voluntary - page 41 - chapter 2

Gravitas - (**grav**-i-tahs) - N - seriousness or sobriety, as of conduct or speech - page 37 - chapter 2

Halyard - (**hal**-yerd) - N - any of various lines or tackles for hoisting a spar, sail, flag, etc., into position for use - page 196 - chapter 11

Hegemony - (**hej**-uh-moh-nee) - N - leadership; predominance - page 82 - chapter 5

Hibiscus - (hahy-**bis**-kuhs) - N - also called China rose, a woody plant of the mallow family having large, showy flowers - page 218 - chapter 12

Holistic - (hoh-**lis**-tik) - ADJ - of or relating to the medical consideration of the complete person, physically and psychologically, in the treatment of a disease - page 19 - chapter 1

Homologous - (huh-**mol**-uh-guhs) - ADJ - having the same or a similar relation; corresponding, as in relative position or structure - page 166 - chapter 10

Horticulture - (**hawr**-ti-kuhl-cher) - N - the cultivation of a garden, orchard, or nursery - page 47 - chapter 2

Hypochondriac - (hahy-puh-**kon**-dree-ak) - N - a person who worries or talks excessively about his or her health - page 19 - chapter 1

Hypocrite - (**hip**-uh-krit) - N - a person who pretends to have virtues, moral or religious beliefs, principles, etc., that he or she does not actually possess, especially a person whose actions belie stated beliefs - page 198 - chapter 11

Iatrogenic - (ahy-a-truh-**jen**-ik) - ADJ - caused by the diagnosis, manner, or treatment of a physician - page 200 - chapter 11

Immure - (ih-**myoor**) - V - to shut in; seclude or confine - page 47 - chapter 2

Impenetrable - (im-**pen**-i-truh-buhl) - ADJ - inaccessible to ideas, influences, etc. - page 82 - chapter 5

Impregnable - (im-**preg**-nuh-buhl) - ADJ - strong enough to resist or withstand attack; not to be taken by force, unconquerable - page 171 - chapter 10

Impresario - (im-pruh-**sahr**-ee-oh) - N - a person who organizes or manages public entertainments, especially operas, ballets, or concerts - page 143 - chapter 9

Impute - (im-**pyoot**) - V - to attribute or ascribe - page 217 - chapter 12

Incendiary - (in-**sen**-dee-er-ee) - ADJ - used or adapted for setting property on fire - page 156 - chapter 9

Incisive - (in-**sahy**-siv) - ADJ - penetrating; cutting; biting; trenchant - page 51 - chapter 2

Inculpate - (**in**-kuhl-peyt) - V - to charge with fault; blame; accuse - page 51 - chapter 2

Indeterminate - (in-di-**tur**-muh-nit) - ADJ - not clear; vague - page 154 - chapter 9

Inexorable - (in-**ek**-ser-uh-buhl) - ADJ - unyielding; unalterable - page 135 - chapter 8

Inflection - (in-**flek**-shuhn) - N - modulation of the voice; change in pitch or tone of voice - page 129 - chapter 8

Infraction - (in-**frak**-shuhn) - N - breach; violation; infringement - page 91 - chapter 5

Ingratiate - (in-**grey**-shee-yet) - V - to establish (oneself) in the favor or good graces of others, especially by deliberate effort - page 112 - chapter 7

Inimitable - (ih-**nim**-i-tuh-buhl) - ADJ - incapable of being imitated or copied; surpassing imitation; matchless - page 88 - chapter 5

Insurrection - (in-suh-**rek**-shuhn) - N - an act or instance of rising in revolt, rebellion, or resistance against civil authority or an established government - page 145 - chapter 9

Intelligible - (in-**tel**-i-juh-buhl) - ADJ - capable of being understood; comprehensible; clear - page 85 - chapter 5

Intermezzo - (in-ter-**met**-soh) - N - a short dramatic, musical, or other entertainment of light character, introduced between the acts of a drama or opera - page 143 - chapter 9

Intermittent - (in-ter-**mit**-nt) - ADJ - stopping or ceasing for a time; alternately ceasing and beginning again - page 168 - chapter 10

Interstellar - (in-ter-**stel**-er) - ADJ - located, taking place, or traveling among the stars especially of the Milky Way galaxy - page 213 - chapter 12

Interstice - (in-**tur**-stis) - N - an interval of time - page 134 - chapter 8

Intractable - (in-**trak**-tuh-buhl) - ADJ - not easily controlled or directed; not docile or manageable - page 38 - chapter 2

Intrepid - (in-**trep**-id) - ADJ - resolutely fearless; dauntless - page 149 - chapter 9

Investiture - (in-**ves**-ti-cher) - N - the act of establishing or ratifying - page 84 - chapter 5

Junta - (**hoon**-tuh) - N - a small group ruling a country, especially immediately after a coup d'état and before a legally constituted government has been instituted - page 123 - chapter 8

Kleptomania - (klep-tuh-**mey**-nee-uh) - N - an irresistible impulse to steal, stemming from emotional disturbance rather than economic need - page 121 - chapter 8

Laggard - (**lag**-erd) - ADJ - moving, developing, or responding slowly; sluggish - page 104 - chapter 6

Largess - (lahr-**jes**) - N - generous bestowal of gifts - page 167 - chapter 10

Latent - (**leyt**-nt) - ADJ - present but not visible, apparent, or actualized; existing as potential - page 106 - chapter 6

Leonine - (**lee**-uh-nahyn) - ADJ - resembling or suggestive of a lion - page 158 - chapter 9

Lethargic - (luh-**thahr**-jik) - ADJ - drowsy; sluggish - page 55 - chapter 3

Lexicography - (lek-si-**kog**-ruh-fee) - N - the writing, editing, or compiling of dictionaries - page 220 - chapter 12

Locution - (loh-**kyoo**-shuhn) - N - a particular form of expression; a word, phrase, expression - page 202 - chapter 11

Lucubration - (loo-kyoo-**brey**-shuhn) - N - laborious work, study, thought, etc., especially at night - page 160 - chapter 9

Lupine - (**loo**-pin) - N - plant having tall, dense clusters of blue, pink, or white flowers - page 212 - chapter 12

Magnanimous - (mag-**nan**-uh-muhs) - ADJ - generous in forgiving an insult or injury; free from petty resentfulness or vindictiveness - page 153 - chapter 9

Malign - (muh-**lahyn**) - V - to speak evil of; slander; defame - page 99 - chapter 6

Malleable - (**mal**-ee-uh-buhl) - ADJ - adaptable or tractable - page 212 - chapter 12

Manifesto - (man-uh-**fes**-toh) - N - a public declaration of intentions, opinions, objectives, or motives, as one issued by a government, sovereign, or organization - page 188 - chapter 11

Marginal - (**mahr**-juh-nl) - ADJ - at the outer or lower limits; minimal for requirements; almost insufficient - page 71 - chapter 4

Matrix - (**mey**-triks) - N - something (such as a situation) in which something else develops - page 207 - chapter 12

Melancholy - (**mel**-uhn-kol-ee) - N - a gloomy state of mind, especially when habitual or prolonged; depression - page 29 - chapter 1

Mercenary - (**mur**-suh-ner-ee) - N - working or acting merely for money or for the reward - page 99 - chapter 6

Metonymy - (mi-**ton**-uh-mee) - N - a figure of speech that consists of the use of the name of one object or concept for that of another to which it is related, or of which it is a part, as "scepter" for "sovereignty," or "the bottle" for "strong drink," or "count heads (or noses)" for "count people" - page 207 - chapter 12

Millefleur - (meel-**flur**) - ADJ - having a background sprinkled with representations of flowers - page 201 - chapter 11

Minutiae - (mi-**noo**-shee-uh) - N - precise details; small or trifling matters - page 168 - chapter 10

Misanthropy - (mis-**an**-thruh-pee) - N - hatred, dislike, or distrust of humankind - page 103 - chapter 6

Misnomer - (mis-**noh**-mer) - N - a misapplied or inappropriate name or designation - page 192 - chapter 11

Mitigate - (**mit**-i-geyt) - V - to lessen in force or intensity, as wrath, grief, harshness, or pain; moderate - page 160 - chapter 9

Modulate - (**moj**-uh-leyt) - V - to regulate by or adjust to a certain measure or proportion; soften; tone down - page 157 - chapter 9

Mortify - (**mawr**-tuh-fahy) - V - to humiliate or shame, as by injury to one's pride or self-respect - page 172 - chapter 10

Multifarious - (muhl-tuh-**fair**-ee-uhs) - ADJ - having many different parts, elements, forms, etc. - page 186 - chapter 11

Necropolis - (nuh-**krop**-uh-lis) - N - a historic or prehistoric burial ground - page 196 - chapter 11

Nescience - (**nesh**-ee-uh-ns) - N - lack of knowledge; ignorance - page 131 - chapter 8

Nestor - (**nes**-ter) - N - the oldest and wisest of the Greeks in the Trojan War and a king of Pylos - page 185 - chapter 11

Non Sequitur - (non **sek**-wi-ter) - N - an inference or a conclusion that does not follow from the premises - page 177 - chapter 10

Nostalgia - (no-**stal**-juh) - N - a sentimental yearning for the happiness of a former place or time - page 86 - chapter 5

Oblique - (uh-**bleek**) - ADJ - not straight or direct - page 219 - chapter 12

Olympian - (uh-**lim**-pee-uhn) - ADJ - majestic - page 54 - chapter 3

Ostensible - (o-**sten**-suh-buhl) - ADJ - outwardly appearing as such; professed; pretended - page 186 - chapter 11

Panacea - (pan-uh-**see**-uh) - N - a remedy for all disease or ills; cure-all - page 19 - chapter 1

Panoply - (**pan**-uh-plee) - N - a wide-ranging and impressive array or display - page 218 - chapter 12

Paranoia - (par-uh-**noi**-uh) - N - baseless or excessive suspicion of the motives of others - page 179 - chapter 10

Pariah - (puh-**rahy**-uh) - N - an outcast - page 178 - chapter 10

Pecuniary - (pi-**kyoo**-nee-er-ee) - ADJ - of or pertaining to money - page 71 - chapter 4

Penumbra - (pi-**nuhm**-bruh) - N - a shadowy, indefinite, or marginal area - page 180 - chapter 10

Per Se - (pur **sey**) - ADV - by, of, for, or in itself; intrinsically - page 208 - chapter 12

Philistine - (**fil**-uh-steen) - ADJ - lacking in, hostile, or smugly indifferent to culture - page 148 - chapter 9

Picador - (**pik**-uh-dawr) - N - one of the mounted assistants to a matador, who opens the bullfight by enraging the bull and weakening its shoulder muscles with a lance - page 149 - chapter 9

Piety - (**pahy**-i-tee) - N - reverence for god or devout fulfillment of religious obligations - page 191 - chapter 11

Plait - (pleyt) - V - to braid something, especially of hair or straw - page 40 - chapter 2

Platitude - (**plat**-i-tood) - N - a flat, dull, or trite remark, especially one uttered as if it were fresh or profound - page 148 - chapter 9

Plight - (plahyt) - N - a condition, state, or situation, especially an unfavorable or unfortunate one - page 37 - chapter 2

Plutocracy - (ploo-**tok**-ruh-see) - N - the rule or power of wealth or of the wealthy - page 223 - chapter 12

Polarize - (**poh**-luh-rahyz) - V - to divide into sharply opposing factions, political groups, etc. - page 83 - chapter 5

Ponderous - (**pon**-der-uhs) - ADJ - of great weight; heavy; massive - page 211 - chapter 12

Portent - (**pawr**-tent) - N - an indication or omen of something about to happen, especially something momentous - page 102 - chapter 6

Preeminent - (pree-**em**-uh-nuhnt) - ADJ - eminent above or before others; superior; surpassing - page 201 - chapter 11

Preen - (preen) - V - to dress (oneself) carefully or smartly; primp - page 127 - chapter 8

Premeditation - (pri-med-i-**tey**-shuhn) - N - sufficient forethought to impute deliberation and intent to commit the act - page 172 - chapter 10

Prescience - (**presh**-uhns) - N - knowledge of things before they exist or happen; foreknowledge; foresight - page 147 - chapter 9

Presumably - (pri-**zoo**-muh-blee) - ADV - by assuming reasonably; probably - page 130 - chapter 8

Prevalent - (**prev**-uh-luhnt) - ADJ - widespread; of wide extent or occurrence; in general use or acceptance - page 221 - chapter 12

Primal - (**prahy**-muhl) - ADJ - first; original or of first importance; fundamental - page 72 - chapter 4

Pristine - (pris-**teen**) - ADJ - having its original purity; uncorrupted or unsullied - page 54 - chapter 3

Proffer - (**prof**-er) - N - an offer or proposal - page 80 - chapter 5

Proliferate - (pruh-**lif**-uh-reyt) - V - to increase in number or spread rapidly and often excessively - page 226 - chapter 12

Propensity - (pruh-**pen**-si-tee) - N - a natural inclination or tendency - page 114 - chapter 7

Propulsive - (pruh-**puhl**-siv) - ADJ - driving or causing to move forward or onward - page 223 - chapter 12

Proscribe - (proh-**skrahyb**) - V - to denounce or condemn (a thing) as dangerous or harmful; prohibit - page 221 - chapter 12

Protean - (**proh**-tee-uhn) - ADJ - versatile; able to play many kinds of roles - page 215 - chapter 12

Protract - (proh-**trakt**) - V - to draw out or lengthen, especially in time; extend the duration of; prolong - page 109 - chapter 7

Psyche - (**sahy**-kee) - N - the human mind or soul - page 181 - chapter 10

Punitive - (**pyoo**-ni-tiv) - ADJ - serving for, concerned with, or inflicting punishment - page 194 - chapter 11

Purgative - (**pur**-guh-tiv) - ADJ - cathartic - page 214 - chapter 12

Quid Pro Quo - (**kwid** proh **kwoh**) - N - one thing in return for another - page 129 - chapter 8

Raffish - (**raf**-ish) - ADJ - gaudily vulgar or cheap; tawdry - page 121 - chapter 8

Rebuke - (ri-**byook**) - N - sharp, stern disapproval; reproof; reprimand - page 116 - chapter 7

Rectilinear - (rek-tl-**in**-ee-er) - ADJ - forming a straight line - page 190 - chapter 11

Regress - (ri-**gres**) - V - to move backward; go back, to return to a previous state - page 104 - chapter 6

Remand - (ri-**mand**) - V - to send back, remit, or consign again - page 110 - chapter 7

Reprimand - (**rep**-ruh-mand) - V - to reprove or rebuke severely, especially in a formal way - page 187 - chapter 11

Resonance - (**rez**-uh-nuhns) - N - the prolongation of sound by reflection; reverberation - page 188 - chapter 11

Retribution - (re-truh-**byoo**-shuhn) - N - requital according to merits or deserts, especially for evil - page 125 - chapter 8

Retroactive - (re-troh-**ak**-tiv) - ADJ - operative with respect to past occurrences - page 175 - chapter 10

Revivify - (ri-**viv**-uh-fahy) - V - to restore to life; give new life to; revive; reanimate - page 100 - chapter 6

Rustic - (**ruhs**-tik) - N - an unsophisticated country person - page 33 - chapter 1

Sanction - (**sangk**-shuhn) - N - authoritative permission or approval, as for an action - page 122 - chapter 8

Sanctum - (**sangk**-tuhm) - N - a sacred or holy place - page 21 - chapter 1

Secede - (si-**seed**) - V - to withdraw formally from an alliance, federation, or association, as from a political union, a religious organization, etc. - page 210 - chapter 12

Secular - (**sek**-yuh-ler) - ADJ - of or pertaining to worldly things or to things that are not regarded as religious, spiritual, or sacred - page 191 - chapter 11

Seethe - (seeth) - V - to surge or foam as if boiling - page 31 - chapter 1

Serrated - (ser-**ey**-tid) - ADJ - having a notched edge or saw-like teeth, especially for cutting - page 128 - chapter 8

Sibyl - (**sib**-uhl) - N - a female prophet - page 190 - chapter 11

Siren - (**sahy**-ruhn) - ADJ - seductive or tempting, especially dangerously or harmfully - page 187 - chapter 11

Skinflint - (**skin**-flint) - N - miser - page 120 - chapter 8

Slander - (**slan**-der) - N - a malicious, false, and defamatory statement or report - page 137 - chapter 8

Solace - (**sol**-is) - N - something that gives comfort or relief - page 31 - chapter 1

Solicitous - (suh-**lis**-i-tuhs) - ADJ - anxiously desirous - page 123 - chapter 8

Solstice - (**sol**-stis) - N - a turning point - page 216 - chapter 12

Soluble - (**sol**-yuh-buhl) - ADJ - easily solved or explained - page 173 - chapter 10

Sonorous - (suh-**nawr**-uhs) - ADJ - rich and full in sound - page 132 - chapter 8

Spartan - (**spahr**-tn) - ADJ - marked by simplicity; avoidance of luxury - page 104 - chapter 6

Spendthrift - (**spend**-thrift) - N - a person who spends possessions or money extravagantly or wastefully; prodigal - page 119 - chapter 8

Staccato - (stuh-**kah**-toh) - ADJ - composed of or characterized by abruptly disconnected elements - page 195 - chapter 11

Steadfast - (**sted**-fast) - ADJ - fixed in direction; steadily directed - page 137 - chapter 8

Stigmatize - (**stig**-muh-tahyz) - V - to set some mark of disgrace or infamy upon - page 125 - chapter 8

Stoicism - (**stoh**-uh-siz-m) - N - a school of philosophy that teaches that people should be free from passion and unmoved by joy or grief - page 32 - chapter 1

Stratification - (strat-uh-fi-**key**-shuhn) - N - the hierarchical or vertical division of society according to rank, caste, or class - page 174 - chapter 10

Stringent - (**strin**-juhnt) - ADJ - rigorously binding or exacting; strict; severe - page 193 - chapter 11

Stupendous - (stoo-**pen**-duhs) - ADJ - causing amazement; astounding; marvelous - page 174 - chapter 10

Subservient - (suhb-**sur**-vee-uhnt) - ADJ - serving or acting in a subordinate capacity - page 207 - chapter 12

Subtext - (**suhb**-tekst) - N - the underlying or implicit meaning, as of a literary work - page 207 - chapter 12

Succor - (**suhk**-er) - N - help; relief; aid; assistance - page 39 - chapter 2

Sumptuous - (**suhmp**-choo-uhs) - ADJ - entailing great expense, as from choice materials, fine work, etc.; costly - page 124 - chapter 8

Superlative - (suh-**pur**-luh-tiv) - ADJ - of the highest kind, quality, or order; surpassing all else or others; supreme; extreme - page 206 - chapter 12

Surmount - (ser-**mount**) - V - to prevail over - page 179 - chapter 10

Surrogate - (**sur**-uh-geyt) - N - a person who acts in place of another - page 32 - chapter 1

Symbiosis - (sim-bee-**oh**-sis) - N - any interdependent or mutually beneficial relationship between two persons, groups, etc. - page 167 - chapter 10

Syntax - (**sin**-taks) - N - the study of the rules for the formation of grammatical sentences in a language - page 210 - chapter 12

Tabula Rasa - (**tab**-yuh-luh **rah**-suh) - N - a mind not yet affected by experiences, impressions, etc. - page 181 - chapter 10

Tenable - (**ten**-uh-buhl) - ADJ - capable of being held, maintained, or defended, as against attack or dispute - page 182 - chapter 10

Tenet - (**ten**-it) - N - any opinion, principle, doctrine, dogma, etc., especially one held as true by members of a profession, group, or movement - page 126 - chapter 8

Trajectory - (truh-**jek**-tuh-ree) - N - the curve described by a projectile, rocket, or the like in its flight - page 151 - chapter 9

Translucent - (trans-**loo**-suhnt) - ADJ - easily understandable; lucid - page 138 - chapter 8

Transmute - (trans-**myoot**) - V - transform - page 106 - chapter 6

Turgid - (**tur**-jud) - ADJ - swollen; distended - page 151 - chapter 9

Tutelage - (**toot**-l-ij) - N - instruction; teaching; guidance - page 114 - chapter 7

Umbrage - (**uhm**-brij) - N - offense; annoyance; displeasure - page 107 - chapter 6

Undulant - (**uhn**-juh-luhnt) - ADJ - wavelike in motion or pattern - page 216 - chapter 12

Venial - (**vee**-nee-uhl) - ADJ - able to be forgiven or pardoned; not seriously wrong, as a sin - page 189 - chapter 11

Verisimilitude - (ver-uh-si-**mil**-i-tood) - N - the appearance or semblance of truth; likelihood; probability - page 177 - chapter 10

Vis-à-Vis - (vee-zuh-**vee**) - ADV - face to face - page 158 - chapter 9

Vulpine - (**vuhl**-pahyn) - ADJ - cunning or crafty - page 182 - chapter 10

Xenophobic - (**zen**-uh-fohb-ik) - ADJ - fearing or hating foreigners or strange customs - page 158 - chapter 9

Zephyr - (**zef**-er) - N - a gentle, mild breeze - page 78 - chapter 5